Praise for Larissa Reinhart's Cherry Tucker Mysteries

HIJACK IN ABSTRACT

"The fast-paced plot careens through small-town politics and deadly rivalries, with zany side trips through art-world shenanigans and romantic hijinx. Like front-porch lemonade, Reinhart's cast of characters offer a perfect balance of tart and sweet."
– Sophie Littlefield,
Bestselling Author of *A Bad Day for Sorry*

"Cherry is back–tart-tongued and full of sass. With her paint-stained fingers in every pie, she's in for a truckload of trouble."
– J.J. Murphy,
Author of the Algonquin Round Table Mysteries

"Bless her heart. Artist Cherry Tucker just can't help chasing after justice, even when it lands her up to her eyeballs in Russian gangsters, sexy exes, and treacherous truckers. A rambunctious mystery as Southern as chess pie and every bit as delectable."
– Jane Sevier,
Author of the Psychic Socialite 1930s Memphis Mysteries

"A true work of art...I didn't want this book to end! I was so caught up in Cherry's crazy life, I wanted to just keep reading."
– Gayle Trent,
Author of *Battered to Death*

"Reinhart manages to braid a complicated plot into a tight and funny tale...Cozy fans will love this latest Cherry Tucker mystery."
– Mary Marks,
New York Journal of Books

"Witty, fast paced dialogue sandwiched between vivid descriptions and interesting characters made *Hijack in Abstract* come to life before my eyes...My recommendation—don't miss this one!"
– Christine Warner,
hor of *Bachelor's Special*

D1738875

"I love this series! Cheeky, clever, and compelling—keeps me reading way too late. This book has one of the most original—and fun—love triangles you'll ever come across."

— Kaye George,
Agatha Nominated Author of the Imogene Duckworthy Mysteries

"Larissa Reinhart has a unique knack of putting her lead character, Cherry Tucker, through a series of obstacles, increasing the pressure until I'm on the edge of my seat... Cherry Tucker mysteries just keep getting better and better. I can't wait for the next installment!"

— Terri L. Austin,
Author of the Rose Strickland Mystery Series

"Cherry Tucker's got an artist's palette of problems, but she handles them better than da Vinci on a deadline. Bust out your gesso and get primed for humor, hijackings, and a handful of hunks!"

— Diane Vallere,
Author of the Style & Error and Mad for Mod Mystery Series

"Reinhart took me on a fun rollercoaster ride. Everyone is a suspect and just when you think you have things figured out, you're forced to reevaluate your theory and modify your suspect list. I haven't had this much fun trying to solve a mystery in a while and it sure beats playing a game of Clue any day! Four out of five stars."

— *Literary, etc.*

"With a well-plotted storyline, witty banter, a warm and friendly feel and a great supporting cast that surrounds Cherry, this was very enjoyable and I am eager to read the next book in this charmingly appealing series."

— Dru Ann Love,
Dru's Book Musings

STILL LIFE IN BRUNSWICK STEW

"Reinhart's country-fried mystery is as much fun as a ride on the Tilt-a-Whirl at a state fair. Her sleuth wields a paintbrush and un-ravels clues with equal skill and flair. Readers who like a little small-town charm with their mysteries will enjoy Reinhart's series."
— Denise Swanson,
New York Times Bestselling Author of the Scumble River and Devereaux's Dime Store Mysteries

"*Still Life in Brunswick Stew* proves beyond doubt that Larissa Reinhart and her delightful amateur sleuth Cherry Tucker will be around to entertain us for many books to come."
— Lois Winston,
Author of the Anastasia Pollack Crafting Mystery series

"Cherry Tucker finds trouble without even looking for it, and plenty of it finds her in *Still Life in Brunswick Stew*...this mystery keeps you laughing and guessing from the first page to the last. A whole-hearted five stars."
— Denise Grover Swank,
New York Times and *USA Today* Bestselling Author

"Reinhart lined up suspects like a pinsetter in a bowling alley, and darned if I could figure out which ones to knock down...Can't wait to see what Cherry paints herself into next."
— Donnell Ann Bell,
Bestselling Author of *The Past Came Hunting*

"The hilariously droll Larissa Reinhart cooks up a quirky and enter-taining page-turner! This charming mystery is delightfully South-ern, surprisingly edgy, and deliciously unpredictable."
— Hank Phillippi Ryan,
Agatha, Anthony and Macavity Award-Winning Author

PORTRAIT OF A DEAD GUY

"*Portrait of a Dead Guy* is an entertaining mystery full of quirky characters and solid plotting...Highly recommended for anyone who likes their mysteries strong and their mint juleps stronger!"
— Jennie Bentley,
New York Times Bestselling Author of *Flipped Out*

"Reinhart is a truly talented author and this book was one of the best cozy mysteries we reviewed this year...We highly recommend this book to all lovers of mystery books. Our Rating: 4.5 Stars."
— *Mystery Tribune*

"The tone of this marvelously cracked book is not unlike Sophie Littlefield's brilliant *A Bad Day for Sorry*, as author Reinhart dishes out shovelfuls of ribald humor and mayhem."
— Betty Webb,
Mystery Scene Magazine

"Larissa Reinhart's masterfully crafted whodunit, *Portrait of a Dead Guy*, provides high-octane action with quirky, down-home characters and a trouble-magnet heroine who'll steal readers' hearts."
—Debby Giusti,
Author of *The Captain's Mission* and *The Colonel's Daughter*

"A fun, fast-paced read and a rollicking start to her Cherry Tucker Mystery Series. If you like your stories southern-fried with a side of romance, this book's for you!"
— Leslie Tentler,
Author of *Midnight Caller*

HiJACK IN
ABSTRACT

The Cherry Tucker Mystery Series
by Larissa Reinhart

Novels

PORTRAIT OF A DEAD GUY (#1)

STILL LIFE IN BRUNSWICK STEW (#2)

HIJACK IN ABSTRACT (#3)

DEATH IN PERSPECTIVE (#4)
(coming Summer 2014)

Novellas

QUICK SKETCH (prequel to PORTRAIT)
(in HEARTACHE MOTEL)

HIJACK IN ABSTRACT

A Cherry Tucker Mystery

LARISSA REINHART

HENERY PRESS

HIJACK IN ABSTRACT
A Cherry Tucker Mystery
Part of the Henery Press Mystery Collection

First Edition
Trade paperback edition | November 2013

Henery Press
www.henerypress.com

This is a work of fiction. Any references to historical events, real people, or real locales are used fictitiously. Other names, characters, places, and incidents are the product of the author's imagination, and any resemblance to actual events or locales or persons, living or dead, is entirely coincidental.

ISBN-13: 978-1-938383-72-4

Printed in the United States of America

To Mom.
Thanks for instilling a love of books within me.
And for letting me borrow yours.

ACKNOWLEDGMENTS

Thank you to Rick and Ann Walker. Rick, thanks for your service as a Special Agent and for sharing all your great stories!

Thank you to Matt and Palmarin Merges. Matt, your gun knowledge astounds me, and Palmy, your creativity inspires me.

Thank you to my special readers, Gina, Diana, Julie, and Linda. You guys rock! And Bill and Erich, you're pretty cool, too.

Thanks to Anise Rae for being such a supportive critique partner and friend.

A big thank you to my partner in crime, Terri L. Austin, and her accomplices, LynDee Walker and Gretchen Archer, for their help, support, and silliness. Gigi Pandian, so glad I can stalk you at the same press now.

A huge thank you to my awesome editor, Kendel Flaum, for pushing me to make my stories better and for making Henery Press flourish.

Thanks to all my supporters in Peachtree City, Newnan, Senoia, Grantville, Savannah, and other parts of Georgia, as well as the folks in Illinois, Texas, and North Carolina. Your love and patronage really motivate me.

Thank you to librarians and Friends of the Library everywhere for your dedication to books, authors, and readers, particularly Peachtree City Library, Geneseo Public Library, Watauga County Public Library, and Newnan Carnegie Library.

And finally, a triple-decker, super gigantic thank you to Trey, Soph, & Lu for everything. Especially for letting me wonder aloud about really strange things that would annoy most normal people. And for understanding my lack of interest in vacuuming.

ONE

There are many places you don't want to be at zero dark thirty, but I've got a personal top three. One is the ER. Second is a police station. The third is your ex-boyfriend's bedroom.

Thank God Almighty I was not in number three. Stupid does catch me occasionally, but not this night. I was nowhere near an ex-boyfriend's bedroom.

At two forty-five in the morning, I found myself in number two. The Forks County Sheriff's Office to be accurate. My cornflower blues were a bit bloodshot and blurry, but my grin matched Shep Peterson's, who also found himself in a similar location. However, Shep had a drunk tank grin. Mine was more of a self-congratulatory grin, born from knowing that finally someone in Forks County had recognized my accomplishments in the art world. Never mind the phone call that woke me from a dead sleep and near gave me a heart attack. Or that I had to drive my sister's Firebird because her vehicle was blocking my driveway. Or that I now sat in the junior officers' room with a cold cup of coffee and had just realized I had forgotten to comb my bed-head designed blond cowlicks in my bleary-eyed haste.

And to put on a bra.

The Forks County Sheriff, Uncle Will, needed my expertise. That's all that mattered. And I was going to get paid.

Needed me for what was still a bit vague. I hoped nothing needing brushed hair and a bra.

"Wha'cho in fer?" called Shep from two desks over. "You a D and D, too?" He pitched forward in his seat, but righted himself before his arresting officer could shove him back in his chair.

"No drunk and disorderly tonight," I said. "I'm here in an official capacity. As an artist."

"Artist? You wanna draw my picture? Wha's your name, darlin'?"

"Cherry Tucker," I grinned. "Mr. Shep, you know me. I'm Ed Ballard's granddaughter. He buys bait from you. I've been to your tackle shop."

"Is very hard to meet new people in Halo," he said, attempting to bow. "My apologies, darlin'. Think I'd remember a pretty, young thing like yourself. Look like my first wife. Even with that crazy hairdo."

I surreptitiously finger-combed my hair. Not that I was trying to impress Shep.

Deputy Wellington slapped him back in his seat. "Shep, stop hitting on Cherry. You're about fifty years too old for her anyway."

"Can't blame a guy for trying," he said and hiccupped.

Deputy Wellington fanned the space between Shep and his desk. "Just sit there and be still while I finish this paperwork."

"That Shep again?" drawled a deep bass. "Wellington, throw him in the drunk tank and let him sleep. This room smells bad enough."

I turned in my seat and saw Sheriff Will Thompson's massive form filling the doorway. Before I was born, Uncle Will had made an easy transition from University of Georgia linebacker to Forks County crime buster with his quick wits, easy smile, and powerful handshake. Some would think having a close family friend as a sheriff would keep you out of trouble growing up. However, the Tucker kids were boundary testers. For Uncle Will, raising my family was as much of an act of community service as his dedication to the law.

As a twenty-six-year-old woman, I felt it my duty to make up for any of the gray hairs my teenage self might have added to Uncle

Will's head. Which is why I had no problem tumbling out of bed and driving across the county to sit in a chair and allow seventy-year-old bait shop owners to flirt with me.

That and I hoped to make a few bucks.

"Hey Uncle Will," I called. "Are you ready for me yet?"

"Bring your paper and pencils," he said.

With my messenger bag bumping my back, I hugged my chest, figuring it best not to give an extra show to Shep and the boys. I followed Uncle Will down the hallway, waiting while he unlocked a door. The door opened and two faces turned to look at us. One I didn't recognize, but judging by his despondent expression, I figured he was probably in a mess of trouble. The other person, another deputy, I identified immediately. Hard not to recognize those brown ochre curls with the highlights I had decided were transparent oxide-red lake. Or the lean, muscled body, much like Michelangelo's *David*. Or by the strong jaw buttressing two adorable dimples that made a rare showing.

Unfortunately, I knew Deputy Luke Harper a little too well.

He gave me a scant nod and turned back to the perp.

My hand snuck back to my hair and yanked on a particularly tall cowlick in back. I gritted my teeth and gave myself a quick lecture not to make a scene. We had aired our irreconcilable differences behind the local roadhouse, Red's County Line Tap, a few months ago and I had not quite recovered.

"That's Tyrone Coderre," said Uncle Will. "He's going to give you a description to draw. We need a composite sketch."

Uncle Will stopped me before I entered the room and pulled me to the side. "Can I leave Deputy Harper in there with you or do I need to call in another officer? Harper's the one who picked up Coderre, so this is his investigation."

"I'm quite capable of separating my personal and professional life," I said, tilting my chin so I could eyeball Uncle Will. "You might want to ask the same of him."

"I trust Luke not to screw up his job. You are another story."

I gave him a "why, I never" gasp.

"I'm going to be watching through the two-way." He tapped my messenger bag. "Lucky for you, I don't know other artists to call during the middle of the night. Wouldn't want to be accused of nepotism. But I want a sketch while the memory is still fresh in Coderre's mind. Don't disappoint me, Cherry."

"So, this is an important investigation?" Excitement zipped through my veins and made my fingers tingle. "I won't let you down. You can even deputize me if you want."

Uncle Will chuckled. "Just draw us a good picture. That's plenty helpful."

"Yes, sir," I said and snuck by him to enter the room. I nodded to the man in the black sweat suit behind the table and held out my hand. "Hello, Mr. Coderre. I'm Cherry Tucker, a local artist."

"Don't shake his hand," barked Luke. "Are you crazy?"

Tyrone Coderre's cuffed hands retreated below the table, and I blew out a hard breath.

Looked like it was going to be a long night. At least the criminal had manners.

Couldn't say the same for the cop.

"How's this?" I held up a page from my sketch pad. After a few false starts, Tyrone Coderre settled on a long, oblong face with a rounded jaw line. The composite had shoulder-length hair, blond and on the thinnish side, and a soft mouth. "Are you sure he's not a girl?"

"Pretty ugly girl," said Tyrone. "His eyes were closer together."

I gummed out the eyes and reapplied my pencil, a sanguine oil, perfect for warm, heavy tones which erased easily on my seventy-pound, smooth sketch paper. Erasing was necessary when drawing a face from Tyrone's memory. His first description began with "a skinny, blond dude."

Tyrone yawned, and as they were catching, I followed with one of my own.

"Maybe you could get us a cup of coffee, Deputy?" I asked in my prettiest drawl.

"And leave you alone with a junkie copper thief? I wouldn't do that to Tyrone."

"You're a copper thief, Tyrone?" I said as I crosshatched shadow lines to emphasize the composite's cheekbones. "Now why would you want to spend your nights stripping air conditioner units when you could be doing something more productive?"

"I don't strip A/C units." Tyrone tapped on the sketch pad. "His nose needs to be longer."

I grabbed my gum eraser and scrubbed at the end of the composite's nose.

"Air conditioners are not enough of a challenge for Tyrone here," said Luke. "He likes to shimmy poles for his wire."

Tyrone smiled. "They call me the Flying Coderre."

"Were you up on a pole when you saw this guy?"

Tyrone cut his eyes to Luke. "Allegedly. At the rest stop on the interstate near the Line Creek exit."

"What was the guy doing?"

"Helping himself to a truck."

"You don't need to know that information," said Luke. "Just draw."

"I'm just curious. It's not like I'm going to look for the guy."

Luke snorted, which was his way of saying "I don't believe you."

We've had some past misunderstandings on the difference between "being helpful" and "interfering with the law." Luke refused to acknowledge I can gain information as good as any cop just through my local gossip network. I call myself inquisitive and creative. He calls me nosy and harebrained. He forgets my interest for crime had been honed from growing up around a county sheriff. I never wanted to be a cop, though. Not unless I could bedazzle my uniform and stonewash the polyester out of the cotton/poly blend. And those cop shoes? Forget about it.

"I don't think the deputy trusts you." Tyrone eyed my drawing. "The dude was wearing a track suit. Shiny blue or black. It was hard to tell the color in the dark."

I began sketching in a track suit collar. "I've given the deputy no reason not to trust me."

Luke snorted again.

"Are you catching a cold or something?" I said. "Do you need a tissue?"

"I need you to finish up and stop talking to the perp."

"Tyrone, let me ask you this," I said. "If you had a girlfriend who was an artist, and you knew she had a painting deadline that involved a life study, and then found her innocently drawing this model, would you accuse her of cheating?"

"Do not talk to her, Tyrone," said Luke.

"What's a life study?" said Tyrone.

"Drawing the human figure using a live model."

"Drawing somebody naked," said Luke. "And not just anybody. Her ex-husband."

A knock sounded on the door and we glanced at the narrow in-set window to see Uncle Will glaring at us. He twirled his finger in the wrap-it up sign and nodded at Luke.

"Dammit," said Luke. "How did you pull me into that?"

"Todd's not really my ex-husband," I said quickly to Tyrone, needing to defend myself despite Uncle Will's strange ban on gossip in the interrogation rooms. "Our Vegas wedding was annulled before it even began. Todd's just a friend."

"Why don't you draw naked chicks?" said Tyrone. "Then everybody'd be happy."

I glared at Tyrone for a millisecond. "The subject had to be male. And the boyfriend refused to participate even though he had the perfect physique for this specific painting."

"Finish your picture," said Luke.

"I don't know about painting, but I do know something about cheating," said Tyrone. "By the way, I'm pretty sure he had a necklace. Something shiny around his neck anyway. Unzip his jacket some."

"So what do you know about cheating?" I kept my eyes on the paper. "How far down his chest did the necklace go?"

"My girl cheated on me. Not with her ex-husband though. She cheated on him, too," said Tyrone. "The eyes still don't look right."

"No more cheating talk," said Luke with a glance at the two-way mirror. "You sure you didn't get a look at the other guys?"

"Luke might know something about cheating, too," I said. "The subject makes him a tad uncomfortable. The grapevine says he has many admirers. They are called badge bunnies and they call him Luquified—"

"That's enough," snapped Luke. "What about the other guys?"

"Naw, they kept their ski masks on," said Tyrone. "This guy was the only one who pulled his off."

"Ski masks," I said. "A hold up? In Forks County?"

"I tell you what," said Tyrone. "I'd never been so scared in my life. Thought I'd fall off my pole. I didn't move until long after they'd gone."

"Poor Tyrone," said Luke. "So scared he didn't even get to collect his wire."

"I thought the driver was dead," said Tyrone. "These guys were pretty bad-ass."

Luke pushed out of his chair and moved behind me. "This is a good likeness."

"Thank you," said Tyrone, as if he had sketched it himself.

The door unlocked and Uncle Will strolled in to stand over the drawing. "Very good," he said. "Let's take this and scan it into the system."

"Yes, sir." Luke bent over me to tear the paper from its perforated edge.

I sat beneath the cage of his arms and tried not to breathe in that specific Luke blend of pheromones and aftershave. That particular concoction can prove deadly to the female libido and I didn't want my libido getting any funny ideas. My libido had already done that dance and lost.

"By the way, Cherry," Luke slid the whisper past my ear as he righted himself. "You might wear a bra next time you visit the sheriff's department."

I crossed my arms and felt my cheeks hit every shade of pink from ruby lake to vermilion extra.

"You done good, girl," said Uncle Will. "I'll cut you a check for your time and service. Tyrone, you sit tight."

Tyrone blew out a sigh and laid his forehead on the table.

The three of us ambled out of the room, the sketch now in Uncle Will's hand. He studied it before holding up the copy to Luke.

"I'm going to make some calls," said Will. "Someone in Atlanta might recognize him. Every county with an interstate running through it gets an occasional hijack. Guess it was our turn to get lucky."

"Yes, sir," said Luke.

I held my breath, knowing that anything exiting my lips could blow any chance of hearing something interesting.

"I know that look. You're not getting any classified information from us." Uncle Will leaned to pop a kiss on my forehead. "Go get you some sleep, sugar. Are you going to have trouble staying awake on the way home?"

"I'll be all right," I said, yawning. "Maybe I'll get some breakfast. It's close to five, isn't it?"

"You go with her," Uncle Will nodded to Luke. "Don't want to hear that broken-down truck left her in a ditch. Might as well swing by the Waffle House on the interstate and see if they recognize this mug."

"I could go for a pecan waffle," I said. My stomach woke from its slumber and made a noise similar to a Harley with an engine knock. "Maybe some grits and bacon, too. And more coffee."

"I'm sure the sheriff wants me to take you home first," said Luke, barely masking his impatience.

"The least we can do is treat her to a pecan waffle. While she's eating you can ask a few questions." Will fished a ten out of his wallet and handed it to Luke. "Son, where's your manners? I pulled Cherry out of bed to do this."

"Yes sir," muttered Luke, "but whose bed did you pull her out of?"

TWO

At the Waffle House, Luke ordered his regular artery clogger and slipped out of the booth to talk to the waitress hovering near the cashier stand. My early excitement had fizzled and I now felt tired and drained. I watched as Luke, holding out a copy of my sketch, strolled to the few customers sitting at the counter. Heads shook. At the last seat, a cadaverous, partially toothed man grabbed Luke's sleeve. Luke slid onto a stool and leaned in to hear the man's story.

I held out my coffee cup to my bottle red-haired waitress. "Did you see that picture the deputy is showing around?"

She nodded and poured. "Yeah, don't think I've seen him before."

"Heard about a robbery around here? Of a truck? At the rest stop?"

"No. What like a hijack?" Her hazel eyes gleamed, and she set the coffee pot on the table for a chitchat.

"Probably a hijack," I said. "At our interstate rest stop. That's all I know. I'm curious, though. Not like we get a lot of hijacks around here."

"No kidding? Truckers will sleep at that rest stop. Ones on a long haul, you know. Sometimes they'll come out to the Gearjammer for a bit of fun. Me and my girlfriend have some good times there."

"That's over in Line Creek, right? I've not been to that particular establishment."

"Sugar, you should go. Them truckers are a lot of fun. We dance and they buy us drinks. Sometimes other stuff. They sure know how to party," she giggled and glanced over her shoulder. "Oh, you're with that cop. Never mind. He's cute, though."

"I am not with that cop," I said, directing my gaze to the broad shoulders enveloped in the starchy, brown uniform. "Not anymore, anyway. I've never hung out with truckers, but that sounds like the kind of fun I could use in my recently single state. I don't suppose truckers are art appreciators?"

Ponytail picked up her coffee pot. "Some of them have unique art on their cabs. And there's always the mud flaps."

"I did pick up some good brushes at a detail shop once," I said. "Okay, I'm in. What's your name anyway?"

"Dona Sullens. Thursday night is ladies' night. Mixed drinks are free for the gals."

"I'll see you there," I said. "Might bring my sister, too."

She frowned. "Don't bring too many girls. I don't want an unbalanced ratio." Her ponytail bobbed behind her as she wandered back to the counter. Approaching Luke and his grizzled friend, she stopped and shoved a coffee pot between them. Luke held his hand up, hopped off his stool, and strolled back to our booth.

"Food's not here yet?" Luke slid onto the seat opposite me. He picked up his coffee, sipped, and curled the corner of his mouth. "Cold."

I felt eager to get beyond Luke's earlier rebuff and soothe the tension between us. I tuned my voice to casual and disinterested. "Did that guy on the end know anything?"

"No," Luke set his coffee down. "That's Clinton Hackley. He's a couple fuses short of running on full power. Poor guy."

"You're getting to know a lot of people on the job, aren't you? And a different picture of Forks County than what you grew up in, I'm sure."

"A high schooler's view of their world is pretty limited. Especially if your stepdad is a Branson." The Branson family had ruled our little neck of the woods for generations. My Grandpa's family, the Ballards, had been around as long as the Bransons, except we didn't have as much to show for it.

"I couldn't wait to get out of this backwater," Luke mused. "Funny how your view changes when you come back. Of course, now much of my meet and greet's done from a patrol car."

"It's not so bad here in Backwater, Georgia," I smiled as a plate full of waffle and bacon slid in front of me. "Thanks, Dona."

"Sure honey," she said. "See you Thursday night."

"What's Thursday night?" asked Luke.

"I'm meeting Dona and her friends down at the Gearjammer. For Ladies' Night."

"You know Dona?"

"Nope. But she seems nice."

Luke ran his hands through his curls, massaging his head. "Isn't the Gearjammer a trucker hangout?"

"Could be," I shrugged. "Never been there. I'm always up for trying something new."

He laid an arm on the table. "We've been through this before. Just because Sheriff Thompson asked you to draw that composite, does not mean you can nose your way into this investigation."

"Did I say I have any interest in this investigation?" I waved my fork at him. "What do I care about truck hijacks and copper thieves?"

Luke's gray eyes narrowed into thin, steel slits. "I never said this was a hijack."

"You said plenty, but Tyrone said more." I grinned and slurped my coffee.

He shoveled a forkful of sausage into his mouth and glared.

"Anyway, if I was going to hijack a truck, I don't think I'd stop by a Waffle House on my way back to the hideout."

"You are actually smarter than most criminals." Luke smiled at my brow raise. "But we need to be thorough. Not many places are open twenty-four hours."

"What about the new gas station at the interstate exit? The SipNZip?"

"Next on my list." He swished his biscuit in the gravy. "After I make sure you get home."

We ate in silence, tension driving us to shovel our food like starving Dickensian orphans.

"Why are you driving Casey's Firebird?" said Luke, breaking the strain.

"It was blocking my driveway. She moved in to get away from Pearl," I sighed heavily on that note of family drama. It didn't do to have your Grandpa stepping out with women who cooked better than my sister Casey. "At least there's food in my house now."

"Casey's living with you, too?"

"Too?" One of those nervous giggles slipped through my teeth. "Why don't we go to the gas station together? I'm wide awake now. They've got a case for donuts at the SipNZip."

I wiped my mouth with my napkin and hopped out of the booth. "I can pick up some donuts to bring home. See you there."

"Who're you bringing home donuts for?"

I waved at Dona and skipped out the door, pretending I hadn't heard Luke. I needed to get to the gas station before he figured out he hadn't stopped me.

And I didn't want to have the conversation about my nekkid picture posing ex, Todd, living with me.

The SipNZip was a new establishment and therefore busy even at six in the morning. New businesses made us locals curious, particularly if we didn't know the owners. Also made us a tad suspicious, but we're willing to give new places the benefit of the doubt as long as they didn't put on airs and gave a senior discount.

The SipNZip definitely didn't put on airs. I roamed the aisles, exploring my favorite preservative laden foods, while Luke spoke to the staff. I loved shops that offered glass caged hotdog wheels and Slushy machines with neon flavored drinks. They had a carnival air that appealed to my inner kitsch. At the refrigerated wall of beverages, I found my favorite junkie copper thief rooting through the soda choices. As Tyrone was out among the public, I figured I could say hello without inducing any restraining orders.

"Hey Tyrone," I said. "You're out already?"

"Hey, the artist lady. Just got out and thought I'd grab some breakfast." He grinned, holding up a bag of pork rinds and a Mountain Dew. "Watch your back, there, hon'."

I glanced over my shoulder and saw a girl in a SipNZip vest pushing crates of soda toward us. She waited while Tyrone and I moved a few paces down the aisle. We watched her prop open the cooler and begin filling the plastic dividers.

"Look at that," I said. "RC Cola and Cheerwine. This place has everything."

"I'm more of a Dew man," said Tyrone. "They didn't give me anything to drink at the station other than coffee."

"What happened? They didn't hold you for stealing copper? Let you off for giving them the composite?"

Tyrone put a finger to his lips while we waited for a customer to move around us and snag a bottle of water from the fridge. We watched the man move down the aisle, toward the donut stand.

"Truth is," a smile indented Tyrone's round cheeks, "I wasn't found with any copper on me, just in a terrible location. I was about to slide off my pole when the po-po pulled in, blueberries and sirens blazing. The truck driver must have dialed 9-1-1 right quick. I was too scared to move, so I held on to my pole. It was dark. I figured someone would see me if I tried to get down and run."

"So Deputy Harper found you on the pole?"

"Yes, ma'am. That he did. And I did my good deed by telling the Deputy what I saw. He just got lucky that jacker took his mask off and looked up. Don't think he saw me, though."

Tyrone pulled at his chin. "'Course he might of, but maybe he didn't have time to do nothing about it. The hijackers had to get out of there in a hurry."

"You sure gave a good description. I've never drawn from someone else's memory. I feel like I know the guy's face as well as you now."

"Sure enough." Tyrone tapped his head. "I've got a mind for faces. Never remember any names, but I always remember a face."

"That means you're a visual learner."

"Well, I'll be. Too bad the teachers didn't know that in school." He saluted me with his pork rinds. "Well, I've got some work to attend to. Better purchase my victuals and get going."

"Where do you work?"

"By work, I mean I'm back to the rest stop," he winked. "I left some valuables behind."

"Tyrone, you should not be telling me this. Besides, the police would have been all over that place. Whatever you left is evidence now."

"We'll see. I'm good at hiding stuff," he waved. "Bye now, girl. You go home and get some sleep. Long night for you, too. Thanks for your help."

With a goodbye wave to Tyrone, I continued my quest for hidden gems in the aisles of the SipNZip. Stopping before a mammoth size coffee machine, I grabbed a giant Styrofoam cup. As I sized up my choices, Luke found me and leaned back against the counter.

"Look at this," I said. "You can get a cappuccino, latte, cocoa, and a half dozen different shots of flavor for your espresso. All for a dollar ninety-eight. I love this place. They've also got a sausage biscuit you can heat up in their microwave. Now that's convenient."

Luke grunted, his gaze swiveling around the room.

"Did you see Tyrone?" I asked.

"Yep," Luke shook his head. "I hope he learned something from tonight. But probably not."

"Did any of the SipNZip folks recognize your hijacker?"

"I didn't say he was a hijacker," he snagged a small cup from the dispenser. "Pour me one, too. Please."

"What flavor?"

"Coffee."

"You can have a latte," I pointed at the choices. "I know you like a little cream."

"Plain old coffee. Please."

"What's bugging you?"

"I don't know," he said. "I don't like this place."

"What's not to like? They don't even have Max Avtaikin's poker machines in here. You don't have to worry about busting them for illegal payouts."

He took his coffee, blew on it, and sipped. "Let's go. I've got to talk to the state patrol before I can sleep."

"I didn't know you were back on nights."

He glanced at me and jerked his eyes back to his coffee. "I'm not. I just got lucky covering a shift for a buddy who got sick. Look, I don't want to chitchat."

"Fine," I said, pretending not to be hurt. "I've got to pay for my donuts and coffee."

I left him standing at the coffee machine and strolled to the cashier stand. Surrounded by cigarette cartons, lottery tickets, and energy drinks, a young woman with light brown hair and a pale face manned the cash register. I handed her my bag of donuts.

"And one small coffee and one large latte," I said.

She nodded and tapped the register keys.

"This is some place. You must be doing good business."

She nodded. "Five dollars and twenty-six cents."

I set the coffee on the counter to ferret the money from my jeans' pocket. "You look a little low on help. Y'all taking applications? I've got a friend who needs a job."

A shrug. This time with an eye cut to Deputy Harper standing by the coffee machine.

"Looks like it'll be another beautiful day."

Nothing.

Either this girl was not a morning person or she didn't harken from around these parts. Friendly chatting was the grease that kept our community from grinding one another's gears. "How about the Dawgs this year?"

"Five dollars and twenty-six cents."

"Hold on," I said, pulling a wad of bills and some change from my front pocket.

Behind me, a line had formed and took my speed as a reason to jostle me. I took a step backward, to give myself some space, and noodled a finger into the tiny, coin pocket of my jeans.

"Luke, you got a penny?" I hollered over my shoulder.

The clerk pushed the penny tray toward me.

"Can you hurry it up?" said the Atlanta commuter with the Ohio accent. "I've got to get to work."

"Just one second," I glanced at the clerk. "I don't think I've seen you around Forks County. Are you new in town?"

The clerk bobbed her head and scooped up the money. The cash register pinged as she smacked a button and tossed the cash inside.

"Did that deputy show you a sketch of a man? Did you ever see him in here before?" I watched her face, curious if the employee recognized the perp. Luke wouldn't tell me if they did.

"What sketch?" asked Ohio, reaching around me to grab a newspaper. "Has there been a hold-up? I moved way out here to get away from all that."

The drawer to the register slammed shut, causing a jar of beef jerky to wobble and threaten to tip.

"No hold-up here," said the clerk.

"Well then, move it along, lady." Ohio said to me and slapped his coffee, paper, and muffin on the counter. He tossed the clerk his debit card. "We finally get a quick stop out here and it's still slow."

"Come on, Cherry," said Luke, grabbing the bag of donuts. "Let's go."

"I swear I don't know what's happened to the art of conversation," I grumbled.

We strode out the shiny glass doors and past the gas pumps toward Casey's Firebird. Luke waited while I unlocked the door, then handed me the bag of donuts.

"Thanks for the coffee." He watched as I slid into the driver's seat. "Are you okay to get home or do I really need to follow you? I have a mess of work to do before I can go home and get some sleep."

"I've got my giant coffee to keep me company. Go do your business."

"I do appreciate you coming out in the middle of the night to sketch the composite. It sounds like you're doing well."

I forced a smile. "Someone bought my so-called 'naked' paintings, so I actually have money in my checking account for once. The gallery wouldn't say who bought them, but I have my suspicions it may be Max Avtaikin."

"You have suspected Avtaikin of everything under the sun and now you suspect him of buying your paintings?"

"He's an art collector and appreciator of talent such as mine."

"That's ironic. I'd think he'd just find you a pain in the ass."

"I believe he does that, too," I muttered.

"I'm glad someone bought your paintings," Luke toed my open door, "though it seems strange someone like Max Avtaikin would want naked Todd McIntosh hanging on his walls."

"The collector sees a triptych of classical subjects. Not naked Todd. Max uses the art as an investment. It's not like he's going to hang them in his bedroom." I took a big gulp of coffee as I ruminated on that idea. "Naw, he sees it as an investment."

"Didn't make you feel weird," Luke continued, "painting Todd naked?"

"He was merely a subject and a muse," I said loftily and buried my mouth in my coffee cup.

"What about seeing Todd naked now? That bother you?" Luke's gray eyes narrowed.

I choked on my coffee.

"See you around." He grabbed his Styrofoam cup off the roof of the car.

"Todd lost his job and needed a place to stay," I said. "I can't turn my back on a friend."

"I know that all too well," said Luke. "I think the exact words were, 'I'd break the law to help a friend.'"

"Those were your words and I just agreed. Haven't you ever watched Les Miserables?"

"I'm the law."

"You used to be my friend."

"I don't date my friends."

Ouch. "That's too bad, because Todd and I remained friends after we broke up," I said, seeking the chink in Luke's armor. "I can rely on him and he can rely on me. Which is a nice feeling and probably why I married him for that millisecond." And Todd's kisses could sear a side of beef in one second flat. But I wasn't going to admit that tidbit to Luke.

My door swung shut on that comment. I prepared to turn the ignition and gun Casey's motor, but was stopped, key in hand, by the knock on my window. I rolled down the window.

"If you go to the Gearjammer don't mention the hijack," said Luke. "I can just see you getting into a load of trouble at a place like a trucker bar."

"I told you, I'm not interested in the hijack," I said. "I've got no dog in the hunt. Other than curiosity."

"Maybe I should go with you to the Gearjammer," he said. "To make sure."

"You are not invited to my girls' night out. Do you hear me, Luke Harper? I'm not partying with truckers and you. You'll stand out like a sore cop thumb and ruin my fun."

"See you there." He smiled with his teeth. "And I'd recommend you wear a bra."

I slammed my arms over my chest, making him chuckle as he strolled to his cruiser.

Dangit. I might have to look into this hijack. Just to tick him off.

THRee

As I stepped through the kitchen door of my ninety-year-old bungalow, my brother leapt into view and snatched the bag of donuts from my hand, nearly giving me a heart attack. Like a retriever with his prize dead duck, Cody carried the donut bag to the kitchen table looking very pleased. I set my empty coffee cup on the Formica counter and leaned against the door, eyeing him. My twenty-one-year-old brother wore loose sweat pants, a wife beater, and bare feet. If that wasn't enough of a hint he'd slept in my house, his shaggy, dishwater blond hair still bore a similar bed-head cowlick to mine. I reached behind my head to tug mine down.

"Don't tell me you're moving in, too," I said. "This house cannot take another occupant."

"I remember Grandma Jo saying five kids were raised in this house. One more visitor ain't gonna shake the foundation." Cody yanked a sour cream donut from the bag and tore off a hunk with his teeth. "Pearl said either me or the vehicles had to leave the farm. I can't sell those cars until I fix them up proper."

"I guess Grandpa's letting Pearl do his dirty work. He's been wanting you to clear out those vehicles for years." I could hear the shower running in the back of the house, which blew my next plan of action. "When did you get here?"

"In time to see you tearing out of the drive in Casey's Firebird. I thought it was Casey until I poked my head into the guest room and found her. Where have you been? Booty call?"

I rolled my eyes, threw my satchel on the table, and plopped into a chair. "Sheriff's office. They needed someone to draw a description for a Forks County Most Wanted poster."

"At two in the morning?"

"Luke Harper picked up a witness to a truck hijacking. They wanted the composite sketch while it was still fresh in his mind."

"Deputy Harper," Cody snickered. "Sure it wasn't a booty call?"

"Booty call?" Todd's country baritone drawled from the hallway.

I surreptitiously eyed Todd's stroll into the kitchen. He wore a towel slung low across his lean hips, and his longish blond hair was slick from the shower. The rising sun streaming through my kitchen window caressed his dewy post-shower skin. Skin stretched over a body riddled with taut muscles and sweet dimples.

I needed to remind Todd that roommates wore robes. Which was hard to do, seeing as how I no longer spoke to my sort-of-ex-husband.

"Dude," said Cody, "put some britches on. You walk around my sister's house like that?"

Todd grinned and hitched his towel higher, making me slap a hand across my eyes. Todd didn't care a stitch about modesty. Literally.

"I'm taking a shower," I said, hopping out of my chair. "By the way, Cody. Tell Todd I just visited the new SipNZip gas station. They only had one girl running the cash register. He should see if they need some help."

"He's standing right here," Cody snagged another donut from the bag. "You don't get my help in the silent game."

"All right, baby," said Todd. "I was fixing to fill out applications today anyway."

"Tell Todd that's a good idea." This was why I tolerated Todd as a roommate. He listened and followed orders even when I wasn't speaking to him. That and he was awfully pretty to look at first thing in the morning.

"By the way, sister," said Cody, "word has gotten out about your nekkid paintings. Better expect some Come-To-Jesus-Meetings."

"What's so bad about painting an Ancient Greek styled figure?" I pushed past Todd and tromped down the hall to the single bathroom. "Someone needs to teach the folks in this town about classical art."

"Someone is. Shawna Branson. And she's the one showing Red's customers snapshots of your nekkid Todd pictures."

"What?" I stopped and spun around. "How does she have photos of those paintings? They went to a gallery in Athens. I don't even know who bought them."

"Dunno," Cody licked powdered sugar from his fingers and grabbed another donut. "Maybe she checked out that gallery when she was up in Athens for a Bulldogs game. She is an artist, you know. Told me so herself."

"Calling Shawna Branson an artist is like calling Ronald McDonald the King of Steaks." Shawna Branson and I've hated each other since the days when we all hung out at the Tasty Dip. When I found out she was sharing her sprinkles with my boyfriend, I wrote her number on the men's room wall. Accompanied by an explicit drawing of Shawna's talents. Pretty good rendering for a cement block wall and a Sharpie. Instead of throwing a hissy, she should have thanked me for making her so popular.

"Shawna's got a gallery in Line Creek now," Todd said. "She fancied up her art shop."

"What new gallery?" I said, forgetting my silence rule.

"Something about art," said Todd.

"Who cares?" said Cody. Powdered sugar dotted his beard. "I tell you what you should care about. Todd, ain't you embarrassed for people to see you in those paintings?"

Todd shrugged, slipped onto a kitchen chair, and reached for the donut bag.

"Why should he feel ashamed?" I said. "The good Lord's seen fit to give him the perfect body structure for a work of the High Renaissance. Anyone who thinks differently needs to get their mind out of the gutter."

"We don't live in High Renaissance," said Cody. "We live in Halo, Georgia, and if you see a picture of a naked dude, your mind's going to be in the gutter."

"You are an idiot."

"That may be, but for Todd's sake and yours, I'd do something to stop Shawna from showing the town pictures of his pecker. Everybody thinks y'all are perverts."

"I don't paint nudes all the time. It was for a show with a classical theme. I do portraits of real people. With clothes on." I waved my hand in the direction of my living room-studio with the wall full of clothed portraits. "And thanks to the friggin' Bransons, I haven't even done a portrait in ages. You know what she's trying to do? Force me to stop painting or move. Run me out of my own hometown."

The bedroom door to my left swung open. My sister Casey yawned, stretched, and rubbed her eyes. "What's all the hollering? I don't want to be up this early." Her eyes took in our scene and fixed on Todd. "Well, good morning sunshine. I can get used to this roommate thing."

"Hey Casey," said Todd. "The town thinks Cherry and I are perverts because of those paintings Cherry did of me."

Casey pushed her long, brown hair over a shoulder and leaned into the bedroom doorway, her eyes roving over Todd's fine musculature. "Told you those paintings were a bad idea."

"That bad idea paid the taxes on this house for the year," I said. "I don't know the patron, but they bought the collection for a good price."

She straightened from her languorous pose. "If I were you, I'd find the buyer. See if they want any more. I'll pose naked for a cut."

"That's disgusting," I said. "You're making my art sound as warped as the rest of the town."

She shrugged and stepped out of the doorway. "Don't see what the difference is between me and Todd."

"Todd is my muse," I said.

She and Cody exchanged a look before they began laughing hysterically.

"What? What's so funny?"

"Muse," she gasped. "Todd's your muse."

"Yes," I turned my back on Cody and Todd to give Casey a full-on stink eye. "Many great artists had a muse. Manet. Picasso. Andrew Wyeth. Stieglitz with Georgia O'Keefe, no less. Vermeer. The list goes on." I ticked them off on my fingers.

"I bet them painters were all guys and they were doing the chicks they were painting," said Cody.

I whirled around. "That is so sexist."

"Am I wrong?" asked Cody.

I screwed my mouth and tightened the grip on my crossed arms.

"Thought so," said Cody. "Todd, you better hope Cherry gets famous. You can go down in history as the first dude muse for a chick painter. And then turn in your man card."

Todd grinned. "I think it's kind of sexy."

I dropped my arms and kicked the shoe molding on the wall. A fine sprinkling of plaster dusted my boot. "Dammit. This means I've got to go to Line Creek and deal with Shawna."

"Hey, maybe she'll know who bought your paintings," said Casey, turning her back on me. She walked into the bathroom and closed the door. A moment later I heard the shower running.

I gave an exasperated sigh and glanced over my shoulder at Cody and Todd. The donut bag had been crumpled and tossed onto the middle of the table. Powdered sugar and frosting coated the wooden tabletop.

"Got any coffee?" said Cody.

"There are entirely too many people living in this house," I said. "If Shawna doesn't run me out of town, y'all will."

FOUR

Later that morning, I parked my little, yellow Datsun pickup in front of the old courthouse square. I gave the girl a pat on the steering wheel for making it the fifteen miles to Line Creek from Halo. When your vehicle is almost thirty years old, she needs that kind of encouragement. Lucky for me, my brother teethed on a crescent wrench. He lacked skills in most other areas, but if you have an engine, Cody is your man.

One of the benefits of Forks County was the loyalty of small town patrons to their mom and pop shops. Line Creek's town square still carried boutiques that allowed women one-of-a-kind dress options and children's clothes featuring smocking and embroidery. The square also had a fancified Southern restaurant for posh people who still liked to eat macaroni and cheese. And a Chinese restaurant run by a family who had lived in Line Creek for fifty years and learned to serve sides of mac and cheese with their lo mein.

I crossed the street and walked down the sidewalk, enjoying the cloudless morning sunshine, which would be scorching by afternoon. Passing a jewelry store, I paused to admire some unique pieces in the window, then stopped in front of Shawna's shop.

Her gallery had once been a stationary store specializing in monograms and garden party invitations, perfect for Shawna's brand of cute, curly-cue graphics. It had served a purpose in the Forks County community, as well-bred Southern women monogrammed the crap out of any piece of loose material that could be carried or worn on her person, home, and child. Sometimes their husbands, too (clothing, not bodies). I thought Shawna had been doing well in the monogram trade and her invitations made from heavy cardstock, ribbons, and printed calligraphy were popular, too.

Notice I am giving Shawna Branson her due. And it's not even a blue moon.

The monograms and pretty stationary had left the storefront window. Hanging in their place was a giant baby head centered on a canvas. That the giant baby head had once been a photo was made obvious by the grainy pixels making up the baby's face. Up close, the effect looked like Pointillism, as each pixel had been covered with a dot of paint. A sloppy daub of paint done with a cheap brush in a hurry.

I backed to the edge of the sidewalk to get a better angle on the floating baby head. The baby had a ruddy complexion from the use of straight-out-of-the-tube napthol red dots on his cheeks. The eyes were orbs of ultramarine blue. Someone had played with an introductory acrylic set. And not very well. The baby head looked like a Cabbage Patch with rosacea.

I shook my head and headed to the front door. As well as the merchandise, the sign had been changed to "The Real Artists of Forks County Gallery," which served as a laughable kick in the pants to me. I gritted my teeth and pushed through the door.

Another baby and a few high school senior heads hung on the brick, whitewashed walls, looking like a Chuck Close experiment gone awry. I scanned for more "Real Artist" art and spied two oils, painted by Gertie Speirs.

Gertie only painted chickens, but she had a fabulous coop with an assortment of fancy breeds. She was also eighty-five years old and a sweetheart. I was glad to see Shawna had considered Gertie in her attempts to bring gallery life to Forks County. Even if it was only two small paintings, a Rhode Island Red and a Golden Campine.

A young girl in all black with a ballerina bun sat behind a glass desk. She stood up and handed me a postcard. Her glance took in my boots, cutoffs, and an American flag t-shirt I had beaded in tangerine, black, and kelly green. From her expression, I assumed her creative eye didn't appreciate my complementary colored patriotism.

I glanced at the card and read aloud, "The Real Artists of Forks County presents Pictograph Portraits by Shawna Branson: a study. For sale or order your own." The red-cheeked baby head had been printed next to the announcement. I flipped the card over and a black and white photo of Shawna's face artfully held between her well-manicured hands stared at me. It was the first time I saw an artist's headshot taking up more space than their works.

The girl gave me a small smile and tucked some stray hairs behind her ears. "Would you like a tour?"

"Tour?" I said. "I think I've seen enough baby heads. I need to talk to Shawna."

"Just a moment," she pressed a button on her phone and adjusted her Bluetooth earpiece. "Miss Branson? Someone to see you."

I glanced out the window to check if I had somehow wandered out of Forks County.

"Your name?" asked Miss Ballerina Bun.

I had hoped for the element of surprise when playing on Shawna's home turf. "I'm with the Bulldog Studio Gallery in Athens," I hedged.

Miss Ballerina Bun relayed the message and point two seconds later, Shawna scrambled out a back door. Her wedges halted in mid-stride, skidding on the polished wood floor and almost knocking her on her butt.

"You," said Shawna and then turned her accusatory eyes on Ballerina. "Shelby, she's not from an Athens gallery."

Shelby's lips made guppy motions. Her bun bobbed and she sank in her chair like she wanted to slide under her table. Which was glass and not helpful for hiding.

"I am associated with Bulldog Gallery, as they recently hung my classical triptych on their fine walls," I crossed the room to meet Shawna. "But I think you know that as you took some photos with your phone and showed them to Red's customers recently."

Shawna's blue-green eyes narrowed into a caustic slant and her long nails tapped the sides of her thighs, currently swaddled in a giraffe print. She wore a wrap-around dress that strangled her torso better than cellophane.

"I was wondering, since you were so impressed with my paintings, are you my newest patron?" I smiled with my teeth and held my arms out in an anticipatory hug.

"I would never in a million years pay a wooden nickel for that trash. A foreigner bought it, which shows you how the good people of Georgia feel about that nastiness you painted," she said. "Don't go thinking your buyer was Max Avtaikin either. I looked and didn't see it in his house. Proving he's a well-bred man."

"Well-bred," I snorted. A year in Halo and Max Avtaikin had garnered a good name for himself while sneaking around the law. I hadn't been able to do that in my lifetime. His accent worked like a slight of hand. Or maybe it was his money that made people look the other way. "What are you doing hanging around Mr. Max's house anyway?"

"If you must know," she sighed with faux impatience. Her eyes betrayed her eagerness to brag. "We're planning my own show."

"Why do you need a show? You've got all these baby heads hanging in here for folks to see." A sting of hurt pricked my pride. Even if I found Max's illegal activities distasteful, he did buy my *Dustin* and hinted he wanted to commission more works. Unlike the rest of the population, I wasn't fooled by his accent or money, but I did respect his knowledge of art. And we had somehow forged a friendship based on our mutual love of baiting one another in cat and mouse style antics.

"Pictographs are my portrait business," Shawna glared at my eye roll. "The show would expose a side of my creativity."

"Expose?" I winked.

Her nostrils flared. "I'm not the one painting obscene trash."

"How are classical subjects trash? I based the paintings on some of the most famous statues in antiquity."

"With a local as the model for all the world to see. I feel sorry for poor Todd McIntosh, who everyone knows is dumb and easily coerced by you. You corrupted that poor man."

"Todd's not dumb. And you think I corrupted him?" I laughed. "Have you even met the McIntosh's? They load their dice and mark their cards. They obtain vehicles by racing for pink slips."

Shawna's plucked and waxed eyebrow rose and she planted a hand on one curvy giraffe-spotted hip. "He was dumb enough to marry you."

I sucked in my breath and stopped myself from taking her bait. "So are you gonna stop discrediting me and flashing those photos of my classical paintings around?"

"Not until you bring back the pictures you stole from me."

That wiped the snark off my face. "What pictures?"

"I've asked you before. Don't play stupid now," she hissed. "Pictures for pictures is a fair exchange. Clock's ticking. I haven't even shown your rendition of Todd's bare behind at church yet. That's next. I'm forming a committee."

"Exchange?"

"You heard me. One of you Tuckers has them. And there better not be copies floating around or I will ruin you for good. Not just in Halo. I'm talking all of Georgia."

"I didn't steal anything. I would never."

"Get out," she pointed a cheetah print nail in the direction of her glass front door. "Or I'll also put copies of those paintings in the feed store where your sorry Grandpa hangs out."

I left.

If the church ladies got wind I had done nude paintings, I could expect a mammoth sized shit storm to blow through my door. Grandpa would have my head for embarrassing the family. He'd kick me out of Great Gam's cottage and not only would I be homeless, I'd also lose my studio space.

My steps from The Real Artists Studio moved from amble to hurry as my panic increased. What kind of pictures would make Shawna go ballistic like this? Did she have her own nudie pics floating around Halo? How did one find something when one didn't even know what one was looking for?

Shawna did leave me with one unrelated but important kernel of information, I thought as I hopped into my truck and backed from the parking space. My buyer was foreign. Which further convinced me it must be Max Avtaikin no matter what Shawna believed. Max already owned one of my paintings, the portrait that marked my art career's surprisingly sharp left turn from child and hunting dog portraits toward the avant-garde. It would make sense he would be the foreigner who had bought my triptych. And if Max owned my classical paintings, he could prove to Forks County I wasn't a degenerate.

However, there was a slight problem with visiting Max Avtaikin, a.k.a. the Bear. The Bear hadn't looked too kindly on my helping him out of the illegal bingo business and into an audit. I didn't suppose he'd want to do me any favors, but I figure, it never hurts to ask.

I could always eat a little crow to get a Shawna sized monkey off my back.

Five

The foyer of Max's palatial antebellum nightmare was a study in cool marble, lofty ceilings, and a colossal sized man looking irritated as hell to see me. As I was used to irritating men to hell, it didn't bother me too much. If Max wasn't so big and brutish, much like his nickname The Bear, it probably wouldn't bother me at all.

"Why do you never call before coming to my house?" he said.

"We're a drop-in kind of folks down here," I replied. "Besides if I had called, would you have answered?"

His glacial blue eyes narrowed for a long moment, and he flung out his hands. "You are the most exasperating woman I ever had the misfortune to meet. You invade my house like the tiny insects of my kitchen. I am busy."

He turned and stalked across the foyer toward his library, where he stashed his War Between the States collection and office equipment. Max moved from his ex-Commie country to the south because of his love of American history and the cheap property taxes. And if collecting the old junk wasn't enough, he also enjoyed giving boring history lessons. I hurried to catch him before he holed himself in his Old South bunker and I lost my chance to make reparations in our mostly civil feud.

I slid through the heavy wooden door as Max turned to close it. His eyes slanted at my entrance, but he continued toward his desk without word of kicking me out. The paneled wood walls of his library were crammed with glass-cased relics of the Old South. The floor held furniture of the manly variety. I took an appreciative whiff of the room's leather and teak aroma and then filled my lungs with a great gulp of the stuff for courage. Ignoring the history, I headed toward the office equipment end of the room.

"You have sugar ants? I can help you. All you need is boric acid and mint jelly."

"Sugar ants," he said. "A good name for such a vexing girl."

I stopped before his desk. "I just need to ask you a few questions."

He collapsed into a leather office chair and grasped the armrests, most likely imagining they were a part of my body he'd like to shake. "You always have a 'few questions.' In my country, people mind their own businesses. Why are the Americans so meddlesome? Always with your talk, talk, talk." He waved a hand at an armchair placed before the desk.

I eased myself into the deep armchair and slid backward. My feet dangled from the edge, and I swung my boots while I thought how to best pacify The Bear. "Wow, this is one comfortable chair. You do know how to pick your furniture. Anyway, did you happen to buy my classical triptych?"

"Another collector bought it before I could," he rubbed his forehead and sighed. "I saw the paintings. Your talent continues."

"What's wrong?"

"Nothing." He leaned forward in his chair and placed a heavy arm on the desk. "Are you finished? I have much work to do."

"Something's wrong with you. I can tell. I know I've gotten you into some hot water with the law, but it's worked out in your favor so far. The town is smitten with your accent and love of poker-themed parties. Water under the bridge, Bear. I'm here for you. Tell me your troubles."

He regarded me with his usual shrewd intensity, but I felt his heart wasn't in it. A melancholic smile passed across his face but instead of pouring out his soul, he picked up his Blackberry to demonstrate his intent of brushing me off. "My troubles are not your concern, Artist. How can I assist you further?"

"Listen, I have a chance for you to assist me, and it would make me feel better if I could do you a good turn."

Max's finger hovered over his Blackberry, but his eyes remained glued to the little screen. "This is new. You have not struck me as one to ask for help."

"Well, in this particular dilemma, I find you might be the only person who can aid me."

"Fascinating." Max set his Blackberry on his desk and eased back in his chair.

Despite my qualms at Max's sudden change in demeanor, I decided to proceed. "I believe you are acquainted with Miss Shawna Branson."

He gave a curt nod.

"Perhaps you did not know Miss Branson hates my guts and would like to stick it to me in a very public way. Like ride-me-out-of-town public way."

Max grunted and motioned for me to continue.

I was getting a Godfather vibe I didn't appreciate, but it was too late to back out. "The paintings which you say you did not purchase are of a sensitive nature to the people of Forks County."

"I would think they would be sensitive to a Mr. Todd McIntosh in particular," said Max. "Perhaps they are a bit provocative, but nothing to cause the censor. You are a classical realist, are you not? A how do you say, throwback, to the Academy Style?"

"Throwback?" I slid forward in my chair. "If I'm a throwback, I would think Halo, Georgia, would be all over my paintings. I may be classical in style, but I can still do edgy."

"This edgy will not sell you paintings in the Forks County."

"Dangit if you aren't right," I sighed and rested my head against the supple leather of the chair back. "When I heard a foreigner bought the paintings, I assumed it was you. I heard you were going to do a show for Shawna Branson, and I kind of thought you might do a show for me as well. Let folks know I'm legitimate and not a pervert." I colored at "pervert" and hoped that word wasn't in his limited English lexicon.

"A foreign buyer?" His eyes flit to mine and he frowned.

"That's what Shawna said. I've asked the gallery to track the buyer down for me, although they might not actually do it. They don't like the artists associating with the buyers unless the gallery gets a cut."

"A public show," he mused, pulling on his full bottom lip. I had a feeling he was weighing the financial benefits. "You have other pieces?"

"Hell, I'd make some up tonight if needed. Pieces aren't a problem. I even have acrylic mockups of that triptych in my closet. Getting Shawna to loosen her restraints on the Real Artists of Forks County Gallery would be the tricky part."

"Venue is nothing," he continued to pull on his lip.

I watched, fascinated by the flexibility.

"There is something you are not telling me. Why does this Shawna Branson have you in such a, how do you say, tizzy that you would come to me for help?"

"You are the only art appreciator in Halo I would trust with this delicate matter," I paused, knowing flattery wouldn't satisfy The Bear. But I hated to admit I had fallen for Shawna's convoluted scheme. "And she thinks I have something of hers. Which I don't. I don't even know what pictures she's talking about."

"Shawna Branson is discrediting you as blackmail. She wants payment in the form of these pictures you say you don't have and know nothing about."

"I guess that sums it up," I chewed my lip for a moment. "I have no chance of finding these pictures if she won't even tell me what they are."

"You are in a bind," he smiled.

That smile gave me the heebies. I don't think I'd ever seen his mouth crack wide enough for teeth.

"You must find these pictures. In the meantime, I will assist you in raising your artistic stature within the community. Which I find both ironic and amusing, considering you've been trying to expose my vices and discredit me."

"I will back down, but you brought that on yourself." I held up my hands. "Now. I've told you my problem, but you still haven't shared yours. Spill."

"Why are you always wondering about the issues which are not of your concern?" He sighed again. "It is no wonder the policeman no longer dates you."

"Hey," I hopped out of my chair. "You don't have to get ugly."

"Your prying nature has caused the man quite a few scares. I merely point out that most men could not handle your type of," he paused, searching his limited English vocabulary, "your type of intensity."

I wasn't sure if intensity was flattering, but I wasn't one to turn down charity compliments. "That may be true of most men, but Deputy Luke Harper has a strong gut. I think it bothers him more that I cramp his style. On the job." And maybe off the job, too. He never did introduce me to his parents as his official girlfriend.

"Now you look the one in need of comfort. Perhaps there is something else I can do for you?" Max rose and circled his desk to stand before me. "How is Todd McIntosh? I miss his friendship."

"I'm trying my best to help Todd," I said, my eyes straying from Max's granite features to my hands. "He's out of work. I told him not to visit you because of his gambling problem. You remind him of poker. I'm sorry. I didn't know y'all would miss your friendship so much."

"He needs a job." Max reached to tuck a strand of hair behind my ear. "Let me see what I can do. I am enjoying this new side of our friendship where you can rely on me, Artist."

I jerked my head up to meet his gaze and untucked my hair. "Last time you gave Todd a job, you used him as a ringer."

"I meant a company job. I know many business men. I also have very profitable, legitimate businesses."

"Most of the business men you know played cards in your basement for exorbitant sums of money. I told Todd to apply at the SipNZip. It's not much, but it'll help him get on his feet. It looks like they're short on employees anyway."

"The SipNZip?" Max shook his head. "Not good idea. No, I find him better job."

"Why?" I noticed his accent became more pronounced. Before I could wring an answer from him, my phone sang a tune from my back pocket. I let it skip to voicemail, but lost my opportunity. Max had recovered his wits and his grammar.

"Trust me, Artist. I will enjoy this new development in our friendship." He smiled, hooked my arm in his, and walked me toward the study door. "Now I must get back to work. You are a distraction. Just like sugar ant. Sweet, but also very annoying."

A moment later I stood on his veranda staring at the door. "Like hell," I muttered. "Sugar ants and I aren't sweet. And I'm only a little annoying."

Mostly I was confused. I had just indebted myself to Max Avtaikin without finding what he wanted in return. I needed his help, but I also needed to find a way to repay him. Quickly.

Before he asked for something I wouldn't want to give.

Six

After running a few errands around Halo, I parked on the street before my house. I gazed at the old bungalow for a long moment, admiring my tropical print cushions on the rocking chairs and ferns hanging from the porch rafters. The paint and pretties could not make up for the sagging foundation, faulty electric, and leaky plumbing. However, I did love this house.

I could not let Shawna Branson run me out of town. Even if it meant entering a bargain with the Bear. Of course, Shawna had mentioned Max also sponsoring a show for her. The Bear worked angles better than a protractor.

With that irritating thought, I readied to hop from the truck, grabbed my phone, and noticed my missed call alert showed an Atlanta area code. An Atlanta call meant opportunity. Or bill collectors.

With another glance to my crowded house, I closed my truck door and hit redial. The tone buzzed twice before a smooth female voice answered with clipped tones. Not a local.

"Rupert Agadzinoff's office," said the voice. "How can I help you?"

I was momentarily stunned. "Who is this?"

"Are you trying to reach Mr. Agadzinoff? Did you need an attorney?"

"I don't think so. I haven't been in an accident."

"He's not an injury lawyer. Immigration law."

"I'm not looking to immigrate," I said. "I'm pretty happy where I am."

The voice cleared her throat. "Were you trying to reach Mr. Agadzinoff or is this a wrong number?"

"Actually he called me, but I didn't know who he was."

"Who are you?"

"Cherry Tucker. I'm an artist. Maybe he had the wrong number."

"Just a moment," the line clicked and my ear filled with a steady stream of Muzak. I sang along with Diana Ross before the line clicked again.

"Miss Cherry Tucker, hello," said the new voice. "I have found you."

Considering the voice was somewhere in metro-Atlanta and I was sitting in my truck in mid-west Georgia, I didn't follow. "Were we playing hide and seek?"

He found that line hilarious, judging by the full thirty seconds of laughter that followed.

"You are one funny lady," he said. "And a very talented artist. I am the owner of your Reconstructing Classicism works."

"That's what the gallery named the show. I call the paintings, *Three Greek Todds*. Or *Greek Todd* for short."

Another string of laughter had me feeling pretty good about my ability to entertain lawyers. Which is always a handy trait to have.

"I'm Rupert Agadzinoff. Call me Rupert. I recently began collecting art. A friend of mine has your work and I became interested. I found your paintings in a gallery, bought them, and here we are."

"Wow. I'm kind of speechless. Which, if you knew me, you would find remarkable."

He laughed again, and I timed it to thirteen seconds. "I want you to come to Atlanta tomorrow to discuss a portrait commission with me."

If I were a cartoonist, I would have drawn dollar signs in place of my pupils. "Tomorrow?"

"I am free tomorrow. Usually Wednesday is my golfing day. Are you busy?"

"Let me check my schedule," I stared at my watch-free arm and counted ten seconds, "I'm free tomorrow. Where do you live?"

"Darling, do you know Buckhead? I can send a car to pick you up."

A car to pick me up? Like a long distance pizza delivery? Buckhead was the ritziest part of Atlanta. Old money ritzy. Home of the governor and folks who tipped with hundred dollar bills. "I don't live in Atlanta. I'll drive up."

"If you insist, my dear. My secretary will email you the directions. This is a preliminary visit. I want to meet you before I decide."

"Of course. I'll bring my portfolio and contract stuff. By the way, who is your friend?" I figured Max, but I had thought Max the buyer. Sometimes my figuring went south.

"A secret." He giggled. "See you tomorrow."

The line clicked off.

Holy crap. I had a possible commission.

I passed the three vehicles lining my drive, stumbled around the junk in my car port, and tumbled through my kitchen door.

"Where is everybody?" I hollered. "I've got great news. Drinks on me tonight at Red's."

At the arched entryway to my living room-studio, I halted. Cody and Todd struggled to hold a large, flat screen between them while Casey stood before the front door, tapping her chin with a fingernail painted Venetian red with bordello fishnet lines. My vintage fainting couch, antique roll top, and easel had been pushed to the middle of the room. A faded, overstuffed sofa featuring a pattern of hunting dogs and pheasants had been shoved against the picture window.

A nerve above my eye began hammering a rapid staccato. "What in the hell are you doing to my studio?"

Casey spun toward me. "What's the great news?"

"Casey, hurry it up. This TV set weighs a ton," said Cody. "What's the occasion, Cherry? Not every day you offer drinks."

"Did you sell a painting, baby?" asked Todd. His muscles barely strained under the set.

"Never mind that for now. How did this TV and sofa come to appear in my studio? Y'all do know I work in this room? Customers come in here."

"Right. All those customers. We've been turning them away all day," said Cody. "If I'm going to live here, I need a decent TV and a better place to sleep."

"Cody, set the flat screen against that wall." Casey pointed to the kitchen-facing wall, currently housing ten by ten inch portraits of friends and family.

"You are messing with my gallery space," I said. "Those paintings are examples for my portrait clients."

"You said yourself you haven't been able to get a portrait customer since you did the painting for the Bransons," said Casey. "Put it there, boys. That wall has a good outlet."

"If I'm going to drill a hole in the wall to splice in the neighbor's cable, we need to use the outside wall," said Cody.

I slapped a hand on the nerve threatening to pop through my skin. "Drill a hole for illegal cable?"

"It's all right, baby," said Todd. "We talked to Mr. Johnson. We're going to split the cable bill and make it cheap for everybody."

"It's still illegal," I said. "That's all I need is the cable cops all over my butt."

"Let us worry about cable cops," said Cody. "And if you do get a customer, we'll just toss a painting in front of the TV."

"Speaking of losing all your customers," Casey paused from shoving a TV stand under my small gallery of oils, "what did Shawna say?"

"Do y'all know anything about some missing pictures?" I explained Shawna's blackmail scheme while I watched Cody and Todd heave the immense flat screen onto the small stand. I refrained from an explanation of basic structural engineering in fear it would lead to more jimmy rigging.

"Sounds like those pictures are worth a lot to Shawna," Cody's brown eyes gleamed beneath his Kobalt Tools cap.

"Don't go getting any ideas, Cody," I said. "If you find any pictures of Shawna, you give them to me so I can get her off my back."

"I'm kind of surprised at you." Todd dropped onto the dead pheasant couch, folded his arms behind his head, and stretched out his long legs. "You're playing defense with Shawna when you're an offensive type of gal."

Casey rolled her eyes. "I think Todd is wondering why you're bothering to look for these pictures in the first place. Knowing Shawna, it's just an excuse to make you look bad. I say you let us deal with Shawna. She's been riding us Tuckers long enough. It's time to make her pay." She cracked her knuckles and gave me a look that would have scared a lesser mortal.

"Good Lord, Casey. That's all Shawna needs is you doing God knows what and adding more fodder to her fire. Let me handle this my own way. I'll look for the pictures, but I think Max's show will do better for my reputation."

"I think you better come up with a Plan B." She flipped her ponytail over her shoulder. "We've got your back."

"Let me think on it." I yawned. The excitement of the commission drained, washed out by the day's events that began at two in the morning.

I dragged down the hallway, threw myself on my bed, and gazed at the painting of Snug the Coonhound hanging above me. Normally that painting made me smile. Now it was a reminder of the kind of local art I had once done and could no longer get commissioned.

Lucky for me, I thought sleepily, rich immigration attorneys found me talented. And funny.

I woke when the bed shifted beneath me. My hand automatically flung over the bedside to reach for my shotgun, but then I remembered I no longer lived alone. I rolled over and stared up at the big, cerulean blue eyes hovering over my head. Cerulean flecked with cyan blue.

"You awake?" Todd asked.

"Get out of here," I yawned. "I need to sleep."

"I need to tell you something. But first, what's your good news? You never told us." He dropped next to me and propped his head on his upraised hand.

"A lawyer from Buckhead bought my paintings and he might want me to do his portrait. I'm meeting him tomorrow."

"That's exciting, baby. You're living your dream."

"Not exactly. Pearl is seriously screwing with my family. I don't get what's going on between her and Grandpa. And I don't understand Shawna," I yawned again and rolled on to my side, facing Todd.

"You never cared what people thought of your art before." Todd reached over me to pull the quilt off the side of the bed and draped it over my body.

I snuggled into the quilt and pillowed my head on my curled arm. "The ladies of Forks County are already steamed at me for shutting down bingo. Now they think I'm corrupting you."

Todd laughed. "That's funny," he paused to smooth my hair. "I'm glad we're talking again."

I frowned. "I'm not talking to you. This is an exception. I'm still mad. You lied to me."

"I didn't lie," he continued to stroke my hair. "I was just protecting my reputation."

"Reputation as the town idiot?" I closed my eyes to better concentrate on his rhythmic hair stroking. The man was a drummer. He did rhythm well.

"You lied to me about playing poker again. You lied to me about helping Max with his illegal gambling consortium. And you lied when you played the ringer in our relationship by acting all innocent and naive, when you knew exactly what you were doing. You helped place the final nail in the coffin of my breakup with Luke and I believe you aren't even sorry about that."

"You can't be that ticked at me." His hands left my hair, trailed to my shoulder, and began to knead. "You're letting me live here."

"It's my Christian duty to help the needy. The same reason I don't kick out Casey and Cody." I rolled on to my front to grant his deft fingers better access to my tight back muscles. "I'm on to you, Todd. You're trying to trick me into a romance, just like you tricked me into marrying you."

He rubbed a particularly hard knot, and I moaned.

"Not going to work," I mumbled. "You're smarter than you act, but you're not that smart."

"I put my application in at the SipNZip," He spoke while his fingers made magic on my back. "And I picked up some stuff for patching your foundation. I'll work on that tomorrow."

"You're trying to woo me with your obedience. Not gonna happen," I licked the drool dribbling from the corner of my open mouth. Dreamy images of SipNZip employees spackling my house danced through my mind.

"I almost forgot the reason I came in here," said Todd. "The Sheriff's Office called."

The SipNZip employees disappeared and I sat up, pulling the quilt around me. "Uncle Will? What does he want? Is he okay?"

"Pretty sure he's fine. Wants you to come down to the station right away. Something about Tyrone somebody," Todd slid off the bed.

"Tyrone Coderre. Maybe they found the hijacker." Excitement pumped adrenaline through my blood and exhaustion fled.

"I don't know for sure, but it sounded serious," said Todd. "I got the feeling something happened to this Tyrone."

"I just saw him this morning," I said. "What could have happened in that short amount of time?"

Seven

"What's going on with Tyrone Coderre?" I asked Uncle Will. "Do you need another composite drawing?"

I had given up my nap to return to the Sheriff's Office, hoping an additional paycheck would accompany news about Tyrone. Tamara, the receptionist, would not give me any hints. She enjoyed watching me sweat. Tamara had a strange sense of humor.

This time I had been escorted to Uncle Will's office. He sat behind his desk, reclining in his creaky chair, his fingers steepled on his belly. The wood paneled walls held various photos and awards. Piled file folders sat in tidy stacks on his desk. A clock ticked above his head, cracking the silence with each pop of the minute hand. His dinner waited in a brown bag, rolled tightly and smelling of barbecue.

I sat on the opposite side of his desk, my sketching bag at the ready.

"Baby doll, I have some bad news." Will leaned forward. The chair sighed at the three hundred pounds of pressure on its joints. "Tyrone's been murdered."

I tried to swallow and realized my mouth was hanging open. "How can that be? I just saw him this morning."

"I know, hon'," Will blew out a long sigh. "If I thought he was in danger, I wouldn't have let him out."

"He seemed happy when I saw him at the SipNZip. What happened to him?"

"Like a fool, he went back to the rest stop to get some wire he had stashed before Deputy Harper picked him up. The hijacker either followed him or had been waiting. If it was the hijacker. Shot him and took off. Looks like semi-automatic handgun wounds, but I'm waiting for a report. Pretty ballsy on both their parts considering it was late this morning. Of course, we're close enough to Atlanta. That rest stop doesn't get much traffic midweek mornings."

"Who found him?"

"Gal who comes to clean the bathrooms. She took the trash to the dumpster in back. She said she didn't know what made her walk farther into the copse of trees behind the rest stop. Found him there."

"I talked to Tyrone at the SipNZip. He told me he was going back to the rest stop." I put a hand to my face. "Oh Lord, what have I done?"

The chair creaked as Will suddenly straightened. "Talk."

"I am so sorry, Uncle Will. I knew Tyrone was planning on recovering that wire. I got distracted and didn't tell Luke." Not only did I withhold information from the police, by withholding it I had gotten Tyrone killed.

Will rubbed the bridge of his nose and didn't respond.

Nauseous and dizzy, I leaned over to rest my head between my knees. "Are you going to arrest me?"

"You were at the SipNZip when Tyrone told you he was going back to the rest stop?" He pulled a legal pad out of a drawer and began writing.

"Yes, sir."

"Anyone else at the SipNZip who might have heard you?"

I left my head resting on my knees and my hands dropped to the floor. "There were a ton of people in there. Lots of commuters. And Luke, of course. He can give you better descriptions."

"Did you tell anyone about your conversation with Tyrone? Obviously, not Deputy Harper."

"Oh crap," I moaned. "I talked to lots of people today."

"I'm listening."

"I can't remember exactly what I said," I sat up and my words ran together as I forgot to breathe. "There was everybody at the Tru-Buy and then Whitney Elbert at the bank. I chatted with a waitress at the Waffle House. Of course, Casey, Cody, and Todd." I chewed a nail and thought.

"Oh wait, I saw Shawna Branson. But I doubt I mentioned the hijack to her. I was too ticked at her for spreading unpleasant rumors about me again." I fell back in my chair and let my boots dangle. "I don't think I told Mr. Max when I dropped by for a visit."

Will double blinked. "Did you sleep yet, hon'?"

"About ten minutes before Todd woke me up to tell me you called. And I came straight here."

Will glanced at his watch. "All that today?"

"I didn't have much going on work wise."

"What exactly did you chat about?"

"A lot of them kept their comments directed toward a certain set of paintings I did." I probably turned three shades of brilliant pink. "If I talked about something else, I asked them if they had heard about the hijacking. You know, to see if they had any information that would help your investigation."

"I see. Did you mention Tyrone witnessing the hijack? Or you sketching the composite?"

"I know I did to my family. To everyone else? I don't rightly remember." I stared at the ceiling and blinked my eyes, causing a pattern of dots to brighten and scatter in my vision. "I don't think I did. I felt safe talking about the hijacking. Most folks would know about it quick enough."

I lowered my head and let my vision clear to study Will's face. "Uncle Will, I'm sorry."

"Sugar, I know you can't keep your mouth shut. It's the risk I took when I brought you in to do the composite. You're just like everyone else in the county, always running their mouths. While you were still at the Waffle House, I fielded calls from the local papers. Didn't tell them about Coderre, of course."

I nodded and chewed a hangnail.

"If word leaked about Tyrone's composite and somehow got back to the hijackers, it would mean the hijackers had a connection to somebody in this county. It's not impossible, but doesn't make a lot of sense. We would see more hijackings than just this odd duck."

Will stood and strode around the desk to pat me on the head. "Don't you worry, honey. You go on home. Leave me to my dinner and a mess of paperwork that needs doing."

"Either way, I need to pay my respects to Tyrone's family. I owe them that." I waited while Will opened his door and ushered me into the hall.

"I'll find out if there's a funeral and call you with the details."

The door to the Junior Officer's room swung open. Luke strode out and seeing us, stopped. "Good evening, Sheriff. What's Cherry doing here?"

"Just come to chat with me a minute," said Will. "I thought you were off duty."

"Officially," Luke cracked a thin smile. "Just checking on a thing or two."

"See that this one gets home safely." Will gave me a small shove that sent me stumbling in Luke's direction. "Casey and Cody can keep an eye on you, Cherry. Why don't y'all stay home tonight. You need to catch up on sleep."

"What's going on, sir?" Luke hooked his hands on his belt.

"I told Cherry about Coderre. She's a might upset," said Will. "She wants to visit his family. I told her I'd call her when I knew the funeral arrangements."

Luke moved his gaze off Will to settle on me. "Visit the Coderres?"

"Not tonight," I said. "And I don't need an escort home either. My truck is full of gas and working fine, all things considered. I've got a big appointment up in Atlanta tomorrow, so I'll just scoot."

"What appointment?" said Luke.

"Some hotshot lawyer bought my recent classical-styled paintings and wants me to come up to Buckhead to meet him for a possible portrait commission."

"Good for you, honey," said Will.

"Guess this is the start of something big for you," said Luke.

"Maybe. I'll let y'all know how it works out." I felt too distraught over Tyrone to accomplish any horn tooting. I trudged to the end of the hall and waited for Luke to unlock the door.

In the parking lot, I climbed into my Datsun and cut on the motor. I heard the growl of another truck, a black Ford Raptor, one I had once snuggled in with the gray eyed deputy driving, and felt the stinging barbs of heartache. Although Luke refused to be the subject of my paintings, I know he'd be proud of me. In the past, I had imagined celebrating a big commission with him. However, it didn't do me any good to wish things had turned out differently. We both carried baggage that didn't fit through one another's doors.

My record with men was about as good as my mouth's ability to stay out of trouble. Poor Tyrone. Lost his life through the one time I held my tongue.

I backed out of my parking space and left the Forks County Law Enforcement Center, tailed by the black pickup. Twenty-five minutes later, I had reached my home and parked on the street. The Raptor pulled even to my door. I stepped out of the truck, and Luke rolled down his window.

"Go get some sleep," he said. "Be careful driving to Atlanta tomorrow."

"I will." I tried on a smile. "You worry too much."

"Well, you don't worry enough." He glanced at the house. "You got a party going on up there? Every light is blazing."

"My home has become something akin to a frat house. There's a couch and a big TV in my living room."

"Shocking," Luke smirked. "A couch and TV in your living room. How many people are living there now?"

"I'm not sure if Cody is permanent or just for the time being, so four," I stopped, realizing where this conversation headed. "Guess I'll go in. You didn't need to follow me home, but thanks."

"Four in two bedrooms," said Luke. "How cozy."

Too cozy. "Night," I waved and inched past his door.

"Listen. Don't go to the Coderres' alone. The Sheriff said he'd contact you with the funeral info, but I know you."

"I knew Tyrone was going back to get his wire, Luke." Guilt caused my eyes to smart, and I rubbed them before they did something stupid like water. "I don't know why I didn't tell you. I could have prevented his death."

Luke cut off his engine and slid out of the truck. As he circled around his bed, I took a few steps back toward the safety of my vehicle. Not that I was afraid he'd be angry. In my anguish, I feared my body would involuntarily bend toward his arms.

Luke noticed my retreat and stopped a few paces away.

"I wish you had told me," he held out a hand, caught himself, and laid his palm on my truck. "The fact is we screwed up, too. Actually, I screwed up."

"What do you mean?"

"I was too focused on questioning witnesses and talking to the State Patrol, when I should have kept a tail on Coderre. It doesn't take a mind reader to know he'd go back to find his wire."

I nodded and focused on the large hand resting on my truck.

"If Coderre wasn't stealing copper in the first place, he wouldn't have returned to the scene of the crime." Luke pulled his hand off the truck, shook off the flaking paint, and reached to pat my shoulder. "You take everything too personally."

"A man died. That's pretty personal."

Luke stared at the ground, kicked a rock, and looked up. "If you want to visit the Coderres, I will take you. No strings."

"Really?" My hands inadvertently reached for Luke's and squeezed. When it came to police business, Luke normally groused about my involvement. Or threatened to serve me with obstruction. This offer touched me. And was actually very helpful. To be honest, I didn't particularly look forward to visiting the family of a copper thief who had been murdered due to my delinquent admission of his whereabouts.

"You're going to Atlanta tomorrow morning." He pulled his hands from my squeeze. "What about tomorrow evening? I can pick you up when I get off work."

"I should be home from Atlanta by then," I shoved my hands in my pockets. "Why the sudden interest in helping me?"

"Kill two birds, that sort of thing." He shrugged and slapped my truck, causing more paint to peel. "Speaking of that, are you still fixing to go to the Gearjammer?"

I had forgotten the Gearjammer in the flurry over Shawna, my new patron, and Tyrone's dead body. "I suppose so. I told Dona I would."

"I'll pick you up at eight. Thursday, right? I want to talk to some of the truckers and they'll be more inclined to chat there." He dodged my disagreement by striding around his truck. Without a goodbye, he revved his engine, shifted into drive, and took off.

I stood in the road with my hands on my hips, watching his taillights fishtail down Loblolly Avenue.

The man was an enigma wrapped in hotness. Unfortunately, the hotness was no longer mine.

EIGHT

I stalked up the rise to my bungalow. Luke had been correct about a party in my house. Through the picture window, I could see a baseball game on the big television.

Taking a deep breath, I opened the front door. My brother's friends glanced over, yelled greetings at my entrance, and turned their eyes back to the game. I waded through the passel of bodies, gritting my teeth at the beer cans cluttering my desk and antique table I used when painting. In the kitchen, more men sat around my table playing cards.

My brother was nowhere to be seen.

Todd stood at the stove stirring a pot of something with the delectable aroma of spices and ground meat. "Hey, baby," he said. "You want some chili?"

"What's going on here?" I said. "I'm in no mood for a party."

"It's not a party. Cody invited some guys over to watch the Braves. I'm making chili for our dinner."

My stomach gurgled, causing the men at the table to lay down their cards and tip their chairs back to glance in my direction. I waved a hand at them to get back to their cards.

"Looks like a party to me. Are you in on that poker game, by the way?"

Todd dropped the spoon into the pot, then jerked his hand up after trying to reach into the boiling mess to grab it. "Of course not, baby. I told you I quit."

"You have a gambling problem." I eyed the empty chair at the table and Todd's fingers playing a tempo on his cargo shorts. I glanced back at the men sitting around my kitchen table. "Did y'all hear about Todd's amateur poker championship last year? Got him a free ride to Vegas."

Two faces glared sullenly at Todd.

I smiled. "Enjoy your chili and your game, fellows."

"That was when me and Cherry got hitched," said Todd, with a quick grin for the table. He slung an arm around my neck and kissed the side of my head. "We had a beautiful wedding with Elvis as our minister. What I can remember of it anyway. That night was a blur."

"Touché," I muttered and shoved off his arm. "That chili smells good. I wish I felt like eating."

"You don't feel like eating?" Todd's snapped shut his dropped jaw. "What happened at the Sheriff's Office?"

"Uncle Will told me someone murdered Tyrone, the guy who gave me the description for the composite. Fact is, I knew Tyrone was returning to the scene of the crime, and I didn't report it to the Sheriff's Department. I am responsible for his death."

Todd took my hand and pulled me to the corner of the kitchen. "Baby, I'm so sorry. If they lock you up, I'll visit you in prison."

"Not that responsible. But I feel horrible about it. Luke offered to take me to visit Tyrone's family tomorrow."

"Where did it happen?" Todd studied the fret lining my face, captured my other hand, and drew me closer.

"The interstate rest stop outside Line Creek." While I focused on repeating the details of the hijacking and Tyrone's death, I talked my brain out of comparing the comfort of Todd's warm grasp with Luke's earlier quick but capable squeeze. I pulled my hands from Todd's to finish the story.

"Damn. So, the hijacker must have seen Tyrone? Why didn't he do anything when Tyrone saw him?"

I shrugged. "Dunno. Uncle Will said maybe he didn't have enough time."

"I guess you probably want to check that out."

"What do you mean? Go to the rest stop?" I dropped my gaze to my boots.

"Baby, I know you. You'll be stewing about this all night, wondering how this happened to Tyrone. You are a curious type of person. You're fixing to drive out there, just to see for yourself, aren't you?"

"I am curious. But I thought it might seem morbid."

Todd pulled me into his body for a long hug. "I don't care what the town thinks. You're a good woman, caring about folks like murdered copper thieves. Let me take you to the rest stop. I love doing stuff like that with you."

I shoved off his chest. "Don't go getting any ideas. I'm still not talking to you. That also means no hugs."

"Sure, baby," Todd grinned. "Whatever you say."

Todd parked his little, red hatchback before the low pitched building holding Georgia travel brochures, soda machines, and bathrooms. We hopped out of the Civic and studied the empty car park area. The evening air had cooled. I shivered in my beaded flag t-shirt, but the goose bumps rose from the lonely setting, not the chill. We could hear the whine of motors zipping down the interstate toward Atlanta or Alabama. Behind the building, the low rumble of a parked diesel truck hummed.

I looked at Todd. "Guess we better head around back. That's where Tyrone would have seen the hijack. Maybe there's still yellow tape marking off the areas. The police would have already scoured for evidence in both crimes, so there won't be much to see."

We followed the sidewalk around the back of the building. A lone Georgia State Patrol vehicle had parked on the edge of the lot. Under the yellow glow of a streetlamp, one semi pulling a long trailer rested near the woods. The GSP car door opened and a tall figure in full uniform stepped out of the vehicle.

"Rest stop closes at ten," he said. "On your way to Atlanta?"

"No, just stretching our legs," I called. "Going to sit at one of these picnic tables for a minute."

"Don't take too long. Stay away from the taped off areas." The officer left his door open and leaned against the car, folding his arms. "I can see y'all from here."

"Yes, sir," said Todd.

We crossed the lot, heading toward the wooded picnic area behind the truck parking. With the dim light from the parking lot lights, we could spy the yellow tape looped around a stand of spindly pines in the distance. I stopped at the edge of the blacktop. My shoulders drooped. Todd laid a gentle hand on my neck.

"Tyrone didn't get very far into the woods," I said. "That perp has balls of steel. If anyone drove up, they would have witnessed the murder."

"I don't get why they didn't kill Tyrone right away," said Todd. "Were there any other trucks parked back here during the hijack?"

"Good question. My guess would be no, unless the drivers slept pretty hard. They would have heard gun fire."

"Maybe the hijacker saw Tyrone but thought it was too late to do anything about him," said Todd.

"If I had just shot someone in cold blood and then saw a witness, I would not let that witness get away."

Todd pulled his hand off my shoulder.

"They must have heard about it after the fact," I explained. "Or followed Tyrone."

"Do you think they know about you?" said Todd. "That you drew a picture of the killer?"

A breeze rattled the leaves on a sweetgum tree and I shivered. "Why would that matter?" My pitch drew high and loud, and I lowered my voice. "As far as anyone knows, that composite was drawn by a cop. I didn't sign the sketch." Did I? I drew my hands in to clutch my arms as I tried to remember if I had. Signing pieces had become a habit from school. Why would I sign a sketch, though?

A breeze carried the sound of someone heavy thrashing through a pile of leaves. I jumped, and Todd grabbed my arm. We backed onto the blacktop, and I glanced over my shoulder to check on the State Patrol officer. A moment later, a giant man and a small jumble of fur popped out of the woods.

"Hey there," the giant called. The man's t-shirt strained to hold his girth, and I caught belly peekage. His toes hung over his flip flops. The fur yapped and strained at the leash, eager to inspect us.

"Hey yourself. Are you the driver of that rig?" I relaxed my stance and Todd dropped his hand. I bent over to let the giant hamster smell my hands. "You're a cute, little thing."

"She's Princess Yapadoodle. I'm Joe, and yep, that's my Bulldog. My Mack truck. Hauling wine through the Bible belt." He grinned. "Y'all stopping through to the Big A? Sorry if I scared you. Princess needed to tee-tee."

"Actually we're local," I said. "I'm Cherry and this here is Todd. Did you know a truck was hijacked here last night?"

Joe's jowls brushed his neck as he nodded. "That news spreads fast. Heard about it at the Flying J outside Birmingham."

"What are folks saying?"

"Most are shocked. I knew the driver from a mutual acquaintance. Got a wife and kids in Chattanooga. You know he wasn't even supposed to be driving? Took the shift when the original driver got tossed in the can for drunk driving. I believe he's from these parts."

"That's bad luck," said Todd. "Pick up an extra shift and get jacked."

Princess barked and turned three circles. Joe glanced down at the mop of fur. "Princess's got to go tooty. She didn't finish her business."

"Be safe, Joe," I said.

"Yes, ma'am," Joe saluted me. "Y'all have a nice night." He pulled Princess back toward the woods.

I glanced at the patrolman, still leaning against his vehicle and watching us. "I'm glad he's there for Joe's sake."

Todd watched the giant clomp through the trees. "I don't think many people would bother Joe. He could crush a person with his thumb."

"I don't think a thumb can crush a handgun." I scowled. "That semi-automatic sure did a number on poor Tyrone. Where was the state patrol when he was getting shot?"

NINE

The next morning, the drive to Atlanta took an hour. And given the confusing lack of signage accompanied with the winding streets of residential Buckhead, finding the home of my newest patron, Rupert Agadzinoff, took even longer.

The trip gave me time to ponder my predicaments including Shawna's missing pictures, the Bear's dubious offer of help, and the hijacking. The sharp barb of guilt over Tyrone Coderre's murder had caught and dug into my conscience. I hoped the police would have some news for the Coderres before my visit with Luke that night. I didn't look forward to admitting I could have prevented Tyrone's death and didn't expect the Coderres to take that fact too kindly.

The tree-lined drive to Mr. Agadzinoff's address curved up a steep hill graced with a palatial antebellum home. My Datsun chugged up the drive, while I squished my mouth to the side and studied the Tara knock-off. Max's house was bigger, but Agadzinoff would have paid more for the zip code. What was it with these Ruskies and their plantation fantasies?

I parked in the donut drive and slid out of the Datsun with my portfolio case. While I waited on the wide, brick stoop, I admired the ornamentals and the decorative metal bracketing on the tall, graceful windows on the first floor. Not the usual plantation decor, but Agadzinoff did live in the city, and I supposed lawyers might need to protect themselves from irritable clients.

After a few minutes, my ding-dong was answered by a woman dressed in a study of gray chromatics starting at her feet with expensive looking charcoal pumps and gradually lightening to her smoke gray blouse. Her white-gold hair had been tightened into a bun, the strands refused release even with their good behavior.

"May I help you?" Her sharp, blue eyes combed over my contract outfit. Boots and an orange tank dress I had decorated with day-glow puff paint. An oversized neon paintbrush, of course. My wispy, blond hair never had a day of good behavior in my life. Luckily, my dress distracted her attention from my hair.

"I'm Cherry Tucker, the portrait artist, come to see Mr. Agadzinoff." I held out a hand she shook with an alarmingly strong grip. I pulled my hand away and slipped it behind my back to wiggle the blood back into my digits.

"Come," she said and held the door open wide.

I entered into a parquet foyer with a blend of wood forming a giant script A in the middle of the floor. Whereas Max's foyer glittered with sunlight and marble, Agadzinoff's was a study of mahogany and teak.

I slid my portfolio case off my back and into my hand, afraid a sudden swing would knock over the fancy vases filled with professional arrangements.

A wide staircase of more polished wood anchored one end of the foyer. On the staircase landing, an older, balding man with a heavy, dark mustache paused his descent to wave at me. For his casual Wednesday, he wore khakis and a polo with an oversized insignia on his left breast. Perhaps so the nearsighted could easily calculate the cost of his wardrobe.

"Miss Cherry Tucker," he called. "I am Rupert Agadzinoff. Please call me Rupert."

"Hey Rupert," I slipped past Miss Monochrome to the staircase. "Nice to meet you. Beautiful digs you've got here."

"Thank you." Rupert stopped on the last stair, making me look up to eyeball him. His brown eyes lighted on my puffy paintbrush. "Ha, ha. You with the sense of humor."

As I did not intend my contract dress to be humorous, I ignored my hurt feelings and braved my best customer service smile. "I brought my portfolio."

"First, let me show you my recent acquisition." He snapped his fingers. "Miss David."

At the snap, Miss David whipped her chromatic self to a set of gilded French doors to the left side of the foyer. She opened the door and held it with her back. I followed, careful with my portfolio case, and wondered how much Miss David was paid to answer to snaps.

As I reached the entrance, our blue eyes met. No friendly, woman-to-woman, "hey, my boss may snap at me, but you'll do fine" passed between us. In fact, her look said, "I can disembowel you with a bobby pin." I fought off a shiver and scooted through the door, then stumble-halted in the entrance.

I had thought no one could surpass Max Avtaikin's love for red and gold accents, but I was sincerely mistaken. This sitting room's decorator had harbored murderous intent by way of stroke-inducing design and color choice.

The blood red walls sported gold molding of every kind, from rosettes to panel molding, chair rails to crown. Delicate Louis XIV furniture in more gilt and red sat in clusters on a richly vibrant oriental rug. Several gold chandeliers and electric candelabras as well as gilt angels and cupids completed the look. A Victorian-Baroque decorating mashup.

My classical triptych had been hung on the wall directly opposite the tall southern exposure windows, shedding angled light over the three paintings.

"You put my *Greek Todds* in here?" The words left my mouth before I could soften them. "I mean, that sunlight is going to fade those paintings. You've hung the bare canvas. You need to put them under glass to preserve them."

I glanced around the room again and received a Tilt-A-Whirl feeling for my effort. My poor *Greek Todds*. This was the problem of visiting the resting place of your creative ingenuity. Sometimes it was better not to know. "I'm sure you've got some ornate gold frames laying around this house somewhere. Stick the paintings in those and they'll match the rest of the decor."

"I see," said Rupert, striding into the room. His white polo glowed amongst the violent reds. "Miss David, take care of this problem."

Miss David's thick lashes flashed in compliance and she exited the room on long, nimble legs. A cool draft followed, more evidence of her frigid personality.

"Of course, I will frame these, darling." Rupert shoved his hands in his pockets, rolling back on the balls of his feet while he studied the paintings. "I don't know much about art, I am sorry to say."

I nodded then blinked, my eyes still dilating from the insanely colored room. "So your portrait? You're thinking of putting it in here?"

"Actually, I think I will hang the portrait in my office. Or my dining room. Which do you think is better?"

"Are they decorated like this room?"

"The dining room. Not my office."

"Office." At his questioning glance, I backpedaled. "I'll style the painting to complement its surroundings. And I'm getting an office vibe from you."

"I see."

I could not imagine eating in a room that looked like a Stephen King set, much less painting in it. "Let's see your office."

We left the red room, crossed the foyer, and traipsed down a hall. The heavy wooden door swung open, I stepped aside and stifled a maniacal giggle. "Gold paneling with brass trim. This is a first for me."

"Thank you. Please sit down, my dear." He waved me toward a hunter green chair before the gold-paneled desk.

I sat and brought my portfolio case to my lap to duck behind. I needed the case to get my face sorted out before Rupert sat opposite behind his desk.

"So, darling," he sank onto the leather chair and spread his hands on his desk. "You're a professional artist."

"Yes, sir," I said, sliding my portfolio case to the floor. "I studied at Savannah College of Art and Design. I specialize in portraits, but I can swing a variety of genres."

Unzipping my case, I pulled out a binder of photos taken of my works. I laid the folder on his desk and Rupert began flipping through the clear plastic pages. He stopped on the portrait of Dustin Branson and looked up.

"I have seen this one." He tapped on the photo, while studying me with shrewd, brown eyes.

"*Dustin* was in an emerging artists gallery show in Virginia Highlands last spring."

"Another gallery show? I am impressed. But I have seen the painting in the owner's home, my dear. Perhaps you know him? Maksim Avtaikin?"

"We're acquainted."

Rupert smirked. "I think you are more than acquainted, darling. He lives in your very small town. I attended a party at his home and he spoke very well of you."

I straightened in my chair. "Did he now?" This was news to me. Perhaps Max could save my reputation.

"Maksim enjoys speaking of his pet interests. He's always had interesting hobbies, even back in the old country." Rupert chuckled and swirled his finger over the painting's plastic sleeve. "He does go on."

"That he does," I said, thinking of the history lessons I'd endured.

"I knew he was looking at collecting more of your works. So I bought your paintings just to give him a kick in his pants." Rupert leaned back and laughed until tears ran in his eyes. "It is if I can steal you away from Maksim."

"It's not like Mr. Max owns me. He just owns one of my paintings." I smiled politely and wondered if Rupert wasn't just a little bit nuts.

"Now," Rupert's loud pronouncement made me jump. "Let us talk about the portrait, my dear. I am thinking of wearing a suit and standing by a Christmas tree."

"Christmas tree? We've got three and half shopping months left."

He barked laughter. "The Christmas tree shows my love for the American tradition, very important in my business, and also shows my reputation as a nice guy. Nice guys like Christmas trees. The suit because I am a business man. Although I had thought my football jersey would be fun."

"How about dressing like Santa?" I kidded. "Kill two birds with one stone?"

He whooped and slapped his legs, giving me the impression I had a chance of success in stand-up comedy.

Rupert was more than a little bit nuts. But it didn't seem to hamper his ability to make money. I could work with nuts.

"If that's what you want, I can paint a Christmas tree. Did you have other family members you wanted in the portrait?"

He rubbed his chin. "I think not. This is for my clients to see. Perhaps I'll do a family portrait as well, if this painting is a success."

My wallet snapped to attention. "Sure, whatever you want."

"Leave your contract with me. I am a very busy man, so you'll have to be available when I can spare the time."

"I'm very fast. The only thing that will slow me down is the time it takes for the oil to dry between coats."

"I am in no rush, but I do expect the people I hire to oblige me." He jumped from his chair and wandered to a gold paneled credenza lined in brass and covered with crystal bottles and glasses. "Let's have a toast."

"Sounds good," I left the portfolio and joined him.

He handed me a small glass and opened a panel, revealing a wine fridge. He yanked out an oddly shaped bottle, spun off the cap, and filled my glass. Topping his own glass, he held it up and clinked the crystal against mine. "*Za zdarou'e.*"

"Bottoms up."

We tossed back the vodka shooters. I gasped at the pleasant, delicate flavor. I had expected something harder to digest.

"This vodka is made from the best Russian wheat. They only make it when the wheat has a perfect harvest," Rupert refilled my glass. "It's good, no?"

"The last time I had a vodka shooter, someone lit it on fire," I said. "This stuff is amazing."

"Drink," said Rupert. "To art."

"To art." I threw back another glass and smacked my lips. "It tastes like biscuits."

I timed Rupert's laugh to thirty-five seconds. He rang a bell and minutes later, Miss David strode in carrying a silver tray. After she scooped caviar on wafers with a mother-of-pearl spoon, Rupert offered her a glass of vodka. Feeling warm and happy, I nibbled at the fish eggs for politeness sake.

Rupert snapped his fingers. Miss David disappeared with the tray, then reappeared, and showed me to a town car. I opened my mouth to protest a chauffeured trip back to Halo, but then thought better. A couple of vodka shots and driving in Atlanta traffic were not a good mix. I climbed into the town car.

"Darling, you should tell Max Avtaikin about our friendship." Rupert leaned into the backseat and patted my knee. "I will enjoy you rubbing it in. Tell him I will have more Cherry Tucker paintings than him."

"Sure," I said, although I had no plans to get involved in an inside joke between friends. However, next time I saw Max, I wanted to get the inside scoop on nutty Rupert.

Rupert laughed, wiggled his fingers in a goodbye, and closed the back door.

I settled into the roomy, leather seat for the drive and watched the mansion disappear behind the trees. Getting used to the lifestyles of the rich and lawyerly might be a little too easy. However, after a day in Atlanta, I already missed Halo.

Even though the hijacking and murder put us too close to Atlanta for comfort.

TEN

The Coderre clan lived in Sweetgum, an incorporated shantytown south of Halo. During the great years of locomotive travel, Sweetgum had been passed over as a whistle-stop for Halo. When the interstate came through, once again Sweetgum had been shunned for Line Creek.

When meth labs came in vogue, Sweetgum was all in. Of course, Sweetgum folks believed in diversifying their portfolios. Plenty of pot heads, alcoholics, and itinerant farmers found Sweetgum a good home base as well.

Again, I felt relieved Luke had offered to take me on this visit. If I had dragged my best friend Leah to the Sweetgum Estates, her mother would have had a conniption, then hunted me down in her crazed state to murder me.

The Coderres occupied a double wide in the back of the small trailer park. Considering all of the trailers were made of corrugated metal and tar paper, propped on cement blocks, and circled with chain link fences of dubious integrity, I felt the term "park" was used loosely. As many of the trailers had pit bulls snarling and barking at the edge of said chain link fences, "dog park" might have been a better term.

"I bet some of these are fighting dogs," I said, eyeballing the scene from the seat of Luke's Raptor. He had parked near the Coderre driveway, and we found ourselves procrastinating the actual departure from the vehicle.

"Probably," said Luke grimly. "They need the dogs to protect their homes, though. You could punch your fist through the walls of these trailers."

"To steal what?"

Luke raised his brows. "Do you even have to ask? You think they smoke all the meth they cook?"

"Too bad we couldn't take the Datsun. I'd hate to see something happen to your fine truck while we're talking to the Coderres."

"These folks aren't known for carjacking. Although I wouldn't put it past anyone here. Where is your Datsun, by the way?"

"In Buckhead," I said. "With the rich lawyer."

"I knew you shouldn't have driven that scrapheap all the way to Atlanta."

"That scrapheap is fine. I was the one who couldn't drive home."

Luke cut off the ignition and turned to face me. "Your art buyer got you drunk? In the middle of the day? At his house?"

"Not exactly drunk. We were celebrating our contract. He's a very jovial kind of guy."

Luke set his lips into a line of disapproval. Before he could settle on a nagging spree, I picked up the casserole I had convinced Casey to toss together and popped open his truck door. "Let's get going."

I didn't wait for Luke, but strode to the trailer's door and knocked. A moment later, the door inched open and a brown eye peeped at me.

"Are you one of those church women looking to help the immigrants? They live on the other side of the park," said the voice belonging to the eye.

"No, ma'am," I said. "I'm here to express my condolences about Tyrone and bring you some food."

The door swung wide and a tiny, shriveled woman lugging an oxygen tank squinted up at me. "You knew Tyrone?"

"Briefly," I said. "I met him the morning he passed."

Luke appeared behind me and placed a hand on my shoulder. "Ma'am. I'm sorry about Tyrone."

A pudgy boy waddled to the door and looked us over. "What kind of casserole is that? Mac and cheese?"

"Chicken and rice, I believe." I clung to the casserole, fearing the boy's ability to share food with the shrunken woman.

"Are you Tyrone's mother?" asked Luke.

"Grandmother," she wheezed. "This is my great-grandson, Jerell. My name is Gladys."

"Mrs. Coderre, ma'am, could we come in and visit with you?" I asked. "I feel real bad about Tyrone's passing."

The elderly woman poked her head out to see around Luke and I. I followed her look. Doors to trailers had opened and people in various stages of undress stood on their stoops, craning their necks at us. She waved us inside and shut the door. "Nosy good-for-nothin's."

"Can I put this in your fridge?" I asked.

At her nod, I walked around a table heaped with newspapers and into the kitchen. The tiny galley had a full size fridge newer than mine, but old by most people's standards. Inside the fridge, I pawed aside a jumble of condiments to make room for the casserole. The tiny kitchen had a sink of unwashed dishes and a layer of grime covering the counter.

"Ma'am," I called, peering through the pass through. Luke sat on the edge of a couch across from Miss Gladys and Jerell. I could tell Luke didn't like the closed doors down the small hallway past the kitchen. He looked like a Pointer listening for the rustle of wings. "You get any help around here? I couldn't help but notice you were a little laid up with the oxygen tank."

She yanked the breathing apparatus from her nose. "I have the emphysema. You'd think they'd take better care of me."

I didn't know to whom she referred, but I agreed with her. "Let me clean up in here a bit. And then I'll come out and we'll talk. You got some tea or something you want me to make?"

"We got Kool-Aid," said Jerell.

"That'll work."

"It ain't real Kool-Aid, though." He left his great-grandmother to accompany me in the kitchen. "It's dollar store Kool-Aid."

"Gets the job done, doesn't it?" I patted Jerell on his frizzy head. "Looks like you enjoy yourself a lot of Kool-Aid. How about milk? You drinking any milk?"

"Kool-Aid tastes better. I can make it."

I set to washing dishes and wiping down the counter while Jerell mixed up the fake Kool-Aid. He poured four glasses of red liquid sugar and placed the pitcher in the fridge. We carried the glasses to the living room and set them on a coffee table heaped with tabloids and video game boxes.

I sipped the lukewarm red syrup and hid my grimace. "Good job, Jerell. Nothing like a glass of juice to make my afternoon sweet."

He beamed and slipped back on the couch, resting his glass on his round belly.

"So how'd you two know Tyrone?" asked Miss Gladys. "Did you hear how he died? I always figured he'd fall off a pole, not get shot."

Luke and I exchanged a look.

"I'm actually a sheriff's deputy, ma'am," said Luke. "I found Tyrone at a crime scene and brought him in for questioning."

"Stealing copper?" she asked.

"Yes and no," said Luke "He witnessed a crime and we needed his statement. Tyrone was very helpful."

"I drew his description of the perp," I said. "Tyrone seemed real nice."

"He was a cheerful boy, but a hell-raiser just the same."

"Daddy Tyrone bought me all these video games," said Jerell. "And my Nintendo DS."

"Did you see Tyrone on the day of his murder, ma'am?" asked Luke. "We talked to his girlfriend, Destiny."

"That girl?" said Miss Gladys. "Don't listen to her. She'd just as soon as lie than look at you."

"Destiny's having a baby," said Jerell. "But she's not tweaking no more until the baby comes. That's what Daddy Tyrone said."

Mrs. Coderre snorted, then fell into a hacking spell. She shoved her breathing tubes back in her nose and collapsed against the faded couch. I hopped up to sit next to the woman and held her hand until the coughing finished. The veins on her hands felt like granite ridges beneath her papery skin.

"Do you know who killed Tyrone?" she rasped. "I don't get much for Social Security. Tyrone helped me out, God bless him. I'm hoping I can sue the killer."

I patted her hand. "We'll find out who did this."

"The Sheriff's Office will find the perp," corrected Luke with a hard glance at me. "We're on top of it."

"I saw Daddy Tyrone yesterday," said Jerell. "Before he was killed, I mean."

"You're lying," said Miss Gladys, "You was in school."

Jerell's plump cheeks reddened. "Oh, yeah. I was in school."

"You was in school, wasn't you?" she said and smacked Jerell. The blow glanced off his chin. Her thin, leathery hand wouldn't have left an impression on a gnat, but Jerell's cheeks darkened.

His eyes dropped to his shoes. "Yes, ma'am."

"Lord, all I need is another delinquent. I am too old for this."

I patted Miss Gladys's hand. "I'm sure the boy was in school. Do you have a bedroom, Jerell? Maybe you want to show Mr. Luke where you play video games? If you did see your daddy, I'm sure Mr. Luke would love to hear about it. You might help catch a bad guy."

Luke nodded and stood. "You like to play football?"

"I like to kill zombies better," Jerell cast Luke a dark glance. "You ain't going to light up in my room are you?"

"No, son," said Luke. "I don't do that. How about you show me how good you are at killing zombies and we can talk about your daddy. Miss Cherry will talk to your great-grandma."

Jerell flicked a glance at Miss Gladys and nodded. He pushed off the couch and wobbled toward the back of the trailer with Luke following. Before reaching one of the plywood doors, he stopped and studied Luke. "You ain't gonna eat my candy stash are you?"

"Nope," said Luke. "Don't want to ruin my dinner."

Jerell's face scrunched in surprise. Evidently, "ruin my dinner" was not in Jerell's vocabulary bank. They disappeared through his bedroom door.

Miss Gladys's breathing grew more labored.

I rubbed her hand between mine. "What are you going to do with Jerell?"

"I don't know. The Family Service people's been here before. Tyrone was in County Jail for a spell. I'll try to keep Jerell with me, but I don't know how much longer I have on this earth."

"Don't say that," I blinked away a tear. "Do you have other family who can take him? What about his mother?"

"She's gone. And the rest of them are down the road," she said. "They's so high most of the time, I don't let Jerell visit no more."

She fell forward, and I pulled her into my body, absorbing the shaking and wheezing. Miss Gladys lifted her head. Tears brimmed in her eyes. "Tyrone was a sweet boy. But he was so stupid. How could he leave us like this? What am I going to do with his son?"

"I don't know ma'am," My eyes grew hot. "Let me come by from time to time. Are you having a funeral? You want some help with that?"

She shook her head. "Can't afford a funeral. There's a pine box for him. That's all he gets."

"Do you have a place to bury him at least? I know some church folks. I'll get you a funeral. And there's Victim's Assistance. Maybe they can help."

"They ain't going to release the body for a while. They said the Medical Examiner's got to check him out."

"I'll make some calls for you. We'll get you a funeral. And I'll make sure we find Tyrone's killer."

eLeVeN

As there was no chicken and rice casserole waiting for me at home and I didn't want to keep my distress over the Coderres to myself, I had Luke drop me off at Red's County Line Tap.

Red provided a one-stop shopping experience to meet all my needs in nourishment and entertainment. All within stumbling distance to my home. The old wooden bar top made a good confessional, and Red took his bartender role seriously. He not only listened, but dispensed advice and medicinal refreshment in the form of beer.

I liked the beer better than the advice most nights.

My sister glanced at my entrance, tossed a basket of fried shrimp on a family's table, and scurried to my side.

She flipped her pony tail off her shoulder and wiped her hands on her apron before hugging me. She had toned down her usual waitressing gear for the Wednesday night crowd. Although they didn't leave much to the imagination, her clothes covered her flesh. For the most part.

"How'd it go?" she said.

I shook my head. "It's not good. Tyrone's family is just pitiful. His son, Jerell, doesn't have a mother or a father now. His great-grandma is raising him and she's a cough away from keeling over."

"Damn," said Casey. "That's bad news. Poor kid. He'll end up in the system."

I bit my lip.

"You can't adopt a kid," said Casey. "We've got no place to store him. And if you think about sending him to the farm, Grandpa will feed you to the goats."

"I want to do something for the Coderres. I called Leah to arrange for her church to do a service for Tyrone and to see if someone can find him a plot."

"Is Leah coming in tonight?"

"No, she's got praise services tonight." Leah played organ, directed choirs in local churches, and cut loose by singing in Todd's band at Red's. We'd been friends since kindergarten after I slugged Brandy Cosgrove who had stolen her Beanie Babies dolphin. I'd received my first suspension and a friend for life. "Leah'll help me with the funeral, but it's not enough. I want to do more for the Coderres."

"Come eat," Casey grabbed my elbow and pulled me toward the bar. "Did they like the casserole?"

I nodded and eased myself onto a bar stool. At one end, Todd and Cody held an animated discussion with Red. Locals filled half the tables, mainly groups of parents escorting kids to and from ball practice. Sports news glimmered from the flat screens covering the walls.

The long, narrow bar and grill would hold different patrons on the weekend. The small stage at the far end reminded the families of the rowdier weekend crowd who packed the one and only social club in Halo. Red did well servicing both groups in the moral juggling act that kept small town taverns afloat.

"How was Luke?" Casey knew my man saga too well. We both had been afflicted with the same gene our floozy mother had passed on to us. When it came to good-looking men, our brains tended to shift into neutral, while our hearts and libido revved into overdrive.

"Just dandy," I said.

"Does he miss you?"

"Didn't act like it. Didn't offer to come in to Red's. Too busy saving Forks County. We found out Jerell had seen his daddy before Tyrone went back to the rest stop. Told Jerell he needed to meet someone. Maybe Luke's checking on that," I sighed and allowed Casey a peek at my pity party. "Or maybe Luke didn't want to come in because he was late for a hot hookup."

"What you need," said Casey, "is another guy to get your mind off of Luke."

"I need another man like you need another tattoo. Just one more regret to figure out how to remove later."

"You're too serious. Just find someone for some fun. You need to think good times, not long time."

"I thought I was doing that with Todd and we ended up married," I said. "Now I can't get rid of him. Good thing I came to my senses while I could still get an annulment."

"That's what I mean by too serious."

Red waved us over, and I hopped stools to move closer to their huddle. Cody gave us a nod.

"Hey Cherry," said Red. He slid a frosty mug in front of me, which I accepted gratefully. "Someone was in here tonight talking about an artist who does pervert paintings. Do you know who that is? I know I'm not into the art scene, but it made me curious."

I slapped my hands over my face and settled my elbows on the bar.

"What's wrong? Someone you know?"

"It's Cherry," said Casey. "She's the pervert."

"Cherry and Todd," said Cody, pulling his Peterbilt cap lower on his head.

"We make a good couple," Todd slipped his arm around my shoulder for a quick squeeze. "Don't be ashamed."

I dropped my hands to glare at Todd. "Only if you're talking muse and artist, not a couple of perverts. Red, my reputation is in tatters and Shawna Branson is holding a lighter and a can of gasoline to what's left."

"What did you do?" said Red. He waved at Casey to shoo her back to her customers.

"Why do you always assume this is something I've done?"

The corner of Red's mouth rose.

Cody smirked, while Todd adjusted his poker face to deadpan.

"I know Shawna doesn't think much of you," said Red, "but this seems a little extreme. Even for Shawna."

"Blackmail," I said. "Once word gets out I'm doing deviant art, the town will paint a scarlet P on our family."

"I'll still serve you," said Red. "It's not like y'all Tuckers have a pristine reputation anyway."

"That's our mother's fault and you'll notice she left town because of it," I swiveled on my seat and nodded to the crowd eating dinner. "You won't want me in here once everyone decides I'm a social pariah. They'll start taking their kids to Line Creek for wings and fries."

Cody hopped off his seat. "I've got to get." He kicked my stool, the brotherly form of a reassuring hug. "Don't worry, sister. It'll all work out."

Red looked up from wiping bar glasses. "I sure hope so. I've never liked Shawna, but I'm in the minority. I've a mind to stop serving her. She called my bar 'quaint.'"

I spun on my stool to face Todd. "Enough about me. Did you hear back from the SipNZip?"

"Not yet," he slapped a spunky rhythm on the bar top. "I feel good about my chances though."

"I'd hire you here," said Red, "but let's see how this whole painting deal shakes out. If people associate you with Cherry, they might stop eating here because of you, too."

"Great," I said. "Another reason for me to find those pictures. Todd won't be able to work in this town either."

"What are these pictures?" asked Red. "Kodak moments? Must be pretty hot if she's willing to blackmail for them."

"I have no idea."

"If you find the photos, I want to see them before you give them back to Shawna." Red gave me a toothy smile and waggled his auburn brows. "Shawna's a pain in the ass, but she's a well-endowed pain in the ass."

I rolled my eyes and wrinkled my nose.

"Have you checked the farm?" asked Todd. "Maybe you don't realize you have them and they're in your old room. Maybe the pictures are from high school or something."

"Good idea, Todd."

Todd grinned and his drumming moved from spunky to ecstatic.

"Tomorrow I'm going to Sweetgum to see the Coderres. I'll head to the farm before checking on Miss Gladys."

His drumming slowed. "Sweetgum? Maybe I should go with you."

"I had no problem in Sweetgum today," I said. "The Coderres need groceries brought. What could happen on a goodwill visit?"

TWELVE

The next morning I sped down the county highway in my sister's Firebird, loving the freedom that an overhauled 350 small block V-eight engine could bring.

I needed to find Shawna's snapshots on this visit, but thought Pearl might have some advice on how to help the Coderres. I also hoped Grandpa might have some word on the hijacking. Uncle Will sometimes slipped him a few nuggets that didn't leak out to the rest of the world.

At the turn to the farm lane, I did my usual scan for goats and other dangerous road blocks and proceeded with caution down the gravel road. At the fork, no bearded monsters appeared. I continued toward the house and parked in the driveway. Hopping out of my truck, I glanced around and scurried to the kitchen door, unslobbered and unchased. For one long masochistic minute, I stood on the stoop, searching the half-chewed azaleas and gardenia bushes for bobbing white tails. Seeing none, I hopped from the stoop and poked my head around the corner of the ranch house. The vegetable garden stood empty except for cages of tomatoes and the long, twisting pumpkin vines opening their blooms for the early sunshine.

"Maybe he sold the herd," I muttered and felt a small pang of sadness. The pang dispersed as my eyes darted to the barbed wire enclosing the back forty. In the distance, other hooved and horned beasts pranced in a pretty Turner-like pastoral.

At the fence line stood the white billy goat, Tater. His amber eyes gleamed in recognition, and he bleated a note of welcome. Or warning. You could never tell with Tater.

"What are you doing in the pasture, boy?" I asked, approaching the fence with my normal goat caution.

He bleated again and shook his gigantic goat head.

"I know. Your life has been turned upside down, hasn't it? Everything was rosy there for a time. Had the barnyard to yourself. Rammed my truck when you damn well pleased. Now fate has intervened and stuck you behind a fence."

He bobbed his head, his beard catching in the fence barbs.

I gingerly extended my hand through the fence and rubbed his head. He nibbled at my shirt and then set his teeth to it. I yanked my hand back.

"Don't go pushing your luck. But I know how you feel. Do you think we'll ever get back to the way things used to be? I had customers who wanted paintings of their newborns and frames for their commemorative NASCAR merchandise. I had a boyfriend who I thought was also my friend. A family who didn't live with me, but I could visit on an as-needed basis. And a nemesis who left our pistol-dueling to potshots about my clothing and family ineptitudes."

Tater stuck his head between the wire and mouthed my jeans, spreading gooey green spittle over the denim.

I hopped back a step. "This is Pearl's doing, isn't it? Did that woman stick you in here?"

Tater pulled back, catching his horn in the upper wire. As he yanked, the barb caught at his beard. He bellowed his angst, and I worked at shoving his horn behind the wire. More hair tangled in the lower barbs and the big goat made a frightened call for help.

"Just a minute, boy." The barbs pricked my skin, but I unwound the long, course hair without ripping.

He jumped back and scuttled away from the fence.

"It's time to set things to rights. I know Pearl thinks she's helping Grandpa by taking control of the farm, but she's gone too far." I walked to the gate, sucking on my pricked fingers. "I'm letting you free, Tater. But next time I drive up the lane and you get in my way, I will not hesitate to ram your thick, dirty hide."

He bellowed his thanks, and I left the goat to do some of my own ramming of Pearl's thick hide.

I entered the house, seeking the vixen who had invaded our home and caged the goat I normally loathed. Pearl had taken over the farm kitchen, once Casey's domain. Chased my brother from his barn full of rusting and gutted vehicles. And stolen the heart of my Grandpa Ed. If that was even possible.

Maybe stolen his stomach was a better way to look at it.

Pearl stood at the kitchen counter. The temptress had one hand splayed on a full hip clad in denim capris. The other hand clutched a tape measure. She wore a black tank top and her iron gray hair had a mussed, spiky style. A cut my Grandma Jo would think questionable for a woman of her age. Normally I'd like it, but this was the seducer of my Grandpa.

Her attention was on the window above the sink, but she turned at my entrance, giving me a view of her boob tattoo and the Harley emblazoned on her tank. "Cherry, what are you doing here?"

"Never mind that. What's with that tape measure?"

"I'm going to make new curtains. I hope you're not here just looking for a meal."

I sucked in my lips and fixed my eyes on the gingham curtains that had hung above the sink as long as I could remember. Considering my siblings and I had been raised in this house after our negligent mother dumped us on our grandparents, those curtains had seen a lot. Which was maybe why they were now stained and faded and the hem had unraveled.

"We don't need new curtains," I said. "Those are just fine." For some inexplicable reason, changing those curtains felt like Pearl was tearing Grandma Jo right out of the house. Which was ridiculous since Grandma Jo had been buried more than ten years ago.

We exchanged a long, frosty look broken by the sound of shuffling steps. At the far wall, Grandpa ambled through the living room doorway and eased into a kitchen chair, an expectant look on his thin, leathered face. "Taking a break from haying. I'm ready for my coffee."

"Hey Grandpa," Turning my back on Pearl, I moved to the table and kissed his raspy cheek. "I need to look through our photos."

"Photos? I don't think we have many baby pictures of you."

"Not baby pictures. Don't worry about it, I'm just going to check my bedroom and see if there's any old snapshots."

"Pearl's been clearing out the back rooms for me. You better ask her."

I sucked in my breath and turned on the Pearl. "You're going through my stuff?"

Pearl dropped into a kitchen chair with a cup of coffee. She pushed another cup toward Grandpa. "I should get you and your siblings to help me. Y'all are pack rats. Don't you throw anything away?"

I gripped the edge of the table. "What have you thrown out? Paintings, photos, pictures? Anything of that nature?"

"Lord knows. I needed a shovel and rake to go through everything."

"I'll go check on the pictures in a minute." Because I'm a quick assessor, I realized the futility of the argument. I would have to look myself. "Did y'all hear about the hijacking, Grandpa? I thought I'd bring you some news."

With a healthy glare at Pearl, I settled into a chair next to Grandpa and patted his gnarled and bony knuckle. He gave me a strange look and withdrew his hand. We weren't a touchy-feely family, and I was freaking him out with my territorial behavior.

"Well, now. Hijacking?" he said and leaned back in his chair. "Just a minute. Pearl, you got some food for us?"

"Sure, Ed." She left her coffee and moved to the fridge. "Good thing my Amy knows how to cook. Don't see her dropping by expecting a meal."

"Considering this isn't her home, I'm glad to hear it," I said, but hopped up to pour Grandpa a refill on his coffee and grab a cup of my own.

Grandpa pulled on his chin. "Now, how do you know about the hijacking?"

"Uncle Will called me in to do a composite sketch of one of the hijackers."

"Will Thompson did drop in for a cup of coffee yesterday," Grandpa smiled, loving that it drove me crazy when he strung a story out. "Heard about that hijacking."

I wandered back to the table as Pearl set down our brunch. A single plate of pimento sandwiches sat on the table. They looked awfully lonely without any sides to join them. I had expected something prepared using the stove. Maybe with eggs, biscuits, breakfast meat, or perhaps even a hot bowl of butter grits. I'd even accept a lunch menu. Leftover chicken pot pie. Reheated corn casserole. Maybe I had gotten accustomed to Casey's spread. Or maybe this was my punishment for sassing Pearl.

Grandpa eyed the plate and took a sandwich without comment. Pearl had outflanked me and I had sacrificed my Grandpa in the process.

She was good.

"So what did Sheriff Thompson say?" asked Pearl, settling into a chair across from Grandpa.

"Dixie Cake truck was hit," said Grandpa between bites of pimento cheese.

"What?" I snatched a sandwich. "What do you mean Dixie Cake truck?"

"I suppose it had more than Dixie Cakes in it. Was a big truck, according to Will. Can't imagine a rig full of Dixie Cakes."

"Who holds up a Dixie Cake truck? The Tooth Fairy?" I licked pimento cheese off my fingers and imagined the wondrous ecstasy that would be a truck full of pastries made by my favorite Southern baking company. My stomach responded in kind.

"Four of 'em," continued Grandpa. "Masked and armed."

"Masked?" said Pearl. "What, like Halloween?"

"Halloween masks?" I scoffed. "Ski masks. Now this is classified information, but one guy pulled his off and was spotted by Tyrone Coderre. They think he later came back and shot Tyrone. Unfortunately Coderre returned to the scene of the crime and the shooter was waiting for him." I skipped the part where I had forgotten to mention Tyrone's plans to the police. "They hear anything from the State Patrol yet?"

"Evidently it's not uncommon for food trucks to be stolen. However, the robberies are generally closer to Atlanta. Will said the State Patrol was glad to get your sketch, though."

"Well that's good to hear. I was glad to be of service, particularly since local jobs have been hard to come by."

"Speaking of local jobs, I recently heard about some paintings," said Pearl. "Haven't seen the photos floating around yet, but the ladies say they are mighty interesting. Did you hear about them, Ed?"

Grandpa's eyes slanted to the empty plate. It appeared I had eaten the remaining pimento cheese sandwiches.

"So this hijacking," I said, internally cursing Pearl for bringing up the paintings. "Any more information? I heard the driver wasn't even supposed to be driving. Bad luck for him."

Grandpa scratched his heavy growth of whiskers. "Don't know anything else."

"I visited the Coderres with Luke yesterday. They're an awful mess. Tyrone and his son, Jerell, were living with Tyrone's grandma. She's got emphysema and doesn't seem long for the world. Jerell's future doesn't look too good."

"Mercy, that's terrible." In true small town fashion, Pearl relaxed off her attitude toward me to sympathize in the Coderres' misfortune. "I'll make you some food to take to them."

"Jerell's going to need a home," I gave Grandpa my brightest customer service smile.

"I'll take him if he's a barnyard critter," said Grandpa, "but don't get any funny ideas."

"Don't they have any more family?" asked Pearl. "Where's his momma?"

"She had an ectopic pregnancy a few years back. Didn't know she was pregnant and bled to death."

"Merciful heavens," exclaimed Pearl. "How can that happen in this day and age?"

"Miss Gladys said the momma was three sheets on meth for most of Jerell's infancy," I replied. "We're talking folks living in the Sweetgum Estates."

"I keep hoping the sheriff will clean out that cesspool."

Grandpa's mouth zipped into a line of discontent. "You stay out of that place, Cherrilyn Tucker."

"I'm just doing my Christian duty, sir. Helping orphans and widows. I'm going to bring them groceries and I'm getting a local church to help with the funeral once they release Coderre's body."

"That's real sweet of you, Cherry," said Pearl. "Particularly since the rumors floating around town have cast you in such a negative light. I guess you need what they call 'spin control.' Helping orphans and widows is just the ticket."

I caught my "Oh, shit" before Grandpa heard it escape my mouth.

Pearl gave me a small, hard smile. "I think you better tell your Grandpa about these paintings. Before he hears about them from someone else."

"Grandpa's not interested in my art stories. He grew up watching me paint." I wracked my brain for a way out of Pearl's mine field. "I think the rumors you're hearing are a malicious campaign seeking to ruin my career and will soon be proven false."

I narrowed my eyes at Pearl. "Unless certain pictures have been destroyed by meddling women who can't leave other folks' homes alone."

"First Baptist is having a consignment sale to raise money for their charity mission. They need your cast offs." Pearl cocked a brow and folded her arms over her ample chest. "This house needs a good clearing out anyway."

"Clearing out?" I looked at Grandpa. "You know what got cleared out? Cody and Casey. My house is getting very crowded."

He squared my look. "Your Great-Gam raised five kids in that house."

"You want me to build bunk beds for them? It was supposed to be my studio. That house has two bedrooms and one bathroom. Todd's already living there."

Grandpa's lips disappeared into his mouth.

Sometimes I forget to tell myself to stop yammering.

I needed to explain that it wasn't just Casey and Cody, but Grandma Jo's memories that might be "cleared out" along with Shawna's missing pictures.

However, like my delinquent mother, Grandma Jo was a taboo subject. Talk of the dead and missing were forever silenced in this house.

Before I could appeal to Grandpa's sense of nostalgia, my phone rang. I yanked it from my pocket and glanced at the caller ID. Rupert. Not what I needed at this moment. But a customer trumped family squabbles.

"Hey, Mr. Rupert," I said, moving toward the door. "What can I do you for?"

He broke into peals of giggles better made for a sitcom laugh track. I tapped my foot counting the seconds for him to finish while Pearl and Grandpa watched me.

"Darling," said Rupert. "I have arrived in your lovely town to bring the contract. Halo is so quaint. Please direct me to your studio."

I swallowed a half dozen curses picturing the degrees of nudity and foolishness that might greet him at my home. Besides the fact my studio now looked like the parlor of a redneck bachelor. I wouldn't have been surprised if Cody had already tacked a muscle car nudie calendar on the wall. "I'm actually away from my studio at the moment."

"Where are you, my dear? Let me come to you. I'm enjoying my provincial tour."

"I'm at my Grandpa's farm," I spun my brain's local rolodex trying to come up with a better option. "How do you feel about a Sonic drive-in?"

Rupert found that suggestion hilarious, but cut his laughter short. "A farm? Wonderful. We'll be there in a moment. Just text me the address."

"I don't have a texting plan. Let me meet you somewhere else."

"I would like to see this farm of your ancestors. If you want the contract, you'll give me the address."

Shit, I thought, glancing at Pearl's expectant face. Grandpa curled his lip at the hint of visitors. The thought of Rupert Agadzinoff meeting Pearl and Grandpa was only slightly better than the thought of Rupert meeting a half-dressed Casey who would itemize his wallet and proceed with a "Capture the Sugar Daddy" campaign.

I needed the contract. Rupert would have to come to the farm.

THIRTEEN

I met Rupert and his driver in the farm yard, ready to defend them from errant goats. No goats appeared, nor did Miss David, for which I thanked the Lord profusely. Bad enough to suffer comments from Rupert on my "quaint and cunning bucolic lifestyle" (i.e. hick), but to also suffer the withering glances of Miss David? No, thank you.

In the farm kitchen, I served everyone a glass of tea. The driver disappeared to tour the farm or, more likely, to sleep in the car. After assessing Rupert as an obnoxious irritant, Grandpa took off to hang with his goats. Or fish. Which left Pearl, Rupert, and I. I seated Rupert at the table and watched as Pearl took it upon herself to make a real lunch.

The lunch I wanted an hour ago, not during a contract negotiation.

"I hope you didn't come all the way to Halo to bring me my contract," I said to Rupert, while trying to catch Pearl's attention. She flitted between the fridge and cabinets, gathering supplies. "Pearl. We don't need to be fed. Why don't you scoot and continue your work on ridding the house of its history?"

"No bother, hon'," said Pearl. "I don't let my guests go hungry."

"Mr. Agadzinoff, why don't we move to the living room?" I said through gritted teeth.

"A light repast would be lovely, Miss Pearl," said Rupert.

Pearl turned and shook a fork at me. "See? I'll get you a nice dinner. Now if you need any help with your paperwork, just let me know. I've done many a contract getting my milkers sired. I can just look over the fine print for you."

I began to regret my decision not to expose him to Casey. "Mr. Agadzinoff is a lawyer," I said to Pearl. "We don't need any of your milking contract expertise."

"It's not a milking contract," Pearl whisked eggs into a bowl. "It's a breeding contract for stud service. I hire a registered buck and need a contract to ensure he doesn't shoot blanks and is free of disease when he visits. Needs a good whim-wham, too. I let them get at it, but I need to make sure I can get the buck back if my doe don't settle. By settle, I mean…"

"Good Lord, Pearl. Mr. Agadzinoff doesn't need the birds and bees of goats."

"I'm paying one hundred and fifty dollars for a good rutting." Pearl slammed her fork onto the counter. "If he's a lawyer, he understands."

Chuckling, Rupert held up his hands. "Yes, yes. I understand. I have signed Cherry's contract, though. Maybe I should have had you check to make sure Cherry's giving me a good whim-wham, Pearl."

Pearl nodded and turned back toward the counter where she added flour and milk to her bowl.

Mortification heated my cheeks better than a BBQ smoker. I took the contracts from Rupert. "You want me to come up to Atlanta tomorrow? I can have my sister drive me."

He shook his head. "I'll send my chauffeur. He enjoys driving. Why don't you just stay at my home while you're working? Much easier than the back and forth of the long commute to Atlanta."

"That would certainly solve some of your problems at the house," said Pearl. "Give you some breathing room. Get out of town and away from the gossip, too."

"The drive does not bother me in the least," I said to Rupert followed by a sharp "mind your own business" look to Pearl.

"I do like my employees readily available, my dear," said Rupert. "And your truck seems unsafe."

"She's plenty safe," I said not wanting to cast aspersions on my poor Datsun. "I miss her. When I go out tonight, I'll have to catch a ride."

"Catch a ride?" Rupert leaned forward, clasping his tea. "I am curious as to what there is to do at night in the country? Surely, you don't have clubs?"

Pearl abandoned her dumpling mixture and turned to listen. "Who are you going with? I thought you got dumped by Luke Harper. You're not taking up with your ex-husband again, are you? That's going to make matters worse, as far as your painting problem goes."

If my cheeks grew any hotter, I might have set fire to the contracts. "Mr. Rupert, I assure you I do not have a painting problem."

"Of course not," said Rupert, patting my hand. "I would be interested if your plans ever include Maksim Avtaikin, though. I love to hear stories about my friend, so I can use them to poke him in the ribs later."

"Oh, we love Mr. Max," said Pearl. "He used to host bingo for us until Cherry ruined that."

I took a deep, cleansing breath and counted to twenty.

"So Maksim is well liked in the community?" said Rupert. "But I thought he and Cherry had a rapport?"

"We have an excellent rapport," I said, glaring at Pearl. "I have been assisting Mr. Max in getting past his legal transgressions and staying on the fair side of the law."

"Legal transgressions?" said Rupert.

"Nothing was ever proven," said Pearl. "Mr. Max is a sweetheart."

"That's true." I didn't want Rupert to use Max's illicit doings as a point of good natured ribbing. It seemed ungentlemanly. "He's never been charged with anything."

"He never is," said Rupert, smiling. "Good old Maks. I'm glad to hear he's settled in such an honest and supportive community."

"Mostly," I grumbled, thinking of Shawna.

"Well, then," said Rupert. "I bid you adieu and will see you tomorrow, Miss Cherry Tucker."

We shook hands and he left to find his driver. Pearl peered through the kitchen window at the town car readying to leave.

"He didn't stay for my chicken and dumplings," she said.

The aroma of chicken, vegetables, and baked biscuits drifted through the kitchen. My stomach's rumble kicked into lumberjack-killing-a-sequoia territory.

Without turning, Pearl said, "Don't even think about it, Cherry. You're not getting any of my fixings while your name is mud. I will not have you embarrassing your Grandpa Ed. Get your ducks sorted out and then you can sit at my table."

I grabbed my contract and headed out the door. "It's not your table," I muttered.

FOURTEEN

When I reached the Coderres' trailer, I found Jerell sitting on the stoop with an air rifle on his lap. He scoped out the Firebird, but seeing me alight from it, he threw the air rifle over his shoulder and climbed down the rotting steps to my vehicle. I handed him a bag of groceries and followed him inside, carrying another casserole.

"How's your great-grandma today?" I asked him.

"About the same. We're taking extra cautions now." Jerell laid his gun on the stoop and from under his shirt, pulled out a key hanging on a yarn necklace. He fitted the key into the trailer door, turned the lock, and pushed the door wide.

I fixed a smile on my face, watching him replace his key and grab his BB gun. I could have kicked in that door easier than unlocking it. "Keeping watch over your great-gam? That's good."

"Daddy Tyrone kept us safe," said Jerell. "Now I gotta do it."

The way Jerell talked, they should rename the Sweetgum Estates to Little Beirut.

"That's real grown up of you, Jerell. I'll just go put your dinner in the fridge."

Miss Gladys lay with her feet propped on the couch.

"How you doing, ma'am?" I asked, making my way to the kitchen.

"Not so good, sugar," she said. "Thank you for coming."

I left the casserole in the fridge. Jerell bumped me to the side and began stacking the groceries inside the freezer.

"Jerell, you don't put cereal in the freezer."

"I got to hide it from the tweaker meth-heads. They can smell sugar and they'll go through our cupboards looking for it. This is some good stuff you brought. I like the ones with marshmallows."

I eyed his gun and swallowed hard. "Me, too."

Leaving Jerell to hide the groceries, I walked back to the living area and sat on the couch next to Miss Gladys. "We're working on the funeral arrangements."

"Thank you, baby." She patted my hand. "I don't know what we're gonna do."

"I'm going to find you a new place to live. I'd move you into my house, but it's full up right now."

"That's all right, honey." She shut her delicately veined lids.

I watched the clouding in her oxygen tube for a moment, then rose from the couch. I walked down the hall and knocked on Jerell's door. "I'm going to talk to your neighbors to see if they know anything about Tyrone's murder."

Jerell yanked open his door. "You're not too smart, are you."

"I'm no brain surgeon, I'll give you that, but I've been to college."

Jerell gave the weary sigh of an eight-year-old who'd seen it all. "I guess I'll go with you. I don't like leaving my gam."

"I'll be fine," I said. "She's sleeping."

"You got a gun?"

"I thought if I came armed, it may do me more harm than good."

"Take my knife." He disappeared behind his door and returned with a switchblade. "You know how to use it?"

Careful not to grimace, I shoved the knife in my back pocket. "Which neighbors do you think will be the most helpful? I've got this picture I want to show them."

"Come on," he threw his air rifle over his shoulder and marched out the door. On the stoop, he pulled out his string and locked the door. Taking a right, he hiked toward a trailer the color of a cinderblock. A feeble line of smoke rose from the roof.

Jerell followed my line of sight to the roof. "They put in their own stove."

"They cut a hole in their roof?"

"It gets cold in the winter," Jerell shrugged. "They don't cook or tweak. Look at their windows."

I looked. "They have curtains?"

Jerell pointed to another trailer down the street. "You see them, smoking in front of that house? Look at the windows."

"They're covered in foil."

"Yes, ma'am. That's a meth house. You pass by and it smells like a cat peed all over it. Also got more trash than the others. Tweakers got lots of trash. Alcohol bottles and such. And not the kind you drink. Kitty litter, but no cats. You stay away from there."

"Got it, Jerell." I knocked on the safe house door. The door cracked and a pair of brown eyes peered out. I held up the composite drawing of my hijacker. "Hey, I'm friends with Jerell and Miss Gladys. Have you seen this guy before?"

The man said something I couldn't understand and shut the door. I heard the rattle of a chain and turn of a deadbolt. I looked back at Jerell.

"They don't speak English there, but they're nice." Jerell pointed to the trailer across the road. "Try that one."

I stalked across the lane, trying not to feel so white and female. This trailer also had curtains, giving me hope. I knocked.

An older woman cracked the door. "What do you want?"

"She's cool, Miss April," yelled Jerell.

"Who's that?" Miss April wedged part of her immense body through the crack to see Jerell.

"That there is Cherry Tucker," Jerell hollered from the road. "She wants to know who killed Tyrone. She's going to show you a picture."

I glanced down the road. The crowd in front of the meth house had grown and they watched with interest. I didn't want to seem impolite, so I gave a small wave. A girl tossed her cigarette into the dirt and waved back.

"I guess you can come in," said Miss April. "Excuse the mess." She widened the door's opening. The fetid smell of garbage and unknown substances assailed my nostrils. Various items stacked to the ceiling lined the doorway. Newspapers, magazines, books, garbage bags, clothing, and old games. More than I could itemize in my head. Miss April backed down the path leading to the door.

I held up the composite and tried to hold my breath. "Have you seen this man, ma'am?"

April took the picture and studied it. "No, never seen him before. Who is he?"

"I don't know, but he held up a truck and Tyrone saw the robbery. He might have killed Tyrone."

"Everyone here thinks Regis killed Tyrone." April shook her head. "Bad news for poor Miss Gladys."

"Who's Regis?"

"Regis Sharp. The Sharps run the show around here. Sell their redneck heroin in Line Creek and farther out. Wouldn't be surprised if they're running that stuff into Atlanta."

"Dealers?"

"More than that, honey. They also pimp and loan. They are dangerous men. Tyrone owed them money." April crossed her heavy arms. "Lucky they leave me alone. Nobody wants to bother me, and I don't want to bother nobody."

"Glad to hear that," I said. "This trailer park doesn't seem too safe."

"If you don't have a dog willing to tear a leg off, you better be armed to live here." April laughed, "Or have a booby-trapped house like me."

"Thanks, Miss April." My skin crawled to be out of her trailer, but I didn't want to seem impolite. "I'm going to show this sketch to more people."

"Nobody in Sweetgum Estates knows this man. I can tell you that. I watch who comes and goes."

I folded the drawing and shoved it in my pocket. "Thanks for your help."

"You watch your back," she hooked a thumb in the direction of the trailer down the street. "Folks have been watching you. They know you're checking on Miss Gladys and Jerell."

I mumbled my thanks and backed out the door. Ducking my head, I hurried to where Jerell waited in the middle of the road and we hiked back to Miss Gladys's trailer.

"I'll be by tomorrow, Jerell. I hate leaving you here," I handed him back his knife and squeezed his plump shoulder.

"I got to stay here. I can't leave my Gammy alone." He cast me a sharp look. "I ain't going to school just yet. Someone's got to keep an eye on things."

"I know, baby, and it's okay." I threw my arms around his pudgy body and hugged. I didn't know whether to mention the Sharps for fear of scaring the boy. I hugged him tighter instead.

He shoved me off with an eye roll. "Calm yourself, girl. Gammy and I were here before you ever showed up."

"See you tomorrow, Jerell."

"Bring pizza."

FIFTEEN

Dressing for a trucker bar can be tricky. Elegance is not required, but a bit of pizzazz is appreciated. So is a decent showing of skin, particularly if you want to drink for free. Too much skin and you're asking for trouble, especially from women like Dona. Such was the dilemma I faced when Luke arrived to take me to the Gearjammer. I stood in my bedroom staring at my closet unable to imagine the appropriate outfit to wear.

Casey strolled through my bedroom door, eager to announce Luke's arrival with an older sister's air of showmanship. "What are you doing with Luke? Hasn't he caused you enough heartache?"

"Not a date," I said. "I'm his beard."

"Beard? I don't think your break-up hit him that hard."

"He's investigating the hijack and needs a cover. Besides, my truck is still in Atlanta. I do need a ride." I yanked a denim skirt fringed in black leather from the back of my closet. "This will do. Do you have my camouflage tank? Gray and perylene black?"

"I wish I hadn't made plans tonight," said Casey. "This sounds fun."

"I'm looking forward to meeting up with my new buddy from the Waffle House, Dona. She looks like she knows how to party."

"I meant fun watching sparks fly off you and Luke. There's ten-to-one odds you get thrown out of the Gearjammer for making a scene."

"What? Who's betting?"

"Me and Cody so far, but I'm taking the wager to Red's and running it there."

"Sister, you need a hobby." I shimmied on the skirt and sat on the bed to pull on my boots.

"It would be helpful if you didn't come home tonight. Then nobody would have to share a room with Todd."

I cast her a look of disgust. "I may be cheap, but I'm not that easy. Did Todd get the job at the SipNZip?"

"He starts tomorrow, but got the graveyard shift. Poor guy. We can rotate beds after he starts."

"This arrangement is not working," I added bangles and dangly earrings before pulling the curlers from my hair. The earring tangled in a lock while I unwrapped a curler. "Grandpa's the one who's going to have people talking if he's shacking up with Pearl."

"I don't think they're shacking up. Yet. By the way, Shawna printed poster-size photos of your naked Todd paintings. I caught her tacking one on the Tru-Buy bulletin board. Ripped it down for you." Casey strolled to where I stood by my dresser to help free my hair. I caught her raised eyebrow expression in my mirror. "The one where Todd's ready to throw the Frisbee."

"*The Discobolus*," I said. "He's fixing to throw a discus. That's an Olympic event. Not Frisbee golf."

"Either way, he's standing and hanging free for all the world to see." Casey shook her head. "I think it will do you good to get out of town for a while. Stay up in Buckhead with your rich lawyer."

"That's what Pearl said, too. And exactly what Shawna wants. Me out of town."

"What are you going to do?"

"Stay in town." I applied some coral lip gloss and turned for Casey's admiration. "How do I look?" I spun around in my boots, making my fringe sway.

She rolled her lip. "Sometimes I wonder if we're even related. It's like we have completely different fashion DNA."

I ignored that comment and sashayed out of my bedroom. Ten steps later I stood in the arched entry to what used to be my studio.

Luke, Todd, and Cody sat spaced apart on the dead pheasant couch, staring at the TV screen across the room. The Braves were pitching and the boys weren't speaking. Their expressions matched their aggressive, wide-legged sprawls on the couch. Except for Todd, who had trained his face to look like a happy Golden Retriever.

Luke glanced up at my entrance and stood. He wore a black t-shirt and jeans that melded to his long legs. He put no thought into dressing and still looked as good as smoked meat on a stick. Hot and tasty.

Not that I cared.

"Don't you want to put more on?" His eyes traveled over my outfit as I grabbed my phone off the desk charger and tossed it in my bag.

"Nope. It's still warm and I imagine I'll get warmer with all the dancing I'm fixing to do." I offered him my customer service smile.

"Dancing?" His frown mirrored my smile.

"You didn't think I was going to follow you around interrogating folks, did you?" I said, crossing my fingers behind my back. "I'm in a celebratory mood and if I hadn't agreed to meet Dona, I would be kicking it up at Red's. I got my signed contract today."

His eyes narrowed. "You don't kick it up at Red's. You sit at the bar and gossip with Red."

I shrugged. "New venue, new attitude."

"I think you look great," said Todd. "I would have taken you to the Gearjammer if you'd asked."

"I didn't ask anybody except Casey and she can't go. This was meant to be a girl's night out. Luke forgot his dress, but I'm ditching him at the door anyway."

Luke eyed me again, but I had no time for his suspicious looks. I strode past him to the front door, making my intentions clear. "Let's get going. I have truckers to meet."

Little did Luke know, besides interrogating truckers, I planned to ply him with adult beverages and question him about his step-cousin, Shawna Branson. I needed to take this woman down and wasn't past milking ex-boyfriends for information to do it.

*   *   *

If you could rate a tavern by the initials carved into the wooden bar, the number of stains marking the cement floor, and the heavy haze of smoke filling the air, the Gearjammer would have passed with flying colors. Or failed, depending on your leaning toward what makes or breaks a bar. The liquor bottles had no fruit or chocolate flavors. The beer was American and provided the decor as neon lighting. Merle Haggard sang from a real jukebox and the trucker hats worn were not meant to be ironic nor hip.

Luke paused in the doorway to do a cursory eyeball cruise of the dive, while I scanned for Dona and her friends. They stood at the bar, flirting with men of various ages, hats, and tattoos.

I took an excited leap forward and jerked to a stop. Swinging my gaze over my shoulder, I spoke to the hand that had grasped my waistband. "We're here. You do your cop thing and I'll do my G.N.O. thing."

Luke yanked me back with his finger and hooked an arm around my shoulder. "They'll talk more if you're with me."

I opened and closed my mouth. I had planned on interrogating Luke and the truckers separately. I had also planned on having some fun first. "What's with you? Every time I've wanted to question folks, you won't let me. And now you want my help?"

"Think of it as your chance to play detective," he said.

I could do tit for tat. "You're buying. And sharing information. And later you're dancing."

We strolled to the bar and squeezed between groups of regulars. Luke held up two fingers and pointed toward the tap. I smiled at my neighbors and waved to Dona.

The man next to me lit a cigarette. Blowing the smoke toward his neighbor, he leaned on the bar and gave me a friendly wink. "Don't think I've seen you or your guy in here before. You local?"

"I'm from Halo," I said. "This here is Luke, and I'm Cherry. Luke doesn't feel comfortable taking me to public places where they know him. Thought we'd give the Gearjammer a try."

Luke jerked his head in my direction and scowled. Before he could speak, the bartender asked for payment.

While he fumbled with his wallet, I turned back to talk to my new friend. "What's your name?"

"Marshall Dobson. So you're the kind of girl a fellow's got to hide from his mother." He winked again.

I winked back. "That's me. I'm an artist. Do you drive the big rigs?"

"Used to," he blew smoke toward the ceiling, "I live in Line Creek. Work as a dispatcher now."

"I bet you hear all kinds of interesting stories," I grasped the beer Luke pushed toward me. "Did you hear about the hijacking yesterday?"

Luke sputtered foam mid-swallow.

Marshall tapped his ashes in the tray before him and hollered down the bar. "Y'all hear about a hijacking yesterday?"

"Smooth," Luke whispered to me.

"Expedient," I said. "Now drink your beer. Then order yourself a shot of Jack."

"Why?"

"You're celebrating my commission. I will soon be spending my days in Buckhead, eating caviar and drinking vodka in between painting sessions."

Luke's brows dropped, but he waved at the bartender to set up a round of shots.

A potbellied, older man in a Gators cap left his stool to approach our group. "What's this about a hijackin'?"

I nodded. "What'd you hear? I figure it must be the hot topic of conversation tonight."

Luke clamped his hand on my arm. "Sugar."

"Yes, honey-pie?" I batted my Maybelline coated lashes at him.

"This one's yours." He scooted a shot glass toward me and muttered, "Slow down."

The woman next to Marshall leaned around his arm. "Are you sure about that, honey? You must be mistaken."

"I think you know I'm not mistaken." I smiled but steadied my eyes on hers. "It's juicy, ain't it? I can tell."

The woman glanced sideways at Marshall and back to me. "Juicy for some, I suppose."

Marshall showed me his yellowing teeth. "Well now, Miss Cherry. Sounds like you've heard more than us."

"That depends on what you've heard," I said. "Did y'all see that composite sketch of the hijacker the Sheriff's Office has been showing around?"

"Can't say that I have," said Marshall with a hard look at Luke.

"Baby, let's dance," said Luke, yanking me off my stool. He pulled me to the space before the jukebox. A couple swayed in a boozy, locked embrace that held them upright. We carefully maneuvered around them. One bump and they'd fall over like dominos.

Luke snuggled me against his chest and placed his mouth near my ear. His breath tickled my hair and his aftershave smelled woodsy and clean.

"Maybe I should've explained something before you started. First, don't piss them off. These aren't your typical rednecks. Second, don't talk about Tyrone's murder."

"I know all that. Is there a third?" I asked, following his drowsy steps to *Your Cheatin' Heart.*

"Yes," he continued. "What do you mean you're going to be spending your days in Buckhead eating caviar and drinking vodka?"

"My subject enjoys the finer things in life, what can I say? Now spin me back to the bar. Dona's going to think I'm rude."

"I made a mistake letting you take the reins on questioning truckers," said Luke, bumping his thighs against mine to shuffle us away from the bar. "Let's keep dancing."

"Nice try." I dropped my hands from his shoulders and stepped out of his arms. "I got the conversation flowing at that end of the bar. You go back and chat to Marshall and his crew. I'm going to hang with Dona and see if she's heard anything. If I learn something, I'll let you know."

I quick-stepped from Luke and circled to the other side of the bar where Dona and her friends reclined on stools. Hopefully they knew more than Marshall's group. "So ladies, what's going on?"

"Kind of quiet tonight," said Dona. "Pickings are slim." She looked across the bar and studied Luke as he slid back onto his stool. "You sure he's not your boyfriend?"

I thought about lying for a second. "He's my ex. Let's pretend he's not here."

"That's kind of hard to do," said Dona. "He's like a double-dip on the hottest day in August."

"Dona, don't push your luck." I switched my scowl to a smile for her friends. They wore pony tails with fluffy bangs and heeled boots with their jeans and tanks. All in various colors, reminding me of a box of crayons.

"Did you hear any more about the truck hijacking? Anybody think that composite sketch looked familiar?"

Dona shook her head. "We taped the copy of the sketch on the door. Nobody recognizes him."

"Too bad," I said.

We watched as two men in ball caps asked Dona's friends to dance. They giggled and paraded over to the jukebox to select a song.

"Dona," I said. "Don't you find it strange that there's been hijackings in the surrounding counties but not our own?"

"To be honest, I don't think much about hijackings. Why would I? You don't normally see them around here."

"True enough," I said. "Don't know why I'm thinking much about it myself."

Two cowboys strolled to our corner of the bar. One tipped his hat toward Dona. The other looked me square in the eye and rolled his toothpick from one corner of his mouth to the other.

"Wanna dance?" he said.

I shrugged and looked him over. He was a rangy guy, without boots he was missing a couple inches on most men, but clean shaven and clear eyed. And young. "Why not."

He took my hand and I followed him to the dance floor. He placed a hand at the small of my back, the other near my neck, and began steering me around.

"How old are you?" I said. "You look familiar."

"Old enough," he rolled the toothpick between his teeth. "You a cougar or something?"

"Do I look like a cougar? I'm twenty-six. How could I be a cougar?"

"That's older than me," he smiled. "I like older women."

"Wait a minute. Did you go to Halo High? Are you friends with Cody Tucker?"

"I know Cody," he said. "Are you one of his sisters? I thought I might know you. I'm Zach Stowe."

"What are you doing hanging out at the Gearjammer, Zach? This crowd seems a little old for you."

With his eyes on me, his toothpick took another trip across his mouth. "I'm saving up for truck driving school. I like hanging out with the guys. Learn a lot."

"Good for you."

He leaned me back in a dip. The lip of his hat brushed my forehead.

My back began to ache, but I kept my eyes on his. "Have you heard about the truck hijacking that happened yesterday?"

We popped back up and began another circle. "Sure. Everybody's talking about it."

"What do you mean everybody? Whenever I mention it, they say they've never heard anything."

The toothpick sucked into his mouth and reappeared on his tongue. "That's because some of 'em are on the take. And we're not sure which and don't want to get anybody in trouble. Everyone also knows the guy you're with is a cop."

"Dangit," I glanced over my shoulder at Luke, but Zach's quick pivot had me looking back at him.

"You're kind of cute," said Zach. "Which sister are you? The wild one or the one that gets married all the time?"

"I don't get married all the time. Just once and only for a minute."

"Either way, you've been around." He dipped me again.

"That line is going to get you absolutely nowhere." I glared into his dark, hopeful eyes. "And no more dipping. It makes my back hurt. Tell me more about these guys on the take."

"I figured it out from a few things they said. It's risky, but you can make serious bankroll. They prearrange a place and time for the hold up. It looks like a hijack except you walk away with extra cash. They take your haul. Insurance covers the company. Everybody wins."

"Everybody doesn't win, Zach. You wonder why your insurance costs keep going up? Or why companies go out of business?"

He twirled me around and pressed me closer. "I didn't say I plan to do it. You want to go out and see the backup moves I've been practicing? These guys will let me borrow a cab for an hour."

A hand clamped on Zach's shoulder and we stopped mid-twirl. I stumbled against Zach and looked above his shoulder.

"I'm cutting in," said Luke.

Zach looked at me for approval, and I nodded. "I'll talk to you later."

He peeled himself off my body and tipped his hat. "Later, darlin'."

His caustic glance bounced off of Luke. Taking my hand, Luke led me closer to the jukebox. *Always On My Mind* played and couples crowded the floor.

"That teenager was getting pretty friendly," Luke remarked, wrapping an arm around my lower back. "Make you feel young again?"

I rose on my toes and wished I had worn heels instead of my boots so I wouldn't have to crank my head back to look at him. "One of Cody's friends. I learned something very interesting."

"What's that?" Luke bent to press his cheek against my hair and pulled me into his lean body, so he could hear me. Or to get to second base without trying.

"It seems everyone knows you're a cop, which is causing an epidemic of amnesia. And I think you better talk to your truck driver again. His hijacking might have been preordained."

"Shit." Luke straightened, dropping his arms and my balance.

I teetered and plummeted to the cement floor, taking out the girl next to me with my windmilling arms.

"Hey." She hollered and grabbed her date.

He followed us to the floor.

The girl, actually a good-sized woman weighing somewhere between one hundred forty and one hundred sixty pounds, fell on my splayed body. With unplanned accuracy, her man landed on top of his date. I felt the crush in my knees and pelvis, shrieked, and tried to kick. Which is impossible with three hundred fifty plus pounds flattening you to the ground. Above me, I could hear the muffled bellows of the woman. Her date's stomach prevented her screams to be clearly understood.

The man placed his meaty hands on either side of my body and glared at me before pushing off. Leaving his date sprawled over me, he chose to draw back a fist and throw it at Luke. I watched from my ground level view as Luke pivoted to avoid the blow. The man followed through with a stumble, tripped over our bodies, and fell on top of us again.

Zach swam in my vision, kneeling next to me on the ground. "Miss Cherry, are you all right?"

I gave him a does-it-look-like-I'm-all-right look. "Get these people off of me."

The fallen warrior scrambled up again and readied to take another swing at Luke.

"Ma'am." Zach held a hand to the cursing woman laying on top of my body.

She raised her head, growled at Zach, then looked at me. The suggestions and names she called me were perhaps impossible to do, but intensely creative. Using my body as a cushion, she pushed back onto her heels and rose to her feet. Her date's lunge at Luke landed her a hairs width from crushing my sternum.

I rolled onto my stomach, pushup mode, and eyed Zach. "Tell me when it's safe to stand."

Instead, he grabbed my armpits and pulled me across the sticky floor toward the jukebox. We hunkered against the glowing panels with our knees folded and watched the brawl. Our backs vibrated to Johnny Cash. I held a handful of torn leather fringe in my hand.

"This is why I shouldn't wear skirts," I said to Zach and allowed him to slip a comforting arm around my shoulder.

Zach tipped his hat back to give me a broad grin and a wink. He had lost his toothpick. "'Cause everyone saw you've got on green panties?"

"Exactly." I winced as Luke took a blow to the chin from a guy in a bass fishing t-shirt and Braves cap.

"You want to get out of here?" asked Zach.

"Thanks for the offer, but it's weird. You being my brother's friend and all. I should take that one home and clean him up anyway." I nodded at Luke as he charged the bass fisherman. "But hey, if you hear anything more about the hijack, will you let me know?"

"Yes, ma'am," said Zach.

Then stole a kiss before I could sock him.

SIXTEEN

Lucky for Luke, a bag of convenience store ice, the kind best used for coolers, sat in my freezer, ripped and readied for drinks. The ice was one benefit of roommates. With a forty-year-old fridge, there was no automatic nothing, and my lazy kin didn't like to bother with the fill-and-break trays. I threw a handful of ice in a washcloth and gave it to Luke for his chin.

He expressed his thanks and did his cop thing, a quick walk-through of my house, checking for the boogie man. Or more likely, Todd.

I pulled a long neck from the fridge, another benefit of roommates, and plunked into a kitchen chair to wait out his inspection. "They're probably all at Red's."

He strode back in, holding the ice to his chin. "I haven't been in a bar fight in about ten years."

"You weren't old enough to drink in bars ten years ago," I handed him a beer.

He flashed his dimples and straddled the chair across from me, the bottle dangling from one hand. "Didn't stop us back then, if I remember correctly."

I wished he'd keep those dimples locked down. And the memories. "You think your truck driver lied about his part in the heist?"

Luke tossed the ice on my kitchen table and took a long draw from his beer. "He was shot and didn't make it. I don't think the charade would have gone that far."

"Did you know your driver wasn't supposed to be driving?"

"What do you mean?" The beer bottle halted before his lips.

"Trucker Joe said the real driver had a D.U.I. and your driver took the route at the last minute. Do you think the real driver had an arrangement with the hijackers?"

"The carrier told us it was a last minute change of drivers. Who's Trucker Joe?"

"A big guy Todd and I met out at the rest stop on Tuesday night," I grinned. "He has a little fur ball called Princess Yapa-doodle. I think she's a dog, but I'm not for certain."

"Princess Yapadoodle?" Luke's nose wrinkled. "You and Todd went to the rest stop Tuesday night?"

"I had just learned about Tyrone and wanted to see where it happened. I couldn't help myself."

"You never try to help yourself," he sighed and scrubbed his curls with one hand. "And you never keep your mouth shut."

"You can be very insulting sometimes." I kicked off my boots and stretched on the chair.

He stopped mid-sip and set his beer on the table. "You think I'm insulting you?"

"Yes."

"I meant it literally, not as an insult. You broadcast infor-mation faster than CNN."

"That is also insulting."

"But true."

We stared at each other for a long moment. Long enough to set my nerves to tingle and my brain to partially shut down. I hopped from my chair and did three laps around the kitchen to encourage my blood to flow to other parts.

"So tell me more about this lawyer who wants his portrait done," Luke said, turning in his chair to watch my tour of the kitch-en.

I noticed his eyes remained on my legs.

"Rupert has horrible taste in everything but me and vodka. By the way, he knows Max Avtaikin. He said he bought my paintings to kick Max in the pants. How do you like that? Spending thousands of dollars just to tick someone off. Rich guys are crazy."

"Your art cost thousands of dollars?"

"He bought three life-size oils from a gallery. He wants a full-size portrait of himself standing by a Christmas tree and maybe one of his family. We're talking serious cash." I wandered into my studio-turned-living-room to look at my rows of portraits hiding behind the big television. "That guy is nuttier than a giant pecan, but he's richer than Croesus."

"That's great, hon'," Luke followed me into the living room. "I guess you'll be moving on to bigger things sooner than later."

"Halo's not a stepping stone for me, Luke. I love my town and my family." My thoughts flashed to Pearl and Grandpa. "Most of the time, anyway. I had always hoped to settle here and have a family. Atlanta's close enough to gallery hop."

"You'd do better elsewhere."

I turned to face him. "Your cousin Shawna..."

"Step-cousin."

"Your step-cousin is trying her best to destroy me," I said. "She thinks I have incriminating pictures of her, which I do not. And she's using my art, the paintings Rupert Agadzinoff bought, to sully my reputation."

"Sully your reputation?"

"Yes. Sully. As in blackmail me. She has threatened to broadcast the paintings in local churches if I don't hand over these pictures. She had posters made to humiliate me. Do you know what will happen? She'll ruin me. I'm not even allowed to eat at the farm now."

"Don't you and Shawna have more important things to worry about? She's got her new art shop. You've got this big painting deal."

"Gallery. Commission."

"Let it go," he said.

"You don't realize how hard I've worked these past five years to establish my studio, Luke. You weren't here. I finally had folks trusting me to capture their children and hunting dogs on canvas. It's not about the money. If I wanted to scramble for gallery shows, I would have stayed in Savannah."

I felt close to tears and I don't do tears, so I stomped my foot. "In a matter of months, Shawna has wiped out everything I've worked for. Now she's ready to deliver a pile driver to my career in local culture. And I don't know why."

"Ever since I moved back you two have been at each other's throats," said Luke.

"Before you arrived she barely acknowledged my existence."

"So you're blaming me for this?"

Luke could be such a man sometimes. I held my outrage in with crossed arms.

"I'm asking you if you know of any reason for your step-cousin to want to drive me from my hometown. Other than her usual snobbery, jealousy, and ugly antics."

He stared at me for a long minute. "You're being overdramatic."

"Thank you for the interesting evening. I hope your chin heals quickly and goodbye."

"Cherry, don't be like that."

He reached for me, but I retreated and bumped into the infernal television.

He shoved his hands in his back pockets and shuffled back a step. "Look, I don't want to get involved with Branson business, whether it's Shawna or anybody else. You know my feelings about my stepfamily. And now that I'm living back at home, I can't get away from the Bransons, particularly Shawna. Don't ask me to get entangled in your Shawna mess."

"Max Avtaikin is willing to help me, but you aren't."

"What does Avtaikin have to do with this?"

"He's the only one in town who will back my art. You see what Shawna's done? She's made me challenge my scruples by getting in bed with Max Avtaikin."

"Getting in bed?"

"You know what I mean."

We were interrupted by the sound of the kitchen door swinging open and banging against the wall. A moment later, my siblings invaded the living room. Casey and Cody ignored us to flop on the dead pheasant couch and shoot the TV with the remote. The TV blared on behind us.

"Take it outside," said Cody. "Y'all make better doors than windows. Can't see a thing."

"You'd think this wasn't my house," I said, fixing Cody with a determined big sister stare.

"You'd think right," said Casey. "Move it along."

Luke snagged my wrist. "Come on. It's not worth the fight."

We exited the living room to find Todd in the kitchen, leaning against the countertop. Pen in hand, he tapped a syncopated rhythm across a newspaper he had spread across the counter.

"What are you doing?" I asked.

"I picked up an AJC on the way home. Looking at jobs in Atlanta." Todd tossed the pen on the counter and turned his back on the Atlanta newspaper.

"Why? I thought you got a job at the SipNZip. I know the graveyard shift is no fun, but I thought your layoff was temporary. It'll tide you over and you won't have to commute."

"SipNZip called and said the job was no longer available." Todd drummed his fingers against the cabinets behind him. "I don't get it."

I sucked in my breath. "How can they offer you the job and then take it back? Who do they think they are? Donald Trump? This is Halo, Georgia. That's just plain rude."

"Someone made a mistake," said Luke. "Sorry to hear it, McIntosh."

"Are you hiring at the station?" asked Todd. His drumming increased. "I'll do just about anything."

Luke shook his head. "Money's tight everywhere. I'll keep my eye out, though."

"Luke, do you know who owns the SipNZip?" I said.

"Don't go getting all self-righteous with the SipNZip, Cherry." Luke folded his arms.

"They're new. They don't know how things work around here," I strode to Todd's side. "I've a mind to go in there and tell them what I think about their treatment of you."

"It's all right, baby," said Todd. "I'll get another job."

"Rupert's car is picking me up in the morning," I said. "I'll just swing by the SipNZip on the way out of town. A friendly inquiry."

"Don't worry about it, baby," said Todd. "No big deal."

"Leave it alone, Cherry," said Luke.

"Do you know who the owner is or not, Luke?"

Luke glanced at Todd. "I'm sure there's a good reason for this."

"Who's the owner?" I repeated.

"Max Avtaikin."

"What has happened to this town?" I exploded. "Why would he refuse Todd a job? I specifically told him Todd needed one."

I began another circle of the kitchen, this time to work off my ire.

"Don't get your britches in a twist," said Luke. "Avtaikin might not even know about the hiring. Probably someone at the store made a mistake."

"I know what's going on," I stopped between the two men. "Max wanted to get Todd a job with one of his business associates. The Bear's trying to pull you into his gambling underworld again, Todd. I thought the Bear had learned his lesson with his audit and almost arrest."

"This is how you give me ulcers," said Luke, pinching the bridge of his nose. "A normal woman would tell Todd she was sorry he didn't get the job and go on with her life. You take not minding your business to a whole different level of crazy."

I folded my arms. "Why would I want to be a normal woman? I don't even know what that means."

"Exactly the problem," Luke strode to the door. "Good luck with her, Todd. If you were any kind of man, you'd stop her."

"She's more fun if you let her go," said Todd.

"I'm not a responsibility to pass off. Especially not to Todd," I stomped after Luke. "I care about people, and I'm willing to do something about it. What's wrong with that? Isn't it a sin to look the other way when a wrong's been done?"

"Not if it means vigilantism." Luke swung the kitchen door open. "Or public disturbance."

"When have I ever made a public disturbance?" I thought for a second. "Outside high school? And college."

"Annoying people is a public disturbance." He slammed the door behind him.

I yanked open the door and stepped into my carport. "I can annoy people without breaking the law."

Luke ignored me and continued his descent to his truck. A minute later, the jacked up tires spun down my street and into the night.

I blew out the breath I held. Luke always brought out my fiercest. He was a stick to my bee hive. Which produced a lot of passionate buzzing and sweet honey when we were a couple, but the results had stung.

I stepped back inside and looked at Todd. "I'm going to Max Avtaikin's and see if I can annoy him without breaking the law. I'll take Casey's car."

"You want me to go with you?"

"It's late. If Luke's right about public disturbance, you better stay home. Don't want that on your record if you're trying to get a job."

He gave me his Labrador impression, nodding with an agreeable smile and expectant eyes. His Cherry Tucker game face. If Luke was a stick, Todd was smoke.

"Don't go thinking just because I'm helping you it means anything," I said. "You snookered me into marrying you once, but it won't happen again."

"I know, baby."

"And I'm still not talking to you."

"Sure, baby." His exit smile made me doubt my words.

I might have lost two battles. Time for a third. Stick. Smoke. How would Max Avtaikin deal with my bee hive? Bears don't care about getting stung. They'll tear apart a nest to get what they want.

SEVENTEEN

I had never been to Max's house at night. Particularly around bedtime o'clock. Although I didn't know Max's late night habits, I didn't figure him for farmer's hours and felt fairly safe in approaching his door this late. The porch lights were off, but the front of the house was lit with security and decorative spotlights. I stood on the veranda, shivering in the cool September night air and wished I had thrown a jacket over my tank top.

The Bear had confounded me once again. I had explicitly told Max that Todd wanted to apply at the SipNZip. Max had warned me off the convenience store. It made no sense. If Max and I were going to work together, I needed to trust him. Never mind he was doing me a favor. He'd find a way to make me pay him back, which was the conundrum that worried me.

Therefore, he needed to hear what I had to say. I pressed the doorbell again and listened for the chime echoing in the cavernous foyer. Locks tumbled, and the heavy, wooden door swung open.

"Artist?" Max stepped on to the porch and glanced behind me. "What brings you to my house this time of the night? Again, you do not call first."

He wore a black, cotton bathrobe. My eyes dropped to his bare feet, traveled up his legs, and landed on the curling chest hair exposed in the open V. I closed my eyes, said a prayer that he wore a pair of shorts under his robe, and opened my eyes. He appeared to be examining my trucker bar fashion with a critical gaze.

"Did I wake you?" I said.

"I am watching movie," he sighed, overcome with Eastern European melancholia. "It's not so good. And my popcorn machine is broken."

"Sorry to hear it. I have a bone to pick."

"Your odd phrases," he said. "Come inside before you start picking the bone."

He led me through the foyer and into a sitting room. Paintings hung in clusters in Victorian style arrangements. Like Rupert's formal room, red and gold pervaded the wall color and accessories. However, Max's room did not appear garish, only cluttered. The art of varied genres, mediums, and sizes was chosen with an appreciation for quality. He waved me to a leather sofa and sank onto a chair opposite.

"You have the artistic temperament and much passion," he quirked a slight smile. "But the necessity of speaking your mind whenever the mood strikes is not always convenient."

I blinked in confusion. "I'm busy tomorrow. This can't wait."

"I speak of my convenience, not yours."

"You said you were watching a bad movie." I waved away his complaint. "I just found out you are the owner of the SipNZip."

He eased back into his chair and crossed an ankle over his knee. I was careful to keep my eyes on his face for fear of robe exposure.

"How did you come to know this information?" he asked.

"Not important. Todd McIntosh tried to get a job at your establishment. He was hired and fired in the same day. Before he even got to try to screw up anything at work."

"I see." He spread his arms over the back of the chair, drawing the robe open and revealing a set of powerful pecs.

I held in my gasp.

"I told you I would help the Todd McIntosh find a job," said Max. "Not at SipNZip."

"And I told you he wanted to work at the SipNZip. Why would you turn down his application? He was willing to take the graveyard shift. Which would have helped our current sleeping arrangements."

"Sleeping arrangements?"

"Four people. Two bedrooms."

"Tomorrow I will make some calls," Max shrugged. "He'll have new job by Monday."

"He would have started at the SipNZip tomorrow."

"What does it matter the when and where? If he's willing to work at this convenience store, he will appreciate my finding him a better paying job elsewhere." He drew forward, dropping his leg and leaning on his elbows. "Where have you been tonight?"

"Me?" I felt thrown off by his sudden segue. "The Gearjammer. Why?"

"Your decorative leather is missing."

"What?" I looked at my crossed legs and realized he referred to my torn fringe. "I was dancing and fell. And sort of took down some folks with me. Then there was a fight..."

"Why do you go to such a place? It sounds rough for a young woman such as yourself."

"I'm a little rough," I smirked. "And we were questioning truckers."

"You are such a strange girl. Why do you question truckers?"

I hesitated, but the hijacking and composite sketch were public knowledge now. "There was a hijacking of a truck in Forks County. I actually sketched the hijacker's face from witness testimony."

"A hijacking?"

"Driver was shot and truck stolen." I dropped my gaze, knowing I should hold my tongue, but the quiet of the room and Max's lack of judgment worked better than a confessional. "I saw the witness later that morning at the SipNZip, actually. He told me he was going back to the scene of the crime. Later he was killed there. I didn't say anything to Luke or Uncle Will. Now his grandma and son are one step from government intervention. I feel responsible."

Max remained silent. I glanced up to find him rubbing his temples.

Noticing my gaze on him, he dropped his hands. "You are not responsible. Evil exists everywhere. Even in your precious Forks County."

I shivered. "I cannot turn a blind eye to evil."

"I have noticed. You refuse to turn the blind eye to anything. However, not all of us are evil."

The Bear wanted to knock down my hive. Or at least get the queen bee to look away while he foraged for honey.

"Speaking of evil," I said, "Shawna has started her attack. But I am no longer comfortable with you promoting my art."

"I am happy to assist in publicizing your talent. It is good for the value of the art."

He rose from his seat and crossed the room to stand before me. "Don't speak nonsense. This county is not big enough for both you and the Shawna Branson. I will enjoy defeating her attempts to humiliate you. She is a nuisance to me."

He chuckled and held out his hand. "Come."

I ignored his hand and tilted my head back to glare at him. "How can I trust you with my reputation? You lied about the Sip-NZip two seconds after agreeing to help me. Your job for Todd is most likely a plan to use him in some scheme. Just like you used him to cheat in your poker games."

"I did not lie about SipNZip. I simply did not tell you I own it."

"Why would you keep such a little thing from me? And why don't you want Todd working there?"

He dropped to the couch, perching on the edge, not quite touching my crossed knees. His size and masculinity unnerved me, but I remained still. Still for me, which included an agitated shaking of my foot. But I did not edge away from his intimidating presence.

"Artist," his voice dropped to a low growl, "you do not need to know everything. We have played this game before."

"Yes, sir. And you lost."

His polar blue eyes honed in on my smirk. "Retreat is not loss. You would be best to remember this."

I leaned toward him and caught the scent of a spicy cologne. "That's not what I've been taught. We Tuckers don't skedaddle in the face of danger."

He placed a hand on the couch near my hip, angling his prodigious body toward mine. The sleeve of his robe brushed my thigh. "Do you even realize when you face the danger?"

My gaze left his icy scrutiny to drop to his lips. They relaxed and curled.

My heart began beating one of Todd's breakneck rhythms. I pressed my hands together, willing the palpitations to slow. My eyes fell to the hollow of Max's throat, then down to the dark, curling hairs of his chest. A thick, hard muscled chest. Barrel shaped, as my Grandma Jo would say.

I blinked Grandma Jo's memory away and realized Max watched me.

The slight tilt to the corner of his eyes revealed his natural cunning, but there were also light laugh lines I had not noticed before. And I couldn't decide if his eye color was closer to king's blue deep or blue light.

Maybe phthalo blue touched with magenta for depth and lightened with white, I thought dreamily.

The lines around his eyes creased, and I pulled in my breath. What was my mother's hand-me-down libido doing messing around with the Bear? I had serious problems with men. I was barely over Luke. If barely meant not.

"You're laughing at me," I said, covering my indiscretion.

"Do you hear me laughing?" he murmured. "I am concerned for your safety. Your pride will be your undoing."

I caught his double meaning and fought the blush that threatened to creep up my neck. The man was in his robe, for heaven's sake. My refusal to retreat landed me practically in his lap. Or maybe he meant something else entirely, and I was the one with the dirty mind.

I really needed to see if there was surgery for removing stupid from my DNA.

"My pride will be my undoing?" I hedged. "On the contrary, I think it's more an issue with being stubborn. Or my mouth. I've got a lot of flaws to choose from."

He chuckled and rose. "Let me show you what I mean."

This time I took his offered hand, allowing him to pull me from the couch. My legs had lost some circulation in that heated moment. We passed through the foyer again, his giant paw still clutching my hand, and he pulled me toward his study. Dropping my hand, he opened the door and ushered me inside.

I followed him to his desk, where he switched on the monitor to his computer and tapped a few buttons on his keyboard.

"Look," he said.

I circled his desk to examine the monitor. The screen had been divided into quarters, each section showing a video shot of a different area of his property. Max moved the mouse to click on one quadrant and the grainy picture enlarged. I recognized the street outside his gate. A German hatchback was parked across from his drive.

"Your neighbor?" I asked.

"The car that follows you," said Max.

"What car that follows me?"

"Sorry. My English. You are being followed. By that car."

EIGHTEEN

"Why is someone following me?" I asked Max.

He looked up from his monitor. "Should I not ask you this question?"

"I have no idea. I'm not really stalker worthy."

We watched the car for a moment, but nothing happened. Max rose from his chair, clasped his hands behind his back, and sauntered to one of his Old Reb cases for an introspective gander.

"Do you think the stalker is a fan of my art?" I said excitedly. "A deranged fan?"

"I suppose anything is possible," said Max. "Perhaps you have other ideas, though?"

I dropped into Max's vacated chair and spun in a lazy circle. "The only deranged person I know is Shawna Branson. But that's not her vehicle. She's got a yellow Mustang convertible. And if she swapped it out, she would have done it at the Branson dealership and I'm pretty sure they're not doing European imports."

"She has the success in your humiliation without the need to follow you. No, I do not believe this is Miss Shawna Branson."

"Maybe it's not following me. Maybe they are stalking you and it's just a coincidence they drove up at the same time as me."

"Possibly," Max turned from the case and faced me. He pushed forward his shoulders and stood with his legs spread apart, head raised. He was in full-on Bear mode. "It would be helpful if you had been aware of them while you were driving."

"Why would I check to see if I'm being followed? I live in Halo. Everyone knows what I do without following me." I took another spin in the chair. "Maybe they are following Casey. I am driving her Firebird."

Max grunted. "That is even more unbelievable than someone following you."

"True," I said. "She's more of the stalker type than the stalkee."

Max unclasped his hands and strode to the desk. "We have several options. I can confront the individual. You can drive home and see if you are followed. I can drive you home in a different vehicle and see if we are followed."

"You don't want to confront one of my lunatic fans. What if they throw paint on you?"

"Why would they throw paint on me?"

"I've just been imagining what a crazy art fan might do."

Max raised an eyebrow. "You must take this seriously."

"Then let's call the Sheriff's Office."

"No," said Max. "No police."

"You're so touchy when it comes to the law. If you'd stop trying to straddle the line, the cops would be your friend." I took his chair for another spin and jerked myself to a stop. "Why don't I sneak out and see if I know them first?"

Max nodded. "Let's see who is this bozo."

"You're coming, too?"

"Of course. One moment, please." He moved around the desk, pulling a key ring from the pocket of his robe. I scooted the chair back as he leaned over me to unlock a bottom drawer. Before I could peek inside, Max pulled out a handgun, slammed the drawer shut, and relocked it.

"Is that a Glock? Forty-five or forty?"

"Forty has a bigger magazine." He dropped the speedloader into his hand, checked for bullets, and then slid it back inside the grip. Satisfied, he nodded at me. "Let us go."

I waved a hand at the robe which now fell open to his waist. "You want to put some clothes on first, Cowboy?"

*   *   *

Max was a lover of security. A gated, iron fence circled his beautifully landscaped lawn. Acres of undeveloped forest surrounded his property on three sides. An inner fence cloistered his pool and backyard. Small security cameras were scattered throughout, and every exit and floor had an alarm panel. There was also a big-ass cannon sitting in his front yard, which possibly worked. However, stealth was not his forte. Max's idea of sneaking up on the stalker? Walk to the end of his drive, cross the street, and stick a gun in his face.

In his robe and flip-flops.

My idea? Don cat-prowler gear and ninja our way to the car.

Our compromise was to exit from a side gardening gate and use the wooded area bordering his property as cover. Once we started, I could tell Max enjoyed playing G.I. Joe. He spoke with his fingers and jerks to the head. He had slipped on a black t-shirt, jeans, and a shoulder holster for his Glock. I could not convince him to wear a ski cap to cover his thick brown hair.

Likely worried about getting hat head.

Hell, I was excited, too. The boys used to let me follow them on deer stake-outs, otherwise known as covert juvenile drinking missions, and we'd play sneak attack while tromping through the woods. Sometimes we brought paint guns, although I often wasted my pellets making designs on trees. Tonight, I had borrowed a dark hoodie from Max, thirty-seven sizes too big, but it kept me warm and covered much of my body.

My vertically challenged legs scrambled after Max. After covering half a football field in long strides, Max halted. I slammed into him and cursed my lack of peripheral vision in the hoodie. He barely flinched, while the brick wall effect ricocheted throughout my body. Before I could slide to the ground, he grasped my elbow and jerked me to my feet. His fingers flew to give me the shush sign, and he jerked his head toward the little Beamer parked across the street.

I rolled my eyes and nodded. I was glad Max found skulking entertaining. However, he seemed to overstate the obvious. I pulled my elbow from his grasp and snuck around a magnolia planted near the street. The broad, thick leaves offered wonderful cover. I peeked around a branch, but was still too far to see anything.

A cluster of pines stood across the street, creating a wooded belt between two properties. If I could sneak across the street, I might have a decent chance of spying unseen. I glanced over my shoulder at Max and made a few finger gestures indicating my intention. He made a few gestures back at me, showing his disapproval. I spun around and showed him another finger.

While we finger argued, the mounting rumble of an approaching vehicle reached our ears. I hopped away from Max and peered around the tree. Headlight beams flickered in the distance. The vehicle would give me a chance to cross the street unseen.

While I watched for the oncoming car, Max crept behind me and breathed into my ear. "Let me speak to this person. While I distract, you see if you know them."

I angled a look back at him. "What if the stalker is coo-coo for you and not me? What if they see you're packing and they pull out a pistol and shoot you?"

"I have more fear of you getting hit by this car than getting shot by a sleepy intruder."

"I'll be careful. I'll run across right after this vehicle passes. The oncoming headlights will give me cover."

"Have your way," he nudged me toward the street. "Just be careful. If you get smashed by car, I will have to call police. They will find our alibi strange."

"Alibi? Why are you worried about an alibi?" I said, but the growing headlights didn't give me time to finish the thought. Across the street, the stalker had cranked his ignition. The BMW readied to leave in response to the oncoming vehicle. I crept closer to the street and squatted within the lower magnolia branches.

The rumble grew louder and the headlights grew brighter. I pulled the hood on my sweatshirt forward to ward off their glare.

The vehicle, a large truck, slowed as it approached, bathing me in light. The tree blocked the stalker's view of my squat and the tall headlights would momentarily blind him. I looked over my shoulder. Max had disappeared.

I rose, stepped out of the tree's cover, and stared into the oncoming headlights. Orange and yellow orbs swam in my vision. I waited for the red glare of the tail lights to pass and stepped off the curb. Light brightened the street, confusing my already spotty vision. I took three springing steps to dart across the street and realized I had a spotlight trained on me.

A squeal broke through the sound of the truck motor, and everything went haywire. I froze. Red lights spun to one side. Bright lights washed over my still form. A motor gunned. I couldn't see what was happening. Exhaust and rubber fumes filled my lungs. The lights grew brighter. I flew off my feet.

Airborne is an odd feeling. Particularly if you're not sure where you'll land.

NINETEEN

Beneath the magnolia, Max clutched my waist while we watched the truck finish its donut spin. The BMW had taken off.

"I understand better the frustration of your deputy," Max panted.

"I couldn't see. I didn't know the BMW was fixing to run me over." I was still sprawled over Max's lap, where I had landed after he had snatched me from the oncoming car. "You just saved my life."

"The truck is stopping," he said and jerked us both to our feet. His arm remained circled across my body. His shoulder holster dug into my shoulder blade.

"I'm not planning on running out in the street again," I said. "You can relax your grip."

"Quiet." His thick fingers tightened on my waist, and he reached across me with his other arm to unsnap his holster, effectively blocking my view. And my mouth.

I inhaled the spicy cologne he wore and thought about biting his arm, but worried about breaking my teeth on the packed muscle.

Brakes screeched and a motor cut off. Max dropped his hand from the gun grip. I could see once again.

His other hand remained positioned across me, but his fingers had relaxed slightly. My body concealed his gun from the driver's view.

I vaguely wondered if all this body clutching was for his protection or mine. However, considering our difference in size, I'd make a crappy shield.

The driver's door to the dark pickup swung open and the cab light illuminated the driver.

"Oh shit," I said. "This isn't going to be good."

"You seem to have more than one stalker," said Max.

"What in the hell," bellowed Luke. He jumped from his cab and stomped around the truck. "You crazy woman. You almost got hit by that car."

He stopped in the street before us, the Raptor's headlights now shining a spotlight on him. "What are you two doing?"

"May I ask you the same?" Max said with a casual air of indifference. He might have spent every night snatching women from oncoming traffic and rolling them under magnolia trees.

"What do you mean? I'm not the one standing in the street in the middle of the night."

"Well," I said, "you kind of are. Standing in the street. In the middle of the night."

The look on Luke's face made me ease back into Max's body. I felt his gun press into my back. At least I hoped it was his gun.

Max's hand released my hip. "Is there an explanation for your decision to drive by my home at this time of night?"

"I don't owe you an explanation," said Luke. "The roads are public property."

"I see," said Max. "Good night, then." He clamped a paw around my hand, pivoted, and walked back through the trees, yanking me behind him.

"Hey," yelled Luke. "I'm not done with you."

Max ignored Luke and trucked along, easing us back to his fence line. I strode triple time to keep up with his pace.

I glanced over my shoulder to see if Luke followed us. "You are making an enemy in the Sheriff's Office."

"I am not a fan of police," said Max. "We did not break the law. We have no reason to talk to him."

"Common courtesy?"

"You speak too much," he slowed and let me catch up to his side. "This is your problem. Too much talking. If we had stayed to chat with your deputy, what would have happened?"

"He would've yelled at me for almost getting hit by a car. Then yelled at me for coming here tonight when he told me to leave you alone. And probably yelled for some other stuff I can't think of."

"Always the yelling," said Max. "Why do you want to be with someone who yells at you?"

"He yells because he cares. He fears for my safety overmuch," I said. "But you do have a point."

Max opened the gate for me to stumble through. "Unfortunately, I did not see the driver before he missed squashing you with his BMW."

"I didn't see him either. Do you think he accidentally tried to kill me or was it more on purpose?"

"Very difficult to tell, given the situation." Max fell silent as we trudged through his yard. Reaching the driveway, he stopped. "Perhaps it is nothing but coincidence."

"I'd like to think so," I yawned. "Why would anyone sign my death warrant? Unless it's some extreme anti-nudist folks who caught wind of my *Greek Todd* paintings."

"You spoke of a hijacking and the murder of the witness. May I see this sketch?"

"I don't see why not. The Sheriff's Office is showing it to everyone." I felt for my keys in my pocket and realized I had left my purse in his house. "I'll bring it by tomorrow. I've got a busy day, so I can't promise what time I'll stop in."

"I would expect nothing less," said Max, giving me his ubiquitous eyebrow raise. "I will drive you home. The perpetrator may wait for you. Tomorrow morning I will bring Casey her car."

"Good. Stop in for coffee and you can explain to Todd why you're rehiring him for the SipNZip. He can start immediately."

Max's mouth quirked. "You are like my childhood dog. He would also not give up the bone picking."

"I'm not sure if that's a compliment, but thanks. I'm glad you changed your mind."

"You are mistaken."

"On which part? The compliment or changing your mind?"

By way of answering, he abruptly turned and strode toward the house.

"I see how you work," I said. "When you don't want to have a conversation, you just walk away. Is retreat the only maneuver you know?"

Max stopped and shot a dark look over his shoulder. "I know many maneuvers. Some of which may surprise you."

That statement gave me a pause. And a shocking flutter through my stomach. Whatever maneuvers he wanted to try on me, that one certainly shut me up.

TWENTY

The next morning, I gathered my sketching supplies and made a hasty exit from the crowded house before anyone complained I used all the hot water. No BMW lurked nearby, but Rupert's town car waited for me. At this hour, the street was quiet. Rather unusual to not have prying eyes about and rather unfortunate, I thought, as I climbed into the back of the vehicle.

I could've used the good press of a chauffeured car.

I made the driver, Nick, drive through the middle of town. The post office was empty, save for a poster of *Greek Todd*, which I ripped down and stuffed in my bag.

I studied the Tru-Buy as we passed, but the early hour left the parking lot empty. Feeling disappointed my brush with a chauffeur did not lend itself to bragging, I allowed Nick to continue toward the interstate exit. I would've loved to have him drive down to Line Creek and park in front of Shawna's store, but I didn't want to push her over the edge. Yet.

As we neared the exit, I eyed the SipNZip sign, looming in the distance between a liquor store and a Motel 8. "Nick, can we stop at the SipNZip?"

Nick nodded. He wasn't much on talking. On the drive through Halo, I had tried my best to pull conversation from him. The back of his buzzed, light brown head nodded or shook. Once he turned his head so he could give me an "are-you-serious?" look. Not a chatter.

We pulled into the SipNZip and I popped open my car door, forgetting that was part of Nick's role. "Are you coming in?" I asked him.

He shook his head, pulled a pack of cigarettes from his shirt pocket, and leaned against the car.

"You want a cup of coffee?"

His eyes cut from the lighter he cupped before the cigarette in his mouth. Giving me a quick head shake, Nick torched the cigarette and blew a stream of smoke in my direction.

I gave up on Nick and wandered past the gas pumps to the store. Max might have shut down my SipNZip line of questioning, but I am a woman who follows through with her intentions. I wasn't quite sure of my intentions, but while I tried to catch some ever-elusive sleep, I had thought about Max's reasons to not want Todd in his store. Max had hired Todd for odd jobs in the past. Like calling bingo and dealing poker and something between the two that dipped into card sharking. Max trusted Todd. The problem wasn't Todd.

The problem was the SipNZip.

Max didn't want anyone to know he owned it, which was also strange considering he didn't hide his presence in the community. What was going on with the SipNZip? I reckoned there was only one way to find out. I would have to get a job at the SipNZip. Without Max knowing. In between my hours of working on Rupert's painting, taking care of the Coderres, and figuring out why Shawna wanted to destroy me.

I'd give the job a week. I couldn't sleep anyway. Not with all these people in my house. I was sharing a bed with my sister, for gracious sake.

The sparkling glass door of the SipNZip banged behind me as I walked to the counter. The spindly, young woman I had met earlier worked the cash register again. She looked up from her magazine, recognition dawning in her eyes. Quickly replaced with irritation. She enjoyed my need to chat as much as Nick the driver.

"I want an application to work here," I said.

She shrugged, pulled a piece of paper from the drawer beneath her, and shoved it at me. With a winning customer service smile and a thank you, I took the form and a pen. Five minutes and one cup of flavored coffee later, I returned with the completed application.

"Cherrilyn Ballard?" She stumbled over my name as she scanned the form.

I bobbed my head, taking a cue from Driver Nick. Ballard was my Grandpa's name and my real name was Cherrilyn, so no real foul there. And using my Grandpa's farm address wasn't really a lie. However, my extensive work in the service and retail industry was a bit overblown.

"I'm willing to work the graveyard shift," I said. "Actually, it's really the only time I can work. And on Friday and Saturday nights, I'd rather come in after the bars close."

"We'll call you."

"Alrighty. Have a good day now." I traipsed back to the car.

Nick tossed his cigarette onto the blacktop and opened my door. I clambered in and noticed the poster sticking out of my satchel.

Yanking it out of the bag, I pressed out the wrinkled paper and examined the enlarged photograph. Shawna had used a Sharpie to draw arrows and enhance some of Todd's features. She had also written, "You Call This Art? Concerned Citizens for Decency in Art," followed by her phone number. Todd's face had been Sharpied out. Which I guess was good for Todd, although he might have liked Shawna's enhancements. Likely would have gotten him some high-fives from the guys.

I shoved the poster back in my satchel, pulled out my phone, and called my sister.

Casey bleated an obnoxious word in my ear.

"I found a *Greek Todd* poster in the post office. You, Cody, and Todd need to drive around the county and pull those posters down."

She repeated the offensive word.

"I'm serious," I said. "Shawna's forming a concerned citizens group about me. The witch hunt has begun. I'm on my way to Atlanta, otherwise I would do it."

I hung up before she cussed again. Casey was not a morning person.

I dialed another number.

"Girl, how are you? I'm on my way to the church for organ practice," said Leah. "Mercy, it's a beautiful day. Don't you think?" Leah was a morning person. Which is why I rarely talked to her in the morning.

"Leah, I need your help." I glanced out the window and saw a sign for the Cracker Barrel. My stomach's resonant growl caused a shriek from Leah and a concerned glance in the rear view from Nick. I held the phone away from my body until my stomach finished complaining. "Shawna Branson is up to no good again. Have you heard her newest campaign plan?"

"Honey, yes. I was in the office yesterday when she tried to reserve a meeting room at the New Order Church for Monday night. Some kind of Concerned Citizens League. Wanted it sooner and got real ugly with the receptionist, Beth Daniels. You're lucky Beth doesn't take any guff and wouldn't move the Boy Scouts to another night. They're getting ready for their pinewood derby. Isn't that cute?"

"I tell you what's not cute. What people are going to think of me after Shawna leads this meeting. She'll get all the Bransons to back her. I'll be blackballed from the Lions' pancake breakfasts, much less sell a pencil sketch or anything else."

"Plus your Grandpa will wring your neck. The boys at the hardware store will not let him live this down."

"He'll likely kick me out of my over-crowded house. Which means I'll really need to work in this town to pay rent," I sighed. "Can you talk to Shawna? See if you can get any sense out of her? Find out what she means by these pictures she thinks I have?"

"Of course, I'll try. This is plain silly. How does this one woman get a whole county to shun you?"

"My family history doesn't help. I've got plenty of friends, but most aren't respectable. With the exception of you and, ironically, Max Avtaikin. He can slip through the fingers of the law and still get a key to the city." I squinted in thought. "You'd think the elderly community would be angry with him for that bingo deal, but they blame me instead."

"Everyone loves Mr. Max. And you're sort of easy to blame."

"Don't start spouting the 'blessed are the meek' lines. I get enough of that from Red."

"You do have a mouth on you, honey. No denying that," Leah giggled. "But you generally use it for the good of others. You have a big heart."

"Almost as big as my mouth," I smiled.

"Some Halo residents see a problem with both. Folks don't always appreciate your public service. At least the public you are serving. Unfortunately, the big folks think the people you like to help deserve their misfortune. People like the Bransons don't like your interference."

"I guess helping the Coderres isn't going to get me a Citizen of the Year award, either. Leah, tell me why I want to live in a town who looks down on the unfortunate?"

"Because that happens everywhere, baby. City, country, suburbs. You want to live in this town because your family and friends live here. And it's a good place to raise children."

"Who said anything about raising children? Lord, Leah. Your mind likes to take some exotic leaps."

"I'm going to hunt down Shawna today and try to talk some sense into her. Are you off to your fancy art job? Don't forget Sticks plays tonight at Red's."

"I'll be there. Unless I have to work at the SipNZip. Thank you, Leah. You're the best." I hung up before she questioned me about the SipNZip.

I felt a little better about Shawna's craziness. However, I was still playing defense. Unless I could stop Shawna's forward motion, I had better hope for an interception.

I needed to find those damned mysterious pictures. Before the Concerned Citizens meeting. I didn't have much time before the tar and feathering commenced.

TWENTY-ONE

Inside Rupert's house, I left my sunglasses on to allow my eyes to adjust to his blinding decor. And the retro, red faux-Ray Bans accentuated my red hombre dyed tank top and gold denim jeans. Couldn't hurt to let the patron think I admired his favorite colors. The outfit also worked well as interior camouflage.

Miss David greeted me in head to toe black. Very classy, although I suspected she used monotones to rebel against Rupert's ostentatious style. I followed her to his office where she left me. Rupert sat at his desk, talking on the phone. At my hesitation, he waved me in and then spun his chair so he faced a window.

A decorated Christmas tree now stood on the far side of the office. Compared to the tacky office decor, the tree was beautiful. Southern ideal, professionally decorated beautiful. In other words, it stood out like a Christmas tree in September.

I dropped my satchel on the floor before the tree and crossed the room to gather my other belongings from the town car. Mindful of Rupert's telephone chat, I closed his door softly and tiptoed into the hall leading toward the foyer. Near the front door, Nick and Miss David stood chatting. He had my easel, tackle box, and portfolio under one arm. The other hand reached for Miss David's ass. I backed up, bumped into a Chippendale table, spun, and caught the porcelain vase before it spilled flowers and water onto the table. My lightening reflexes saved the arrangement but had broken the butler-chauffeur dalliance.

Assuming Miss David was a butler, of course. Which didn't matter, because they looked miffed either way.

"May I help you?" asked Miss David, striding to the table. She adjusted the vase three centimeters from where I had just righted it.

"I was coming to get the rest of my things."

Carrying my gear, Nick schlepped past me and into the office.

"Thanks Nick," I said to his back.

"Anything else?" asked Miss David.

"You know, I don't care if you have a thing with Nick. I'm here to do a job, same as you."

"Then go do your job."

"Mr. Rupert's on the phone. I've got a minute. So, where are you from? I can tell it's not Atlanta."

Her pale lips clenched. "Do you want to see my passport?"

"No," I wrinkled my nose, wondering yet again what had happened to the art of pleasantries. "I'm just making conversation. Are you Canadian? You have a teeny accent."

"No," she said with a sneer that would insult most Canadians. "I'm not the one with the accent. Mr. Agadzinoff is expecting you. He's a busy man."

Miss David didn't realize snubbing me tended to have the opposite effect intended. Now I was dying to pull her into a conversation even if I humiliated myself. And use the opportunity to learn more about Crazy Rupert. "What does an immigration lawyer do?"

"Helps immigrants file their citizenship papers."

"Must be lucrative," I leaned against the table and the vase threatened to spill again. Hopping off, I righted the vase and saw Miss David's consternated look. "Does he pay you pretty well?"

"That's an impertinent question."

"I don't mean to be impertinent," I said, honestly. "I'm just curious."

"You know the fable about the curious cat?" She folded her arms over her black suit jacket.

"The one where the cat dies?"

"Mr. Agadzinoff is paying you well for your artistic services. Extremely well so he can truthfully tell his Buckhead friends his art is expensive. That is all you need to know."

"In order to paint a realistic portrait, I need a sense of the person I'm representing. Their personality is reflected in the painting. My curiosity helps me to do my job well."

"Then I'd advise you to ask Mr. Agadzinoff what he pays his employees and not me."

She stalked down the hall. I waited until she was out of sight to shudder off the chill left behind. As I turned back, Nick opened the office door and sauntered toward me.

"Hey Nick," I said, seeking further opportunities for humiliation and information. "Do you think I'm impertinent?"

Nick shook his head and tried to move past me.

I hopped in front of him. "Miss David thinks I'm impertinent. I think I'm giving her the wrong impression. What can I do to smooth things over with her?"

He shrugged.

"Do you have a stutter or something? If you do, I don't mind. I have a cousin who stutters. You can sing your answer if you like. Or write it down."

"I don't have stutter," he said. "You are fine. Miss David doesn't like anybody."

"I think she likes you. And you don't talk to me either."

"She don't like me. I don't talk for my English is not so good."

Aha, I thought. Maybe Miss David's English was also poor. Although she did know the word impertinent. "Are you one of Mr. Agadzinoff's immigrants?"

"Yes." Nick's gaze moved to his shoes. "My name is Nikolai, but Nik sounds American."

"Nikolai is nice, too." I smiled. "Welcome to America, Nik. Hope you like it here."

He blushed, shrugged, and toed the Chippendale table. "I better wash cars. Mr. Agadzinoff likes to ride in clean car. He wants me to wash your truck, too."

"No need for that, Nik. If you wash the Datsun, her paint might peel off. She's one rinse from completely rusting out."

Nik gave me a half-smile and stepped to get around me. I stopped him with a hand to his arm. "Listen Nik, if I talk too fast, let me know. I'd hate for you to think I was being rude."

"You are not talking fast. You just talk much." Nik's grin broke wide.

"So I've heard," I dropped my hand from his arm and grinned back. "I'll see you later."

Nik gave me a nod and continued toward the foyer.

I returned to Rupert's office. He had finished his phone call and paced before the Christmas tree.

"Where have you been, darling?" he asked. "I have some free time now. Let's begin."

"I'm going to start with some quick sketches," I said, hurrying to the Christmas tree. "I'll work at my easel. Feel free to talk and try different positions. Would you like to be seated or standing?"

Rupert turned to examine the Christmas tree. "Sitting will be more comfortable, but I will have better lines if I stand. Don't you agree? And sitting might appear aggrandizing. Like I'm a king on a throne."

I looked up at him from my squat before my tackle box. Rupert put a lot more thought into posing than anyone I ever met. "Whatever you want to do is fine with me. We can try both and you can look at my sketches before you decide."

He strode to his desk and picked up his phone. "Miss David? Can you get the full length mirror from my dressing room and bring it in here?"

This was probably why Miss David hated me. My appearance caused her more work. A butler's job is never done.

Grabbing a good piece of charcoal and my sketch pad, I placed both on my easel and set to work sketching Rupert as he fretted about his pose. I concentrated on getting his relative proportions before worrying about detail and composition. The head is amazingly symmetrical. Pupils are your center. You can actually draw a line from pupil to pupil and use that line to make a perfect square to help find the lines for the mouth and nose.

I find that aspect of the human face amazing. And I don't even like geometry.

Once you understand the shape of a face, drawing becomes much simpler. However, everyone but super models have quirks to their symmetry. Those small faults had to be noted, too, without drawing too much attention to them. People with a crooked nose don't want to see a crooked nose in their portrait. But the painting still has to honestly reflect their face. Tricky.

As I told Miss David, in order for a portrait to look realistic, it needs the personality of the sitter. Portraits are all about nuance, not geometry. A tilt to the head, an uplift at the corner of the mouth, or a slant in an eye's gaze makes all the difference. Otherwise you end up with a robot face.

Or a paint by number project by Shawna Branson.

Miss David returned with the mirror. We set it up next to my easel so Rupert could pose himself as Father Businessman Christmas or whatever look he was going for. He tried standing, leaning, and sitting, then settled on standing.

"So how long has Miss David worked for you?" I waited to ask that question until she had left the room. The less Miss David talked, the more I wanted to know.

"A few years," he picked a piece of lint off his suit jacket. "Do you think I should wear a black or blue suit?"

"Blue. It'll pull out some of the colors from the tree decorations and work better with the undertones in your skin."

I flipped a page in my sketchbook and worked on a close up of his small, bushy mustache. It would not do to have him looking like Hitler.

"So what did Maksim say when you told him I hired you?" asked Rupert. He smiled at himself in the mirror and straightened his tie.

"Mr. Max?" I looked up from my mustache. "I forgot to tell him, actually."

"You must tell him, my dear," Rupert shook a finger at me. His eyes twinkled. "And be sure to report the look on his face. It will make me laugh, I know."

I began working on a set of Rupert's eyes, trying to capture the "I bested Max Avtaikin" twinkle. That look was pure gold. And Rupert liked gold. "Yes, sir. How long have you known Mr. Max?"

"A long time." Rupert's gaze drifted to his gold and brass coffered ceiling. "I helped him immigrate. Did you know his mother was an artist?"

"He told me that once," I said, eager to learn more about the Bear. "Didn't she go to art school before she got married?"

"She was very talented. It's a shame she didn't amount to much."

"Max turned out pretty well. His mother must be proud of him."

"She died long ago." Rupert paused, then shrugged. "Didn't see Maksim amount to anything more than a gangster."

I bit my lip. "I am sorry to hear that. Must have been hard on him."

"Maksim is a hard man." Rupert glanced back to the mirror and slicked down a stray hair. "Before she died, I believe he was involved in some kind of crime organization. Luckily, he eluded the law, otherwise he would still be back home. No immigration for convicts. Legally, anyway."

"Really?" I set my charcoal down. "Tell me more."

"I would think Maks would have told you these stories," said Rupert.

"Max is really good at avoiding reports on anything he doesn't want me to know."

Particularly anything personal or illegal, I thought. Next to the mustache and eye sketch, I drew a bear. A bear with expensive cologne, giant pecs, and a small scar above his eyebrow. A bear who knew maneuvers.

It had been a long while since I had experienced maneuvers, I thought. My old maneuvers were embarrassed to be seen with me or busy telling me I'm overdramatic. My other old maneuvers had tried to trick me into thinking they were someone they were not.

Of course, Rupert's stories weren't doing much to win me over to the side of new maneuvers. And I had to remind myself I had never trusted Max, with or without interesting maneuvers.

I realized I had missed part of our conversation during my bear sketch. "Sorry, what did you say?"

"Maksim Avtaikin is a difficult man to read. What do you think?"

"Yes, sir," I said and flipped the page on my sketch book to hide my little bear. "Real difficult."

"He only has one of your paintings. But you have spent some time with him. He hasn't commissioned you for a portrait yet?"

"Max's mentioned it, but we never talked about it officially. However, he's helping me out with a show in Halo."

"A show? He's commissioning a show?" Rupert's mustache made a peevish dance above his lip.

"Not commissioning. I'm sure he'll take a hefty cut of anything that sells. But more than likely nothing will. There's a," I could not call Shawna an artist, "gallery owner who thinks the *Greek Todd*s are immoral. Or at least she'd like the town to think they are."

"Immoral?" Rupert started a laughing attack that allowed me to capture his likeness in charcoal. Bent over. Wheezing. Tears.

I flipped to a clean sheet. I was saving that to show him later.

"How could you consider those paintings immoral?" Rupert wiped an eye. "Is that what your mother hinted at earlier? Will it increase their value if the public thinks they are immoral?"

"Pearl is not my mother," I shuddered. "It won't increase the value in the public she was speaking of. They don't spend much on art."

"But the paintings are representative of classical antiquity works."

"Doesn't matter to Forks County."

"You need to have these paintings in your show. So this town can see their beauty."

"I don't know if that's a good idea anymore. Forks County is seeing that beauty all over town. Shawna Branson has posters of the paintings hung all over the place. Embellished with a Sharpie."

Rupert tapped his lips. "I want to be involved in this show."

"We could use any sketches I do of you," I said. "I could use colored pencil. Forks County would like the Christmas tree."

"Brilliant," Rupert clapped his hands together. "I must come to this show. Have you changed your mind about staying at my house? You can work on more sketches for this show while you stay here."

"No," I said. "In fact, I'm trying to get a graveyard shift at our local SipNZip."

"Darling," Rupert laughed. "You are a wonder. The graveyard shift at the SipNZip." His body shook as he tried to contain his mirth.

Not that I didn't love a good compliment, but I couldn't figure out why I was wonderful for wanting the late night shift at the Sip-NZip. Unless it was one of those jabs at country folks soaked in irony so we wouldn't know city people were making fun of us. I gave him a good redneck glare just in case.

"Have you told Maks you plan to work at the SipNZip?" asked Rupert.

"No, and I'd appreciate you not mentioning it to him."

"Well, well. This is interesting. I think you've sketched enough for today. I have work to do. You may go home. We'll keep the Sip-NZip our little secret," Rupert giggled. "But don't forget to tell Maks about our portrait commission."

Rupert was making fun of me. Therefore, I might not tell Max diddly. And I didn't like the idea of Rupert crashing in on our show. Or Rupert and his entourage coming to Halo again. That was all I needed. More fodder for gossip. A chauffeured car was one thing. Rich people looking down their noses was another.

I needed to find those pictures fast. Not just to save my reputation. Now I needed a preemptive strike against a Max and Rupert showdown in Halo.

TWENTY-TWO

I left my easel and other supplies, but packed the sketchbook in my satchel. Rupert would go through the sketches, of that I was fairly sure, and I didn't want him seeing my bear next to his mustache. Although he'd most likely find it a riot.

In the hallway, I sought out Miss David. She carried a tray with a glass teapot and dainty mugs of etched glass set inside gold filigree stands. I jogged to catch up and then walked back toward the office with her.

"We're done for the day," I told her, careful to annunciate my words.

"Good-bye," she said and juggled the tray to free a hand to enter the office.

I grabbed the doorknob for her, but didn't open the door. "Let me ask you something," I said. "Do you know Maksim Avtaikin?"

"Why?"

"He's a," I hesitated. What was Max to me? Business associate? Friendly adversary? Friendly adversary with benefits? I stopped on that thought, annoyed with myself. My rebound symptoms were out of control. "He's a friend. Rupert seems to have a competitive relationship with him. I get the feeling this portrait is all about showing Max up."

"What is it to you?" She laid her tray of tea things on the Chippendale table. "Are you in a position to care about the reasons why someone wants to buy your paintings?"

"Not really," I admitted. "However, I feel like I'm in an odd spot. A bit stuck between the two men."

"I'd unstick and get your job done. You have a contract for a portrait and you're getting paid extremely well. Let the men work their issues out without your interference."

"Good point." I cocked my head, fascinated by Miss David. "How do you know Mr. Max?"

Her delicate nose flared. "I work for Mr. Agadzinoff. Maksim Avtaikin was a client. I'm familiar with all the clients."

"Why is Rupert so interested in besting Max? Rupert's rich and successful. I wouldn't think Max would be a threat to his manhood."

"Men," Miss David snorted. "Everything is the pissing contest with them."

"True. Sometimes I wonder if Luke and Todd are really interested in me or only trying to settle some old high school score. I'm like a ten point buck. They both want the kill, but in the end I'm the one mounted on the wall with the glassy eyes. While they're cleaning their guns, getting ready for the next deer season."

"Who is Luke and Todd? They want to murder you?"

"Sorry, thinking out loud. I have a poor view of marriage at the moment. My mother's fault. Just ignore that."

She picked up her tray. "You are very odd."

"Just chalk it up to artistic temperament. Makes it easier on you to think of me that way." I adjusted my satchel and eyed the front door. "Is my truck nearby?"

"You will have to ask Nik. I will call him after I deliver this tea. Wait in the foyer."

"Yes, ma'am." I pulled my phone from my bag and walked down the hall. No calls from Luke.

However, I didn't think much of it. Luke wasn't a phone guy. He would rather confront me about my irrational behavior in person. I knew I had become a burr in his saddle, but I couldn't think of how to change that fact. We had broken up. I was trying to move on. Our last relationship was in college, and he broke up with me by joining the Army. If we were going to live in the same county, he would have to learn to ignore me. Not take me to trucker bars and trailer parks.

Although I liked it when he took me to trucker bars and trailer parks. I rubbed my chest and wished my heart would stop hurting.

I searched for a roll of Rolaids in my satchel, found an old toothpick, and my thoughts drifted to Zach and the hijacking. I realized I should check in on the Coderres again. Thinking about Jerell and his great-grandma revved up my heartburn. I couldn't think what else to do with them other than solve Tyrone's murder so they could take the killer to civil court and sue for damages. Even then they'd have to wait for the criminal trial and I didn't know if Miss Gladys would live that long.

I hoped I didn't have to work at the SipNZip tonight. I was a busy girl. Find the elusive Shawna pictures and save my reputation. Help the Coderres. I also needed to bring Max the sketch and question him on his background in organized crime.

I should make a list. And find an antacid. The people in my life had my heart in a vise clamp.

In the foyer, I hauled open the front door and stepped on to the porch. The town car waited in the donut drive, but I didn't see Nik or my truck. I glanced behind me. The hall was empty and quiet. To my left, the French doors of the red room stood open. To my right, a closed door. A bathroom possibly stocked with over-the-counter medications?

The closed door beckoned. Seeing another example of Rupert's god-awful decorating style had become akin to poking a sore tooth.

With a quick glance outside and down the hall, I approached the unexplored room and grasped the lever, waiting for an alarm. Pushing the door open, I sucked in my breath, surprised by the simplicity of the room. Royal blue and gold pervaded, but the extra molding and accessories had been left out. Not a bathroom. A desk with the usual filing and office apparatus had been tucked in one corner. A sofa and chairs lined the walls and a coffee table laid with magazines sat before them.

I strode to the table, hoping for a peruse through a *People* or *Us* while I waited on Nik. A foreign language with extra punctuation and funny letters adorned the magazine covers. I abandoned the illegible magazines for the desk. Neat, tidy, and impersonal. Obviously Miss David's hang out. Apparently butlering wasn't her only duty. She was also a secretary. Or maybe only a secretary. I had assumed Rupert's office was somewhere in the city, but doubling your home and office had nice tax benefits. I knew that from personal experience. Although, if audited tomorrow, the IRS might have issues with the dead pheasant couch and mega-television in my studio.

Photos in tasteful gold frames covered the two long walls. I strolled the room studying the pictures of immigrants holding their citizenship papers. In each snapshot, Rupert grasped the new citizen around their shoulder, flashing his toothy grin. It warmed my heart to see Rupert helping so many people. I didn't care for his snobbery, but I figured when you were a successful attorney, that went with the territory.

I moved to leave the office when a picture hung in the middle of a grouping caught my eye. I doubled back to study the photo of Rupert and the Bear. Rupert had the same plastered smile. Max didn't look as pleased. He clutched his papers at his side, unlike the other immigrants who held theirs for the camera. He looked impatient to be done with whatever scene had just finished.

Maybe the pissing contest started in this photograph. Max didn't give Rupert the due that Rupert thought he deserved. The other immigrants had the cheap clothing and hungry expressions typical of the Statue of Liberty's "give me your tired and poor." Max wore a fine suit. Hand tailored, not bought off the rack at the Big & Tall store.

I heard Nik call my name, and I left the Bear's citizenship photo with additional questions floating in my mind.

Rupert had been correct. Max Avtaikin was a difficult man to read.

*   *   *

I hastily exited Miss David's office, closing the door behind me, and went in search of Nik. He stood on the porch, smoking. The Datsun was nowhere in sight.

"Hey Nik," I said, slowing my words. "Is my truck ready?"

He stubbed his cigarette out in a portable ashtray and slipped it into his pocket. "No. Your truck is not working."

"What do you mean she's not working? She was running like a top. The wind-up kind, but running anyway."

Nik shrugged. "I take you home. Mr. Agadzinoff said I drive you."

"I want to see my pickup."

Nik jerked his head toward the drive and stalked off the porch.

I hurried after him. "You didn't try to wash her, did you? I told you soap is no good for that truck. The grime holds her together. She gets rained on occasionally."

"You need new car," said Nik.

"I need a ton of new things. The Datsun and I've been through a lot together. I'm not putting her to pasture in Atlanta, I can tell you that. She needs to make it home so Cody can look at her."

Nik strode off the donut and began following another drive around the side of the house. We slowed before the garage, a three door. The far side had my little, yellow pickup. Her entrails were spilled all over the garage floor.

"What have you done?" I cried, rushing to the truck. "Why are you taking her apart?"

Nik followed me into the garage and leaned against a Jaguar in the opposite bay. "She no run. I am mechanic. Checking her parts."

"Baby, I am so sorry," I said to my truck. "I'll bring Cody up to take care of you."

I turned on Nik. "How could you dismantle her engine without talking to me first?"

"I take care of cars. It's what I do." His eyes fixed on my truck and refused to glance in my direction.

"That's bullshit. You aren't my mechanic. You don't work for me."

Nik shrugged. "Your truck is here. She no run. I take care of her."

"I can't believe it," I said. "What am I going to do this weekend for a vehicle?"

My look stopped his shrug.

"Sorry," said Nik, his eyes falling to the floor where my carburetor lay.

"Is there a problem, darling?" said Rupert.

Nik and I turned to peer into the interior of the neat garage. In the far corner, Rupert stood in a doorway. Leaving the door open, he stepped onto the garage stair landing and leaned on the railing.

"Your chauffeur has taken it upon himself to dismantle my truck," I said.

"Oh yes," said Rupert. "He told me it was having some difficulty with starting."

"I find that very odd considering it has a brand new starter."

"Maybe you need a new battery? I know nothing about cars. Don't fret, dear. Nik is an excellent mechanic."

"So is my brother. And if it's all the same to you, I'd rather Cody fix my truck. At home."

"Nik will take you home."

"And what do I do for a vehicle this weekend?"

"I'm busy tomorrow, but I'm available on Sunday. We'll set a time, and I'll send Nik to pick you up. You can always just stay here."

"Don't you get a day off?" I asked Nik. I had a feeling Rupert had ordered the disabling of my vehicle. The control freak wanted me under his thumb just like Nik and Miss David.

"Don't worry about Nikolai," interrupted Rupert. "I will see you Sunday, Miss Tucker." He turned and disappeared into the house, shutting the door behind him.

I wasn't sure if I liked painting rich people. Actually, I was pretty confident I didn't.

"Come on." Nik pushed himself off the Jaguar and left the garage.

"I can't believe I'm at the mercy of a chauffeur. This is just crazy." I huffed after Nik, pumping my arms to help my legs move faster. "You listen to me, Nik. First of all, I call shotgun. I've had enough with playing princess riding in the back. It doesn't suit me and anyway, nobody notices."

Nik shoved his hands in his pockets, searching for his smokes. He jammed a cigarette in his mouth, lit it, and began smoking furiously.

"Second, we're stopping for lunch on the way back," I continued. "You can just buzz into the Varsity, because I'm mad enough to eat two dogs. And a peach pie. And maybe some chili fries. Third, once we get to Halo, I've got errands to run and you're running them with me."

I felt no sympathy for Nik. My poor Datsun had been disemboweled and left for dead. Someone had to be punished.

Before Nik could open a car door for me, I yanked on the passenger handle and set off the alarm. With a smirk curling around his cigarette, Nik pulled his keys out of his pocket and cut the alarm. While he stubbed his smoke in his ashtray, I scrambled into the front seat, belted myself, and folded my arms over my chest.

"I don't like being controlled like this, Nik."

"I can tell," Nik smiled and floored the car, racing down the steep drive.

My hands flew to grasp the door handle. "I'm not talking to you until we get to the Varsity."

"Good," said Nik.

Which was not what I wanted to hear. "Have you eaten at the Varsity?"

"No."

"It's an Atlanta tradition. You need to eat at the Varsity. Every time my family comes to Atlanta, we eat at the Varsity."

Nik sighed and cut his eyes to me. "Why is Varsity so special? What is food?"

"Chili dogs, burgers, fried pies, frosted orange. It's delicious and cheap. And the building is huge. Filled to the brim during Georgia Tech games. You'll be impressed."

"I can get burger anywhere."

"You'll like it. Trust me."

Nik shrugged.

I swear I would smack him the next time he shrugged. I stared out the window and glared at the Buckhead mansions we passed. Luxury cars surrounded us at the intersections. I felt itchy and out of sorts. The way I used to feel when I first visited the Bear's house.

"Nik, do you know Maksim Avtaikin?" I asked. "And don't shrug or you'll be sorry."

"No."

"How do you feel about Mr. Agadzinoff? What kind of man is he?"

"He is my boss. He is rich and powerful."

"Do you like him?"

Nik glanced at me. "No."

"Why?"

"He cheats." Nik rattled off a rant in a language I didn't recognize. However, curse words are evident in any tongue.

"He cheats at what? Cards? Is he one of Max's deep pocket poker patrons?"

"Sure, cards. Anything. I don't know Max pocket poker." His English had broken down and he rubbed his forehead.

"It's okay, honey." I patted his shoulder. "It must be hard to think in two languages." I should have known Rupert's issues with Max might stem from the Bear's underground high stakes poker games. I felt disappointed. Everything with Max seemed to boil down to padding his pockets with poker chips.

I sighed and cupped my hand around my chin to lean against the door and watch the downtown traffic snarl around us.

"What is wrong?" said Nik. "This sigh is not your style."

A BMW pulled around us to pass, and I straightened in my seat. "Nik, have you noticed a BMW hatchback following us?"

"BMW hatchback? Why would One Series follow us?"

"I don't know." I turned in my seat to look out the back window. "You didn't see a BMW this morning when we drove into the city?"

"This is Atlanta. Of course there are BMW One Series on the road. Also Three Series, Five, Six, Seven, X, Z, and M. Which series you interested?"

"A silver one. Must be my imagination," I said. "But if you notice a hatchback, let me know."

"Okay, crazy lady."

"You are going to love the Varsity," I told him. "And you're going to love Red's even more."

"What is Red's? Communists?"

"You're sticking with me for the rest of the day. I'll buy you wings and beer for dinner before sending you home."

Poor Nik, I was taking him to the mother tiger's den and he would need the reward. After fueling at the Varsity for strength, we would stop in to see Shawna Branson's mother. Nik was going to need a beer after that visit.

TWENTY-THREE

By the time we reached Forks County, the town car smelled of grease from the crumpled white and red bags tossed in the back seat. Red cups half filled with melted chocolate shakes sat between us. I patted my contented stomach and tried to erase the sleepy stupor of chili dogs with a yawning stretch.

"Now Nik," I said, pointing him down a Line Creek subdivision street. "I'm going to warn you. The woman you're about to meet has spent her days living vicariously through her daughter's failed cheerleading and art careers. Her husband took off some years ago, although some would say she's better off. Billy Branson's disappearance allowed Delia to leech off her husband's family in style. Some thought Billy might have made it as a golf pro, but he enjoyed shagging his female students more than he did golf balls. Don't bring that up."

"Why would I bring this up? I don't know this woman."

"This is Shawna Branson's mother. Shawna is the enemy. Remember this."

"I do not understand why we are here."

"Reconnaissance mission, Nik. Miss Delia might know about these pictures her daughter thinks I hold."

"I still do not understand."

"Nik, just stand still and look pretty. You'll do fine."

We pulled into the driveway of the two story brick and stucco house. The yard was small, but the landscaping lush and serviced regularly. A ruby red Taurus SHO sat in the driveway. Another gift from JB's dealership.

I rang the bell. Nik stood behind me. After a long two minutes, the front door opened and a blowzy strawberry blond swung into the opening wearing a tiger print silk robe and matching silk pajamas.

My tiger's den comment hadn't been far off the mark.

This was not roll out of bed ware. Her hair and makeup had been done up and her copper lipstick looked fresh. Her blue-green eyes tripped over me and landed on Nik. She stroked a diamond pendant that hung between the lapels of her pajamas. At the sight of Nik, the gleam of her eye matched the stripe of her robe.

The Shawna apple didn't fall far from the mother tree.

"Mrs. Branson," I said. "I'm Cherry Tucker."

Her eyes dropped off of Nik and she stopped salivating to flinch. "What do you want?"

"Well, ma'am, could we come in?"

Delia pulled the door open and waved us through. "Don't think you've ever called on me before, Cherry." Her voice dripped honey and antagonism.

Nik followed me into the living room tastefully decorated in a style that would make any genteel Southern woman proud. I breathed a sigh of relief.

The decor wasn't original and tended toward a golf theme, but at least I didn't have to shade my eyes. Delia waved me to a side chair and pointed Nik toward the couch. She sank beside him, angling her crossed legs toward Nik.

"Who's this?" she asked.

"Nik," I said. "He's my driver. He's kind of quiet."

Her penciled eyebrows rose fractionally, but she kept a better poker face than her daughter. She pointed at a tray with crystal glasses and a pitcher sitting on the coffee table. "Y'all want some tea?"

"Thank you," I said, not wanting to start the visit on a rude note.

She smiled prettily and leaned forward to pour the tea. "I always keep glasses out for company. You just never know who will drop by."

I wondered if the droppers-by liked to find Delia Branson in her PJ's, but didn't think it appropriate to comment. "Thank you, ma'am. I suppose you know who I am?"

"I should think so," she rose from the couch to hand me my glass, careful to stick her hind end near Nik.

His poker face was better than Delia's.

"Your family is quite notorious in the county," she said. "Bless your heart." Which translated as "everyone knows your skank mother abandoned her kids and your grandparents were too old to take a belt to you and your wild siblings."

I was used to such comments, but took a hefty sip of tea to calm my nerves. And came up coughing.

Delia smiled without her teeth. "I picked up this recipe in Charleston. They make delicious sweet tea."

"A sweet tea martini," I said. "Your guests must enjoy this beverage after a round on the links."

"Vodka not gin," she said.

"All the better. Gin has a stronger odor. You can drink this all day and no one would be the wiser."

She frowned. "Why are you here?"

I set my tea glass on the side table next to my chair, careful to use a coaster. "Actually, it's about Shawna. She is looking for some pictures and thought I might have them. I would like to help her, but I don't know what pictures she means. I thought you might have an idea."

"You'd like to help Shawna? She hasn't mentioned any pictures to me." Delia curled her legs on the couch, draping an arm over the back. "She's very busy, though. I've been hosting Pictograph parties for her all over town."

Delia's hand landed behind Nik's neck. He straightened and gulped his tea, allowing Delia another reason to scoot toward him to refill his glass.

"Pictograph parties?" I said.

Delia giggled. "Isn't Shawna clever? I do jewelry parties to make a little mad money. We convinced that client list to also host parties to show Shawna's art."

"Very clever." Shawna had a foothold in every soccer mom's house in the county.

"Didn't you also have a little art business, Cherry?" Delia's fingers dallied with Nik's collar.

Nik scooted forward, finding sudden interest in the coffee table.

"If I don't have these pictures, can you think of someone else who might have them?" I said, ignoring the cut about my failing art studio. "Would Shawna have lent them to a friend and forgotten?"

"Shawna has an excellent memory. I doubt that."

"Could she have misplaced them and thought someone took them?"

"If Shawna says you have her pictures, then you have them."

Delia made Nik look like a brilliant conversationalist.

"I don't have them," I said. "That's why I've come to you for help. I don't even know the subject of these pictures. Or if they are even drawings or photos."

"Shawna doesn't draw. Of course, they're photos."

At least someone admitted Shawna couldn't draw.

A phone rang in another room. Delia glanced behind her. "Excuse me."

I waited until she left the room to stand. "This was a waste of time."

"The tea is good," said Nik. He tipped back his glass and swallowed the remaining liquid.

"How many glasses have you had? I'm driving to the next stop." I circled the room, agitated. "How can these people ruin my reputation? It's akin to the patients running the psych unit."

Nik rose and crossed the room to join me before the fireplace. He pointed to the photographs on the mantel. "Which one is Shawna?"

"She's in nearly all of them. Giant red head with boobs. Take your pick of age." I wrinkled my nose at the frames. Her prom photo featured one of my high school boyfriends. Next to it was a framed, faded snapshot of a red haired toddler with a younger version of Delia and a dark haired man. They stood next to a set of clubs, the Line Creek golf course recognizable in the background. "That must be Billy Branson. Shawna's daddy."

"The golfer," said Nik.

"Yep. That's one thing Shawna and I have in common. Neither of us had a daddy growing up. Which should make us get along better. 'Course, mine passed and hers left." I cast an eye toward the entry Delia had disappeared through. "At least Delia stuck around to raise Shawna. Not that she did a very good job."

"Let's go," said Nik. "This woman make me nerves."

"She makes me nerves, too. You're right. Miss Delia's not going to help me stop Shawna."

We didn't wait for Delia to return, which would have gotten me a talking-to from my Grandma Jo. Politeness requires you to say your goodbyes and thank yous before leaving. However, I didn't respect Delia and was starting to feel my effort to be polite in this county didn't make much of a difference anyway. The people of Forks County, at least the ones who could be paying customers, had formed an opinion of me twenty years ago.

I wasn't sure if there was much I could do to change their minds now.

TWENTY-FOUR

"What am I going to do, Nik?" I said while adjusting the driver's seat to accommodate my lack of height. "Shawna's mother has a voice in the Tupperware community. I had hoped to live in this county for the rest of my life. Now in every shop I enter, people point at me like I walked off a Most Wanted poster. I can't count on Mr. Max's show to prove I'm not disreputable. Controversy kills deals in this area."

Nik slouched in the passenger seat, put out that I made him turn over the keys. "You are born, you live, you die. You drink vodka and forget."

"That is a horrible attitude," I said. "My family history makes living in Halo an uphill battle. I had finally made some progress. I went to college and returned to start my own business. Last year at this time, I was hand lettering wedding announcements and painting studio portraits. I wasn't getting rich, but at least I was getting by."

"So now you paint my boss and get rich. Who cares what these people think?"

"I care. They're my people. I could do without the Bransons, but most in this county are decent folks. Problem is, the Bransons set the standard for acceptable behavior. At least one of them is on every blooming committee and town council. Plus they own a lot of property and businesses. People respect the name and like their money."

"So find the Branson who will help you."

I pumped the brakes and cranked the wheel, spinning a U-turn in the subdivision street. "Nik. You are a genius."

"You are still crazy lady."

Twenty minutes later, Nik and I popped out of the town car in another subdivision, this time outside Halo. Stone and stucco house. Bigger, manicured yard. More money. The big house of Branson, belonging to JB and Wanda. Also the current residence of Deputy Luke Harper as he stockpiled his meager salary before getting his own place. He also liked to please his mother, Wanda, and after seven years in the service, she wanted some family time with her only son.

"Nik," I said, pressing the doorbell. "This visit will be even trickier."

"Will this woman have hands on me, too?"

"No, of course not. Miss Wanda was my Sunday School teacher. She's a sweet lady and Luke's momma."

"Who is Luke?"

"My ex. Except he never told his mother and stepfather we were dating, so Miss Wanda doesn't know he's my ex-boyfriend. She just knows me from town."

"This is tricky part?"

"Tricky part is I once did a painting of her deceased stepson. It's complicated and her husband, JB, doesn't like me. Not sure if it's because I remind him of his son who passed or because he didn't have a high opinion of my family before I did the portrait."

"Your town politics are very confusing. Worse than Communists."

Behind the wavy, leaded glass of the front door, a blurry form approached. A moment later, the door opened and Miss Wanda stood before us in a capri pant set featuring beach umbrellas and pink flamingos. Her short, wavy hair had been covered in a ball cap that didn't jive with the rest of her outfit. Upon opening the door, her blue eyes grew wide. She snagged my arm and dragged me inside. Nik followed, shutting the door behind us.

"Thank the merciful Lord," she said. "Look." She pulled off her ball cap and turned around. Her blond hair had been highlighted with multicolored streaks of paint.

"What happened?" I said, fingering her hair. The paint had dried in a lovely pattern. "I like these colors. What are you working on?"

"Oh honey, this is why I always hire out." Tears welled in Wanda's eyes. "Shawna asked me to help her with a project, but I'm no good at crafts. I had hung some posters up to dry. I got paint all over my clothes, but didn't realize it was also in my hair until I went to run a brush through it before going out."

"You can get this out easily, ma'am," I said. "I've had paint in my hair many times. If it's water-based, it'll wash out. For oil based paint you can use olive oil. Rub it in, leave it on for a while, then comb it out. But how exactly did you get paint on the back of your head?"

"I backed into the poster when the danged dog jumped up to lick me. I have no idea what kind of paint it is."

I giggled. "Let me see the paint you used. By the way, this is my friend Nik. He's driving me around while he works on my truck."

"Nice to meet you, Nick," said Wanda, blushing. "I am so sorry you had to see me like this."

Nik bobbed his head at Wanda and followed us through the foyer to the back of the house and into the kitchen. We stepped through a sliding glass door onto a screened porch where Wanda had taped a line of poster board against the wall of the house. Two posters were a smeary mess. The rest advertised the Concerned Citizens Committee for Decency in Art. At least, that's what I picked out from the drippy lettering.

I cut my eyes to Wanda. "Decency in Art?"

She was too concerned about her poor painting job to pick up on the intended victim of the campaign. "Some Arts Council meeting, I suppose," she said. "I cannot paint or draw worth a lick. Look at these. I'm going to have to tell Shawna that she needs to find someone else. Oh, dear."

"Usually folks use markers for posters. Or poster paint," I walked to her patio table and examined the cans of paint she had used. "This is wall paint, ma'am. At least it's latex. You can wash it out."

"I didn't have anything else and no time to run to the Crafty Corner," Wanda patted her cheeks and shook her head. "Mercy, what a mess."

She clutched my arm. "Cherry, can you please help me? I'll pay you."

"Miss Wanda, I'm not sure." I didn't know what to say. Should I clue her in to what this meeting was about?

"Please, Cherry. You do such a good job. I feel so bad about what happened with Dustin." Her voice broke and fresh tears welled in her eyes. Her stepson had been laid to rest only six months earlier.

"Miss Tucker has commission now with Rupert Agadzinoff, famous lawyer in Atlanta," said Nik. He stood with his back to us, looking out upon the backyard vista that included a pool and garden.

"Please, honey," said Wanda. "I know it won't take you but a minute. And you have all the supplies at home."

"Cherry should help this fascist, Shawna?" said Nik, shaking his head. "No."

"Stop it, Nik." I made a mental note to not let Nik drink sweet tea vodka anymore.

"I don't know Shawna's politics," said Wanda. "But I don't believe the arts committee has any political affiliation. It would mean so much to me personally."

"How many posters?" I said, sighing. I could not turn down a woman as sweet as Miss Wanda. Or humiliate myself by explaining the true subject of the posters. Even if it meant digging my own grave.

Wanda pulled me into a soft hug. "Thank you so much, honey. I'll pick them up."

"I'll drop them off," I said. I didn't want Miss Wanda showing up at my house and greeted by Todd in a towel.

"You are too sweet," she said and released me from her hold. "Don't you go to too much trouble. Shawna said I just need the time, date, and title. She gave me a folder of photos to glue to the bottom of the poster."

"Did you look at the pictures?" I couldn't believe what I had just agreed to do. Maybe I could swap photos.

"Not yet," she said. "I had a hard enough time with the lettering. I thought it would be pretty to use different colors, but then it got all runny and I forgot to use a ruler. Well, you can see for yourself." She waved at the messes on the wall.

I glanced at the table and scooped up the file folder before Wanda could peruse it. "I'll just take this with me."

"Thank you, honey," said Wanda. "I have choir practice and a garden club committee yet today. Looks like I'll need to run to the salon, too."

"Whatever you do, don't let them use turpentine or mineral spirits. If you color, those chemicals will ruin your hair."

Wanda patted her blond, streaky locks. "Of course I color, honey. But thank you for not mentioning it in public."

She drew my arm through her elbow to walk me back through the kitchen. "Where are my manners? I didn't even ask why y'all dropped by."

Nik trailed behind us. "The fascist Shawna believes Cherry stole photos."

I glanced behind me to shoot Nik a "shut-it" look. "Excuse Nik. His English is not so good. What he means is Shawna has mistakenly gotten the impression I have some of her pictures and she's a tad miffed. I had hoped you might dissuade her from thinking this."

"You mean you have some of Shawna's Pictographs?"

"I don't know what pictures are missing," I said. "It would be helpful if you could ask her. A Pictograph is awfully hard to misplace. I know I don't have one of those. I got the impression that the missing pictures are photos."

Lord help me, I'd put my eyes out before possessing a Pictograph.

We sauntered arm in arm down the hall and into the foyer. Hanging on the wall was a grouping of family portraits. A few matted and framed photographs from Wanda and JB's wedding. An oil of Dustin as a youngster grasping a bunny. And a photo of a young Luke, clutching a football. His smile didn't feature dimples, which saddened me. He had mentioned to me his unhappiness with his mother's remarriage to JB and gaining Dustin as a stepbrother. It seemed evident even at this young age.

Wanda glanced at the photos. "I could never get Luke to sit still for a painting. I felt lucky enough to get a few shots of him."

I knew how she felt. Luke refused to model for me even when we were going out. "He was such a handsome child. Those gray eyes and that thick, wavy hair. I would kill for those eyelashes."

"He always was an old soul and so serious. My baby is too handsome for his own good," she said, shaking her head. "The way women throw themselves at him."

What women? I bit my tongue before I could ask. "Good luck with your hair, ma'am."

Nik gave her a brief bow and strode out the doorway, muttering something about the bourgeoisie. I followed and opened the passenger door for him. "What happened to stand still and look pretty? You can't call Shawna a fascist. You don't even know her."

"You call Shawna names," he said. "Why can't I call her names?"

"Because I have earned that right, growing up around her. You have a lot to learn about America, son."

TWENTY-FIVE

After dropping off a pizza at the Coderres, I felt Nik had earned a reprieve from errand running. Jerell had held the air rifle on Nik while I carried in the pizza and checked on Miss Gladys. She had been agitated and the house looked messier than usual. My worry had augmented when a woman in the next trailer leaned out her front door to screech at us. Miss Gladys had patted my hand and told me, "not to trouble myself."

Miss Gladys's hand pat did not reassure me. In fact, it doubled my worries. But at least being held at BB gunpoint by an eight-year-old had stopped Nik's ramblings about political despots. After a stop at home to change my clothes, I rewarded him with a trip to Red's. Sticks played at Red's County Line Tap on Friday nights. The bar would be packed, and Red's was a safe haven from the Branson ugliness. I needed to bask in the warmth of friendship.

We arrived early. Most of the stools lining the old, wooden bar were empty. The local youth and barflies would show later when the dinner crowd dispersed. However, at the far end of the long, narrow bar, a rabble of women crowded around the small stage, shrieking and laughing.

I hadn't realized the Sticks fan base had grown. But between Leah's golden chops and an improvement in the coherency of Todd's lyrics, perhaps word had gotten out. And Todd's hiney did look good in his black leather-like pants. I put that thought away and searched for my buddies.

Leah sat at the bar, sipping a Dr. Pepper and chatting with Red. She had unbraided her extensions to cascade down her back in dark waves. Seeing Nik and I, she waved us over. I cast a critical eye over her choice for performance attire. Tonight she wore belted, high-waisted mom-jeans and a lacy, formless blouse, but her red stilettos sauced up the frumpy style. She and her mother would still buy Leah's clothes from the Miss Modest Line at the local department store if the line produced sizes above age twelve.

Of course with my shrimpy size, I could possibly squeeze into a Miss Modest. But I wasn't into smocking and Peter Pan collars. I had my own line of Cherry Tucker clothing, mostly pieces from Walmart retrofitted with bling, dye, and a pair of scissors. Tonight's ensemble included a gossamer-thin blouse worn over a tube top decorated with multi-colored, micro-beads spelling out my name. Nik's expression proved him impressed. Or disturbed. Sometimes it's difficult to tell those expressions apart.

Hauling Nik with me, I plunked my poster materials on the bar, snagged a stool next to Leah, and introduced Nik to the surrounding folks.

"You're a chauffeur?" said Red. He leaned a freckled arm on the wooden bar top and studied Nik. Red turned his cobalt green eyes on me. "Why do you have a driver? Did your truck die?"

I cast a scathing glance to Nik. "I hope not. My new boss is a little overprotective of my choice in transit."

"Can't blame him there," said Red. "The Datsun could leave you stranded in the city."

"I'm stranded in the country. The Datsun's lying in pieces in my patron's garage."

"Heavens," said Leah. "I guess you'll be staying home tomorrow."

"Are you kidding?" I said. "I've got things to do. I need to visit the Coderres. I also might have to work at the SipNZip."

Red shoved Nik a beer and placed a frosty mug before me. "You got a job at the SipNZip?" He didn't bother to take the incredulousness out of his voice. "I thought Todd was looking for a job."

"Where is Todd, by the way?" I said. "Did he squeeze into his pleather yet? I seriously fear those pants will inhibit his ability to produce offspring. However, that might also be a blessing."

"He's signing autographs," said Leah, "over by the stage."

"Autographs?" I leaned back in my seat so I could see the stage. The crowd had swelled and a few women on the outer ring jumped up and down to catch Todd's attention. I could barely see the top of his sun-streaked blond locks over the gaggle of women.

"I don't know where this surge in his popularity came from," said Red. "To be honest, I'm a little annoyed. These fans aren't buying anything. I'm going to have to start charging a cover."

"I am not paying a cover to see Todd," I said. "I see enough of him as it is. Rarely clothed, too. I swear he was raised by nudists."

"Who is Todd?" asked Nik.

"Cherry's ex-husband," said Red. "Don't get hooked on Cherry. She will break your heart. She has issues with committing."

"I am not hooked on Cherry," said Nik. "She is crazy. Not my type."

I glared at Nik and then Red. "I do not break hearts. They break mine. I thought y'all were my friends."

"Friends keep it real," said Red. "We want to help you."

"I don't need that kind of help. I get enough of that kind of help from everybody else."

"We don't want to see you end up alone," said Leah. "You had two men willing to put up with you. We were surprised you got that many."

"She's feisty," said Red. "Some men like cute and feisty. They think they're going to get the milk for free with this one. You can tell she's not ready to settle."

"Hey," I said. "I don't give away milk."

"She could have a pet. A dog. A cat will not listen to her always talking," said Nik. "A dog is more forgiving."

"Both Todd and Luke have their own issues." I swigged my beer and glared into the mirror. "I might just try someone else out. Casey said I should have some fun." I thought about Max and this time didn't get the nauseous feeling that had previously accompanied thoughts about his maneuvers. Of course, the beer probably helped.

"Another one? You still haven't gotten over Luke. Would you like me to replay your dramatic scene from two weeks ago when sweet, little Tara Mayfield asked Luke to dance, Miss Jealous Much?" Red looked at Leah. "She's going to try rebound dating. Always a bad idea."

"I know, Red." Leah shook her head at her Dr. Pepper.

"Hello, I'm still here," I said. "And now I'm changing the subject to Shawna Branson."

"Not again," said Nik. "I am not liking this subject."

"No one asked you. Red, please get Nik some wings. I bragged on them, so make sure they are extra tasty."

"I did visit Shawna at her shop for you, honey," said Leah. "Those are some scary baby heads she has hanging in there."

"Shawna has baby heads hanging in her shop?" asked Red. He waved at Casey and made the international sign for ordering wings. He pointed at me and twirled his finger to hurry her up.

Even at the other end of the room, I could feel Casey's eye roll.

"Not real baby heads," I said. "Shawna hasn't gone that loony. Yet. Did she tell you what kind of pictures she is looking for?"

"Some snapshots. That's all I could get out of her before she started ranting," Leah shook her head. "Shawna is horribly jealous of your new commission. I shouldn't have told her."

I couldn't help but smile.

"Fascist," said Nik into his beer.

"Whatever you do, Red, don't give Nik any vodka," I said.

"Did you know Mr. Max has hired out her gallery?" said Leah. "She is very happy about that. Ecstatic, in fact. And would like to rub it in your face."

"I thought the Bear was going to help me, not Shawna," I pouted.

"I thought you found Mr. Max suspicious," said Red. "Why would you want him to help you?"

"He is the only person in Halo willing to buy my art at the moment. I don't really have a choice. I'm not sure if I trust him, but he seems very willing to help."

"But what does he want in return?" said Leah.

"Good question," I said. "The Bear does nothing for free. But he hasn't suggested anything yet."

"You be careful," said Red. "There's got to be other people in this town willing to back your art."

"There is posters," said Nik. He pointed to the signboard paraphernalia I had left on the bar.

"That's good news," said Leah. "Who's having you do posters?"

"Miss Wanda." I gulped my beer. "The posters are for Shawna. I didn't have the heart to tell Miss Wanda the announcements are intended to decimate my career. They advertise Shawna's Concerned Citizens brigade."

"You're helping the enemy?" said Red. "What's wrong with you?"

"I couldn't tell Miss Wanda no. She's too nice." I wiped a drip of beer off a piece of poster board. "However, I thought I could put a positive spin on my artwork while still including the information Shawna wanted."

"A Trojan horse poster?" said Red.

"Subliminal advertising," said Leah, reaching for the folder of material.

"Something that would make people not want to go to this meeting," I opened a notebook and drew a pencil from my bag. "I thought y'all could help me brainstorm."

My stomach sensed approaching food and called out to claim it. I clamped a hand over my belly as a few of Todd's fans turned around to search the room for the source of the bee swarm sound.

"Who's this?" said Casey, plunking two plates of steaming wings on the bar before us. She cocked her head and eyed Nik, who straightened from his slump and eyed her back. Casey looked particularly fetching in her Daisy Duke's and County Line t-shirt with the sleeves and bottom hem line hacked off. Her bar apron created the only shield between her belly button ring and Red's public. Considering Red's public was mostly women at the moment, I couldn't help but fear for her tips.

"I am Nik." Nik held out a hand to capture Casey's and kissed it. "And you must be the angel sent to save me."

"Good Lord, Nik," I said, "You can't come up with a line better than that?"

"Hush," said Casey. "I'm taking a break, Red." Before Red could open his mouth to stop her, she had dragged Nik from his stool and they had exited the premises.

"I swear I'm going to fire her, Cherry," said Red.

"You said yourself the Todd fans aren't ordering anything. She'll be back after she and Nik," I coughed, "get to know each other in the parking lot."

"Red, calm down," Leah patted his arm, "you look apoplectic."

"Your face is so red, your freckles have disappeared," I added. "Anyway, Nik needs some cheering up. I don't think he likes working for Rupert. Nik's a very gloomy person."

"Let's work on your posters and take Red's mind off Casey," said Leah. She flipped open the folder of copies. "Lord help us. Have you looked in this folder?"

She held up a photocopy that featured an enlarged section of Todd's anatomy. "This is what Shawna wants stuck on these posters? How could Miss Wanda approve of this?"

"Miss Wanda hadn't looked at the copies yet. Let me see that," I snatched the paper, which caught the eye of two women striding toward the autograph signing. They turned fifteen shades of pink, but slowed their walk and halted before us.

"Are those flyers for the Sticks drummer to sign?" asked a woman with a dark haired bob and carrying a purse that looked suspiciously like a diaper bag.

Before the "what?" could fly from my mouth, the older of the pair snatched the flier from my hand. "I recognize this from the other posters. It has to be him."

"What's wrong with you?" I said. "Give that back."

The older woman shoved the flier into the diaper bag. "I know we're late, but my daughter needs a night out and wanted to see him for herself. Me, too."

"See what for yourself?"

"The man in the posters. Word has spread the model performs in Sticks. We've got one hour before Sissy needs to get home and feed the baby." She gave Sissy a shove and they sped to the far end of the room.

Red shook his head. "I bet they're not ordering anything, either."

I scanned the other copies. "I can't believe this. Shawna has made Todd into a porn star and turned the female population of Forks County into a bunch of degenerates. And she's trying to make me look depraved?"

Leah shoved the copies back into the folder. "This is horrible and wrong. I don't want to see Todd like this."

"Todd's image has been sliced and diced and corrupted," I said. "Shawna has taken an object of beauty and turned it into an object of lust."

"This kind of notoriety might bring in customers now but will doom my business." Red leaned over the bar to reexamine the crowd. "Folks will think I support this kind of smut."

"You have to stop her, Cherry," said Leah with a lethal glare at Red. "I'm sure Red is just as concerned about what these posters would do to you and Todd as much as his business."

Red's ruddy complexion brightened. "Well, of course, Leah. Maybe I should disperse this crowd."

"I'm getting out of here. I'll work on these posters at home." I hopped from my stool, slung my satchel around my shoulder, and turned toward the door. "Actually, I'll go out the back way. I think seeing my sister and Nik getting acquainted in the breezeway may turn my stomach."

"She better not be in my foyer," called Red.

I eased past Todd's groupies, hoping not to be recognized. The bingo crowd still had it in for me and there was no sense in riling that group. Women addled with Todd-induced hormones and deprived of bingo were a dangerous lot. I caught the gleam of Todd's tight, faux-leather tush and pushed through the swinging kitchen door. I waved a "hey" at the staff and scooted toward the back door where the cooks took their smoke breaks.

Slamming through the door, I hooked a right toward the parking lot, remembered I didn't have my truck, and stumbled to a stop at the edge of the building. I scanned the lot for Rupert's town car and couldn't find it. Todd's Civic was also missing. However, Casey's Firebird had been parked in a prime slot in front.

I thought about returning to Red's kitchen to look for her keys, when I spotted a familiar BMW parked across the street.

"Shit."

TWENTY-SIX

I watched the BMW for a good five minutes, or at least a long thirty seconds as I wasn't wearing a watch, and again nothing happened. The parking lot grew busier as women juiced up on Todd's splendiferous form left Red's and the regulars who knew Todd and didn't care to see his all-but-nothings arrived for the usual Friday night party. I needed to see who drove that silver hatchback. Calling the police would mean scaring the vehicle away, and danged if I would let this sonofabitch follow me around town and not know who he was.

The BMW had parked to watch Red's from across the street. Behind the vehicle, a steep hillside led to a vacant lot and an abandoned building used by local high schoolers for practicing their spray painting skills. Red's gravel parking lot, bare of trees and bushes, didn't provide much cover. The sun hadn't fully dropped either. On my left lay the old railroad tracks, marking Halo's town limits. Here, the tracks ran in a depression created by a ditch that banked and grew into the hillside on the other side of the street. If I could get to the top of the hill, I could spy on the Beamer. The ditch wouldn't hide much more than a rabbit on this side of the road, but following the tracks was my only chance to cross the road unseen.

Dropping the poster board at the side of the building, I darted toward the tracks and hunker-walked the shallow ditch, hoping the busy parking lot would keep attention focused on Red's. At the street crossing, I squatted and waited for a minivan to cross the tracks to use as cover to scurry across the road unnoticed. The raised tracks and rutted road had a jarring effect on most chassis's, so locals knew to ease over the crossing before accelerating into Halo where the potholes were filled with asphalt on a more regular basis. The minivan crept toward the tracks. I popped up from my squat, startled the driver into braking, and hurried across the road to drop into the deeper embankment.

There I waited while another minivan and an SUV left Red's and bumped over the tracks. The embankment rose past my head. At the top was the abandoned, crumbling brick building once used for storage by the railroad, currently decorated with graffiti tagging and crude penis drawings.

Flipping my satchel onto my back, I climbed up the hill on hands and knees. I gladdened in my effort to dress in jeans and boots, although the tube top hadn't been so smart. It had worked its way toward my navel by the time I reached the top of the hill. I reached under my shirt to yank it up, knocking off beads in the process.

I hurried toward the vandalized building and peered around the side. The BMW was parked below me. From this vantage point, I had a bird's eye view which did me no good. The sun roof appeared as a dark rectangle. I dropped to the ground, Army man style, and wormed my way hand-over-hand to the edge of the hill.

Across the street, more vehicles pulled into Red's. A hefty engine growled and a yellow, convertible Mustang with a GAPCH license plate charged down the street toward the bar. I froze. The tires sprayed gravel as Shawna took a tight corner into Red's. I assumed she had heard about the Todd extravaganza going on inside. She revved through the lot, forcing a cowboy to back into his tailgate, and stopped before Red's front door.

Hopping out of the car, she turned to cast a caustic eye on the man she almost hit, then trailed her eyes over the parking lot. Her automatic money-seeking sights trained on the BMW. She cocked her head, and I imagined an android read-out blipping the model, make, and market value of the Beamer in her brain. Her face lost its mad-as-hell look and grew puzzled. I held my breath and let it out as her eyes left the BMW, traveled up the hill, and stuck on my face hovering Wizard of Oz-like above the hatchback.

My cover blown, I didn't know what else to do but smile. Shawna shrieked and pointed. The cowboy turned and looked. The car engine spurted to a start below me. I thought but didn't say a few expletives and started my hand-over-hand backwards crawl. Shawna darted across the parking lot, screaming my name and all the things she'd like to do to me. Max's words about "danger" and "retreat" popped into my mind as I scrambled through the weeds.

Taking his advice, I jumped to my feet and ran.

I gunned Todd's Civic through town, swerving on to side streets toward the county highway to confuse the BMW. I had run home, discarded my ruined chiffon blouse, grabbed Todd's keys, and headed out the door. Once again, my house had been full of young bachelors enjoying a self-proclaimed "happy hour" on my porch. They had moved the dead pheasant couch outside where they lounged with their feet on the rails and coolers at their sides. I hadn't stopped to kick them out. I had hoped the BMW didn't know where I lived, and I wasn't going to stick around for it to find me.

Once out of town, I made straight for Max's Nouveau Antebellum estate. Amid Shawna's screaming about my moral ruin were boasts of Max's financial support of her. He had been my last hope in proving the witch hunt false. I needed confirmation if I really indeed should "abandon hope of living in Halo."

According to Shawna, I did.

At this point, faith in my local art business's success had already snuck out the back door. I might have to make a career of the graveyard shift at the SipNZip. I'd live. But if I were run out of Halo, who would check on the Coderres? I needed to stick around to keep up the momentum of helping that family. Finding a way for Miss Gladys to care properly for Jerell and breaking the family pattern of drugs and robbery seemed paramount.

With so many thoughts about stalkers, Shawna, and the Coderres circling my brain, I passed the black pickup parked down the street from Max's drive without thinking.

I had pulled the Civic's grill before Max's closed gate, ready to hop out and speak to his intercom, when I did my double take. I shoved the gear shifter into reverse, backed into the road, and parked across the street from the truck. A cab light flared. I hopped from Todd's hatchback and strode across the road to the jacked-up pickup.

Luke rolled down his window. "What are you doing here?"

"I have business to discuss with Mr. Max. What about you? This looks like a stake out."

"Get in," Luke rolled up his window.

I circled the truck and climbed in through the passenger door. "This is the second time I've found you hanging around Mr. Max. What's going on?"

"I could say the same to you."

We scrutinized each other for a long moment. Luke cut off the overhead light, breaking the tension.

"Why are you watching his house?" I said. "Shouldn't you be out looking for Tyrone's and the Dixie Cake truck driver's killer?"

"The hijacking is bigger than that. And don't ask me for details because that's all I'm telling you."

"Bigger than what? Are there more dead people?"

"Lord, I hope not." Luke rested his head on the seatback.

I ticked off points on my fingers. "Let me see if I can figure this out. You've got a hijacking where there's normally no hijacking. The driver was shot, but he's the wrong driver. You have a witness to the shooting, who is later killed. It doesn't sound that complicated to me. But you're watching Max Avtaikin's house."

"Yep."

"Did you know I was coming here?"

Luke sat up. "Why would I know you were coming here?"

"I told you Mr. Max was going to help me absolve my name in the community by financing a show. You were clear about not supporting that decision. And seemed pretty irate to find us together under that magnolia tree."

Luke folded his arms. "Your little game of Frogger had me irate."

"It didn't bother you at all to see Max's arms around me?"

I felt that statement detonate and sensed the sizzle of Luke's blood beginning to steam.

I backed off. "I've been bringing food to the Coderres. Got them a funeral, too. Do you think the M.E. will release the body soon? I imagine Miss Gladys is getting anxious to have Tyrone buried. I know she's anxious to have his killer caught so she can proceed with suing the perp."

"About that," Luke's tension ran out, and he unfolded his arms to slip one across the back of the seat. He took my hand. "I have some news. Family and Child Services visited the Coderres this afternoon. Did Miss Gladys tell you?"

"No." I blinked, feeling a sting behind my eyes. "I just saw them a few hours ago. Nik and I dropped off a pizza."

"Nik?"

I began to explain my chauffeur when Luke interrupted me.

"Never mind that for now." Luke stroked his thumb across the back of my hand. "Miss Gladys and Jerell already had the visit by that time. They probably didn't want to upset you."

"Why would I be upset?" I sniffed and swiped at my nose with my shoulder. "I'm sure if they had some news they would have told me. The little man was doing a good job of protecting his great gam. Used his BB gun to force Nik to stay in the car while I brought in the pizza. Their house was a disaster. I said I'd come over tomorrow to clean it up."

"Sugar, that's real sweet of you."

I yanked my hand from his, scrubbed a weepy eye, and raised my chin. "What are you trying to tell me? Just say it."

"Jerell's been taken to a foster home."

"What?" Hot tears bubbled and clouded my vision. I swept them away and pounded the seat with a fist. "That's not right. He's got his great-grandma. I'm checking on them every day. Did they tell you that? I'm working on finding them another place to live."

"You take everything to heart. I love that about you, but you can't help everyone."

"I thought you cared, Luke. I saw you with Jerell. You were so sweet with him. You can't let this happen." I banged on his arm, and he captured my hand to bring it to his lips, but I yanked it away.

"Honey, it's for the best. Sweetgum isn't safe. Think about Jerell's future if he stays there."

"He wasn't going to stay there. I was going to find them another home. Now he'll be in the system. He's eight, Luke. He'll get passed from family to family."

"He might be adopted. The families will make sure he sees Miss Gladys. There are some very charitable parents willing to share their home with a child like Jerell."

"It's too soon." My lip trembled.

Luke slipped his hand off the seat and on to my shoulder.

I pushed it off. "I don't trust the system. People fall through the cracks all the time. And what about Tyrone's funeral? Will they let Jerell attend? What about Miss Gladys? She's all alone now. Jerell was protecting her."

"An eight-year-old boy shouldn't have to protect an old woman."

Luke was right, of course. I hugged my chest and took deep breaths to stop the tears.

"Baby, I'm sorry," He scooted toward me but was blocked by the center console. "Don't cry, sugar. I didn't want to make you cry."

"I'm not crying. I'm fine. I'll just see Miss Gladys in the morning and talk to her about this. We'll figure out what to do."

I fumbled in my pocket for a tissue, then flipped the passenger visor down to check my makeup in the mirror. I blinked at the bright light and swiped the mascara off my cheeks. Not my best look. I pulled up my tube top and patted the flyaways in my hair.

"I have some business to attend," I said. "I'll just see you around. You can mark Todd's car in your little notebook as a visitor to the Avtaikin household."

Luke laid his hand on my forearm. "Don't. You're still worked up. Why don't you just sit here for a little while? Maybe we'll see something interesting."

"No, thank you. Have a good evening."

"Cherry, I don't want you visiting Avtaikin," Luke stroked my arm. "Please."

"Will I be arrested for visiting Mr. Max?"

"Of course not," Luke's brows fell. "You should stay clear of Avtaikin right now, that's all."

"How else am I going to stop your cousin's campaign of hatred against me?"

"Don't be ridiculous. There's no campaign of hatred."

"Talk to your momma about the posters I'm doing for her. A Concerned Citizens group has formed to run me out of town. The meeting is Monday night. You can join them with your own tar and feathers."

His hand slipped off my arm as I turned to open the door and slide out of the truck. When my feet hit the ground, I yanked on the tube top and looked over my shoulder.

"By the way, if you happen to see that silver BMW hatchback that tried to run me over the other night, you should check its plates. It's been following me around town. Might be a stalker. Or might be one of Shawna's minions. Or both. Have a good night."

And kiss my ass, you child abandoner, I thought as I strode back to the Civic.

TWENTY-SEVEN

Back at Max's gate, I climbed from the Civic to buzz his intercom. Instead of the sound of gate locks tumbling, Max's disembodied voice told me to go away.

"I'm in no mood for this," I said. "Open the friggin' gate or I'm climbing over it."

I felt his long sigh but had already climbed into the car to wait for the gates to open. They slowly swung back. I gunned the motor, glancing in my rear view to see if I could spot Luke watching. I lurched through the gate, burned rubber up Max's drive, and squealed to a quick stop before Max's house. The Bear stood in his doorway, waiting.

He wore clothes. No more robe with pec cleavage for me.

"You are going to talk to me," I said, marching past him and down the hall to the sitting room. "No subterfuge tonight."

He followed me but halted in the sitting room doorway and shoved his hands in his pockets. "It's a bad time, Artist."

"You got a dinner party or something? Poker game in your basement?" At the brief shake of his head, I continued. "That's what I thought. I figured it was a bad time, considering the local po-po are watching your door."

"You noticed." He scrubbed his thick, brown hair, then strode into the room and collapsed on the couch.

I remained standing, but gave my tube top a small hike before pulling a sheet of paper out of my satchel. "Who is this?"

Max took the copy of the composite sketch and studied it. He tossed the paper onto the couch and pursed his lips. "Your hijacker?"

"He's not my hijacker. You are tied to this crime somehow. Why else would the deputy in charge of the hijacking investigation stake out your house?"

"Are you sure Deputy Harper's still in charge of this investigation? Perhaps he has a personal vendetta?"

I opened my mouth to dispute his accusation and then closed it. If the crime was bigger than a hijacking, would a lowly deputy be in charge? Would he even remain on the investigation team? How big was big?

"Dammit," I stomped my foot. "I'm tired of all this secrecy. What is going on? I need to help the Coderres. The state took away Jerell. I've got to do something. What do you know?"

Max snagged my hand and pulled me to the couch. Clasping my hand in his, he studied my face. "You have been crying."

"So what? Sometimes it happens." I struggled to pull my hand free, but he held tight.

"Listen to me. The Coderres have the bad luck. No effort to catch the killer will help that family."

"I don't believe you," I said. "Justice should serve everyone."

"You are too idealistic. Justice doesn't serve everyone. That is life. You know this personally. I do, too."

"What are you talking about?" I scrubbed my eyes with my free hand and tried not to sniffle.

"Go home. Stay away from me. As you say, I'm watched by the local po-po."

"That's just Luke. I don't care what he thinks."

"You should. You were very worried about the town's opinion of you a few days ago."

"Too late for that." I jerked my hand away. "You turned on me, too. Shawna said you're doing a show for her now. Thanks a lot."

"I hired her gallery." He stood. "Now go. No more drop-in visits."

I sucked on my bottom lip, then took a deep breath. "You can count on that. I knew I shouldn't have trusted you. Rupert was right, you're impossible to read."

"Rupert? You have been talking to Rupert?" Max grabbed the strap of my bag and jerked me to my feet. "Get out of my house."

Amid my curses and threats, Max drug me from his sitting room, through the foyer, and out the door. Breathing hard, his icy stare caused ripples of goosebumps to prickle my skin.

"Stay away from me," he growled.

The door slammed shut.

I kicked the door. "Tell your maneuvers they can go to hell."

Spinning around, I flew down the porch toward the red hatchback. The hijack was bigger than two murders? That meant finding Tyrone's killer had been bumped down the Sheriff's Office to-do list. Looked like I had been left alone to continue my quest to bring the murderer to justice.

I was going to the SipNZip tonight. To hell with Max Avtaikin and the rest. I knew that store had to be involved. The coffee was too good to be that cheap.

Even at night the SipNZip had the bustle of early morning accompanied with the smell of coffee, cleaning formula, and simmering nacho cheese. I pulled in an appreciative deep breath at the door, then strode to the counter.

"I'm Cherrilyn Ballard," I said, sticking my hand at a guy with a short, brown mohawk working the cash register. He wore a bright yellow tracksuit with a red stripe and several chains around his neck. I admired his choice in color.

"I am Anatoly," he shook my hand. "You call me Little Anatoly."

"Nice to meet you, Little Anatoly," I said. "You're not from around here are you?"

He winked. "You are good judge. How can you guess? You haven't even heard my rhymes yet."

"What rhymes?"

"I'm dope rapper, yo." He dropped back to swing his arms and move to an internal beat. "Freestylin' rhymes to score more dimes. I've got lyrics so good you'll think you're in da hood. Beeyatch."

I stood on my toes and leaned over the counter. "You listen to me, Little Anatoly. I don't want to hear any of that ugly talk. You call me a bitch again, and I'll teach you some American whoopass you won't forget."

"Chill, woman."

"And don't call me woman. I hate that." I looked around. "Now who else is working here?"

"Just me and Sam." Anatoly hopped back on his seat. "Why you so crazy?"

"Let me talk to Sam," I said. "I'm not getting much from you."

"Sam's busy right now." Little Anatoly glanced toward the back of the store. "He's unloading."

"Sounds like a good place for me to start. I can stock while he unloads."

"What you mean 'start'?"

Little Anatoly leaned over the counter to gawk at my tube top ensemble. He mouthed the name written on my top. "Who are you? What is Che y? Spanish?"

I glanced down at my top and gave it a tug. "I lost some beads earlier. I'm here to work the graveyard. I filled out an application the other day."

"Elena did not mention a new worker," said Little Anatoly, still trying to work out the lettering on my top.

I crossed my arms over my chest. "That scrawny girl is the manager? Is she here?"

"No." He sank back on his stool and studied my face. "I think she will not hire you. You must be mistaken."

"I just came from Max Avtaikin's house." I watched for his reaction. "He owns the SipNZip."

"Don't know him." He leaned back against the cigarette case and put his hands behind his head. "I only hear from Elena."

Just my luck the woman who didn't seem to take to me was in charge of hiring. Elena reminded me of a sloppier version of Miss David.

A small light bulb winked on in my brain. "Do you know Rupert Agadzinoff?"

"Sure," said Little Anatoly, "he is my lawyer, yo. 'Cause when you're def like me, you can't keep no peace. Keepin' lawyers on retainers, no repercussions later."

He grinned. "How do you like that?"

"Your English vocabulary is suspiciously large when you freestyle," I said.

"I watch MTV all the time in my country. Also MTV Live, VH1 Europe, MTV Dance, MTV Hits, MTV Rocks, and Nickelodeon. I like the SpongeBob SquarePants."

"Now that you live here, I hope you realize Americans are not portrayed at our best on those shows."

"Living here has been disappointment," he sighed. "But I can drive to Atlanta to go to clubs someday. Maybe I will become DJ before I make it big as rapper."

"Sounds like a good goal. You should meet my friend, Todd. He's a drummer."

"I want to meet this Todd drummer. But I work all the time. Can't get no rest--"

I interrupted before he started another freestyle block. "It seems like you need more employees at this store. How many work here?"

"Me, Sam, Dina, Gleb, Elena. Twelve hour shift. Every six day."

"That's ridiculous. Why would you agree to those hours? Why couldn't Todd or I get hired?"

Little Anatoly's gaze drew to the back again. I followed his look. A tall man with a bad crew cut and determined stare stood in the doorway of the stock room. He also wore a track suit, kelly green with a white stripe. I wondered if they exercised in the stock room when the store was empty.

"Sam," whispered Little Anatoly.

Sam honed in on us, but planted his feet before the door. He nodded to Little Anatoly and gave me a curt, once-over.

"I'm going to introduce myself to Sam," I said. Sam had some of the same features as Tyrone's hijacker. Long face and nose. Rounded jaw. High cheekbones. Pretty mouth. "Did he cut his hair recently?"

"No." said Little Anatoly. "You do not want talk to Sam. He is psychopath. Look at his eyes. I cannot sleep for fear that Sam may cut my throat. He does not like freestyle rap."

"Seriously? You think he'll murder you?"

"He has told me this himself. 'Anatoly, cut the shit or I cut your throat.'"

"You live together?"

Little Anatoly nodded. "We all live together in the Line Creek Apartments. We have the two bedroom. Not so bad with our shifts, but Elena always complaining about my clothes on floor."

I knew the Line Creek apartments. A step up in pay scale from Sweetgum Estates, swapping the meth-heads for rock bottom alcoholics, unwed mothers, and twenty-somethings who spent their rent money in bars. "I am experiencing that problem myself. Is Elena your sister?"

He shook his head, keeping his eyes on Sam.

"You sure you don't know Max Avtaikin? Does Elena or Sam?"

"Sam doesn't know anyone. He is at home or in this store. Sometimes he goes to movie. That is all."

Creepy Sam. "Well, nice talking to you, Little Anatoly." I wandered to the coffee station and began to prepare a cup while I covertly watched Sam's sentinel position. He seemed rather territorial about the stock room.

I needed to see the stock room.

The door jangled and a man and woman came in. They began to browse the aisles. I glanced at Little Anatoly, but he had turned his attention to a magazine. Sam disappeared into the stock room. I stirred a packet of sugar into my cafe au lait and strolled toward the back of the store. I tried the store room door. Locked. I knocked.

The door swung partially open, blocked by Sam's lanky form.

"Hey Sam," I said, trying to peer around his body. "Max Avtaikin told me to help you in the back."

"Who is Max Avtaikin?"

"The owner?" Why didn't these people know the Bear? "Maksim Avtaikin? Signs your paycheck?"

Sam snorted. "What do you want?"

"To help you."

"Are you with the church women who visit the apartment?"

"No," I glanced at my tube top. I wasn't usually mistaken for a church lady. "So you don't know Max Avtaikin? Or heard about him?"

"No. Go away." He slammed the door shut.

Sam's shorn locks had grown out from a buzz that looked more than a week old. He had a scar on his chin, but Tyrone might have been too far away to see it. Sam was also taller than the hijacker Tyrone reported. One call to Uncle Will and I could report Sam as someone matching the hijacker description.

Couldn't hurt to bring the fuzz down on the SipNZip. Maybe Max would take notice.

And maybe I needed to learn more about the Bear. There was too much mystery surrounding that animal.

TWENTY-EIGHT

The next morning, I shot awake, partially because Casey's foot was embedded in my armpit, but mainly from an overwhelming sense of dread I'd forgotten something important. I climbed over Casey, stepped over Todd's snoring form on the floor, and tripped over a gym bag left in the hall by Cody. As I brushed my teeth, I examined the anxiety squeezing my nerves and realized it stemmed from the unresolved mess left by the hijacking.

According to Luke and Max's hints, the Sheriff's Office had apparently moved on from their investigation into something grander than the death of a truck driver and a two-bit junkie copper thief.

Jerell had been swept from his family. Miss Gladys now lived alone and unprotected in something akin to a cardboard box. I had failed them. I had spent the greater part of my week trying to clear my own name when something more significant was at stake than local petty prejudice.

I spat toothpaste in my Pepto-pink sink, stared at the blond frizz flying around my head, and thought hard. Which didn't work. At the kitchen table, I pushed aside Miss Wanda's poster art and tossed down a small pad of newsprint and a Berol number three. I doodled a Dixie Cake truck, a handgun, and a driver who was not the real driver. Next, I drew a circle of copper wire, the small pipe of a meth user, and a cracker box trailer. Why had Tyrone decided to steal wire in a spot where truckers slept and minivans stopped for tee-tee breaks? Why had the robbery happened at a spot unusual for hijacks? Was Tyrone supposed to meet his dealer at the rest stop?

Lord help me, but I didn't want to speak to any Sweetgum tweakers. If Tyrone's death didn't have anything to do with the hijacking, or the "bigger than the hijacking" crime, his murder might never get solved. I put aside thoughts of the Sweetgum mafia and thought about how Max could be tied to the hijacking.

I tapped my pencil and drew the SipNZip logo and a cranky bear. Did the police's interest in Max relate to the truck hold up? Why did Max try to hide his ownership? Why were all the employees foreign and living together in an apartment?

Why did I care?

Finally, I drew a little hatchback. That particular vehicle stumped me. While Luke watched Max, who watched me? I sketched Shawna's face next to the car, then added horns and a mustache.

I heard a shuffle of feet, looked up, and found Todd standing in the kitchen entrance watching me. He wore plaid pajama pants and had slipped a soft gray t-shirt over his sculpted body. I wasn't sure if I should feel thankful or deprived for his coverage.

"What are you doing?" he asked.

"Trying to understand what's going on," I said. "The government has intervened. Jerell has been placed in foster care. Miss Gladys is sucking on oxygen all by her lonesome. She needs full time care and her main source of income is dead. Never mind that source of income came from larceny and illegal drugs. Miss Gladys is still living in a cardboard box surrounded by cookers and crankers and barely strong enough to heat a can of soup."

"What are you going to do?" Todd slipped into the chair next to me and examined my drawings.

"Now that Shawna has muddied my name, no one will listen to me. At least Leah's asking the churches to help Miss Gladys. I can't find Shawna's photos. And it doesn't look like Mr. Max is going to help us. I'm sorry you've been dragged into this."

"I like being your muse," he smiled and drew a happy face on my pad. "It looks like you're figuring more than a charity call. Your bear wants to rip apart the SipNZip."

I studied my drawing. "You're right, Todd. Why does the Bear hate the SipNZip? It must turn a good profit. There's barely any employees."

"The overhead is cheap, too."

I studied Todd's face bent over the paper as he drew a dollar sign. "What do you mean?"

"When I went there to apply, I went around back to watch them unload a truck. You know, that used to be my job."

"I know, honey," I said and squeezed his hand. "You'll get re-hired as soon as the economy picks up."

"Anyway, they were bringing in cases of stock from the back of a U-Haul."

"What does that mean?"

"I was only a brown box, front door delivery guy. But generally, stores get their stock delivery from company trucks. You've seen the commercial where the beer truck drives up to the store and everyone cheers? At the SipNZip, two guys were unloading boxes of beer from a U-Haul." Todd drew a big U on my sketch pad. "Something's wrong with that."

I leaned over and kissed his cheek. "Todd, you're brilliant. I don't know why you try and hide it. You need to call Uncle Will and tell him what you saw."

"I'm pretty sure he knows. Deputy Chris Wellington watched them from his pickup. Like he was doing the plainclothes detective thing."

"Hot damn," I slipped from the chair, avoiding Todd's reach for another kiss. "That's why the cops are watching Mr. Max."

"Probably why Mr. Max doesn't want me working there, too." Todd strummed the table surface, tapping out a happy rhythm.

"You are right again. Max is protecting you." I felt so energized, I didn't bother to stop Todd's annoying drumming. "And me. He wants me to stay away from him in order to protect me."

I ran to the door to grab my boots. "Can I borrow your car? You want to tag along?"

"Sure, baby," said Todd. "Where are you going?"

"The Gearjammer doesn't open until later and the Sweetgum meth-heads are likely still asleep. My first stop today is Atlanta. Rupert was Max's immigration lawyer. I bet he's got a file on Max that will tell me something. Max is somehow tied to this hijacking. All this interest in him and the SipNZip didn't start until that truck was robbed. If I can't do anything else for Miss Gladys, I can tell her who killed Tyrone so she can sue them."

"She doesn't care about the killer going to jail?"

"Prison justice is for folks with money. People like Miss Gladys would rather use the court system for economic retribution."

"You think Mr. Max did this?" asked Todd. "I like Mr. Max. I can't see him robbing a truck or killing anyone. Although I wouldn't want to mess with him."

"I agree, Todd. The Bear is a dangerous beast, although his criminal activity seems to be contained to cheating at cards and rigging roulette wheels. Rupert mentioned Max worked for a casino in his younger days. Vice tends to flow to other realms. I hope this is not the case."

"If they are stocking the SipNZip with jacked goods, Max is going to prison for a long time," said Todd. "What if he doesn't know they're doing it?"

"Dammit." I yanked on a boot. "Am I going to have to help the Bear, too? I swear I don't know why I care so much, Todd. It's not like I'm accumulating any accolades around here."

"I'll clap for you, baby," Todd said and winked. "But I'd rather kiss you instead."

At Rupert's Buckhead McMansion, Todd rang the doorbell. He glanced at me, a smile curling his soft lips.

Todd's fondness for adventure almost outweighed his fondness for performing in tight, faux-leather pants. Playing poker gave him a similar adrenaline rush. Todd didn't need drugs. His body made his own.

Maybe we should offer this wisdom to the Sweetgum crew.

"I forgot to ask you how your set went last night," I said. "I had some trouble with a vehicle following me."

"That silver hatchback you mentioned?" asked Todd. "I haven't seen it, but I think Casey mentioned seeing one yesterday."

"Dammit," I said, then closed my mouth as the door swung open.

Miss David wore a pale blush velour yoga set. Her impassive expression barely registered the shock of seeing me, but wavered a bit upon taking in the hunk that is Todd.

"You are the model for the classical paintings," she said to Todd. "Amazing."

"So you're not a robot," I said. "I was beginning to wonder. Mind if we come in?"

"I don't believe Rupert needed you today," she said, but stepped aside to allow us entrance. She gave my cutoffs and Daytona Beach t-shirt a sneer. I supposed she didn't care for stock cars and dolphins.

"You have come all this way for nothing."

"We were in the area. Todd wanted to see where his paintings hung," I said, hiding my crossed fingers behind my satchel.

"I've never seen myself hanging on a real wall before," said Todd.

Miss David's lower lip dropped. She closed it quickly. "Of course."

"Is Mr. Rupert in?" I pointed down the hall. "I left my tackle in his office and need it for another project."

"Not now. Shall I fetch the box for you?"

"Don't bother, I'll go grab it," I said. "You go along and show Todd the paintings. He'll enjoy that."

I waited until they entered the red room and closed the French doors. Running down the hall, I flung open the door to the office and snagged my supply box from its spot near the Christmas tree.

I tore back down the hall, dropped my tackle box on the floor, and cracked the door to Miss David's office. I headed immediately past her desk to the file cabinet, opened the first drawer, and began leafing through folders. Avtaikin popped out quickly, and I blessed Max for his convenient initial. Grabbing the folder, I shoved it in my satchel and scooted out of the room. I pulled the door closed and reached to snatch my tackle box from the floor. As I straightened, I found Miss David watching me from the doorway to the red room.

"Find everything you need?" she asked.

"Yep," I said. "Where's Todd?"

"Here I am," he said, slipping around Miss David. "I noticed the frame was crooked and while I straightened it, Miss David disappeared on me."

"I thought I heard something," she said, studying me.

"I think I hear something, too," I said. The growl of a car engine grew louder. I peered through the bracketing on the front door's adjacent window. The town car zipped around the donut toward the rear garage. "That's Nik. What happened to him last night?"

"Don't know," said Todd.

"Let's find out." I didn't like the way Miss David eyed me. Any woman who wouldn't stay to watch Todd's backside stretch over a sofa to adjust a painting had something wrong with her.

We hustled out the front door and walked down the drive to the rear garage. With a cigarette dangling from his mouth, Nik wiped the car down with a wet rag. Seeing Todd and I, he dropped the cloth and took a deep drag before pulling the cigarette from his mouth.

"You have ruined my life," he said.

"How's that?" I halted my gait toward the garage.

"Your sister."

I nodded. Casey was the boll weevil to the cotton hearts of men. There was no hope of recovery once she struck. "Sorry about that."

Todd placed a hand on my shoulder. "Too bad, man."

I twitched off Todd's hand. "It's our momma's fault. I advise you to move on quickly."

Staring at the sky, Nik sucked on the stub of his cigarette and blew a tendril of smoke toward the clouds. "'Like a spirit of the purest beauty. In the torture of hopeless melancholy,'" he quoted. "Pushkin."

"Lord help him," I said to Todd. "Let's get out of here before he pulls out a bottle of vodka and starts singing."

Nik nodded. "Leave me to my pain."

"Maybe you can focus your pain on rebuilding my truck."

I pulled on Todd's hand to reverse our walk to the front of the house. "I picked up some interesting materials. I'm going to read to you on the way home."

"I liked Nik's poem," said Todd.

"It's better than a poem. It's background information on the Bear."

TWENTY-NINE

On the way home, we stopped at the Varsity. Todd drove and munched on fries and onion rings while I flipped through the thick file on Maksim Avtaikin. I rummaged for photos first. His passport pictures disappointed me. No smiles.

"Keep your eye out for little BMWs, Todd," I said, taking a sip of Varsity Orange.

"Do you want me to count them? Two just passed me." He gave me a lazy smile, and I thought about the plague of Cherry Tucker chomping away at Todd's heart.

"Todd, do you feel like you have something in common with Nik?"

"I think my English is better," he said. "But we both seem to enjoy driving you around."

"Nik does not enjoy driving me around," I said. "Anyway, that's not what I meant. Just like Casey and Nik, I'm no good for you. I love being friends, but you should think of moving on, too."

"I know what I'm doing," he grinned and winked. "You just started talking to me again."

"I can fix that right quick," I snapped and turned to the file to assuage my feelings of guilt. I studied Max's passport copy. "Holy crap. Max is only thirty-five."

"Wow, he's old," said Todd.

"Thirty-five isn't old. Maybe he seems old because he plays golf with the middle-aged set. Maybe money ages you."

I turned over a copy of a diploma I couldn't read and found a photo of a young, smiling Max in a suit and tie. An older man in flashy threads stood next to him. Max's thick, brown hair had been longer and his cheeks rounder, but he still towered over the man next to him. His smile had the rakish smirk of an eighteen-year-old who thinks they've figured out the world. I knew that feeling. Lost it around twenty-two when I started paying off my student loans.

I glanced at Todd, shoved the picture in my back pocket, and flipped to the next document. "I can't believe this. Max went to Emory."

"Emory University in Atlanta?" Todd glanced at me before accelerating around a chicken truck. "He never mentioned that to me. I thought he liked the Bulldogs."

"No football at Emory. They prefer country club sports." I glanced through his class listings, mainly history and business. "No diploma."

"I guess he didn't graduate."

"No college photos either," I said. "Unfortunately, most of the interesting parts of Max's file are written in that alphabet with the crazy letters. Looks like he went back to his home country between Emory and Halo."

"Cyrillic," said Todd.

I glanced sideways at Todd before leafing through the oodles of citizenship forms. "Found his social security card," I said and almost gagged upon reading the receipt for Rupert's filing. "No wonder Max hates Rupert. You should see what he was charged for immigration. There's processing, courier, visa, fingerprint, and application fees. Those are just for the government. Some are up to six hundred dollars each."

"I guess that way immigrants get used to the government taking away their money before they even move here."

"The government fees aren't as bad as these other costs. Rupert's office charged him for more consultation, filing, courier work, and processing. These receipts begin in the thousands and work their way into double digits."

"Damn," said Todd. "It's a wonder he has any money left."

"No kidding," I said. "This can't be normal. How can America open her arms to the 'tired, poor, and the yearning to be free' for close to fifty thousand dollars? I can't imagine the Vietnamese family that runs the nail shop in Line Creek paying fifty thousand dollars for their green cards."

"Probably used a different lawyer."

"Seems to me there's only a couple reasons to charge that much money. Either Max is so rich he didn't care what it cost to get his paperwork squared away. Or Rupert offered a special service."

"Like the kind you get at the Happy Massage Spa?"

"What is wrong with you? No, not that kind of service. One where Max didn't have to wait in line as long as other people. Or one where the United States government wouldn't find out about Max's past and reject his entry."

"Oh," said Todd.

"Just drive and watch out for silver BMW hatchbacks." I closed the folder and noticed a name written on the bottom left corner, M. Hawkins. I flipped back through the file, but couldn't find a match.

"Do you think I should give this file to Uncle Will?" I said.

"Didn't you steal that file?" said Todd. "He can't use it if you stole it."

"Dangit if you're not right. I might just have to do an anonymous tip." I tapped my Stargazer blue nails on the folder. "I'll slip this back when I go to work on Rupert's portrait. I'm sure nobody will miss it between now and then."

"I suppose I should visit with Miss Gladys," I said to Todd as we turned off the interstate and onto familiar roads. "I am ashamed to admit that I don't want to face her now that Jerell's been taken."

I examined the SipNZip as we passed. The shiny, new exterior dulled in my eyes. Not even the thought of microwavable sausage biscuits could make me think positively about the SipNZip.

I wondered if Little Anatoly could freestyle about sausage biscuits.

"Are you worried Miss Gladys will be angry?" asked Todd.

"I think it will break my heart if she's not angry," I said. "I don't want to go to that old, rundown trailer and not see Jerell. Maybe I can get Miss April, the nice hoarder in the next trailer, to check on her today. If I had good news to bring Miss Gladys, I wouldn't feel so bad."

"What kind of good news?"

"At the very least, I wish I could say I found her a new place to live. I've got Leah working on that. What I'd really like to tell her is Tyrone's killer is in prison and she can start researching lawyers." I pondered that thought.

"Tonight I'll go back to the Gearjammer. There'll be new truckers there. I can flash around the composite drawing. I just don't know what else to do."

"I'd take you to the Gearjammer," said Todd. "But I've got another gig at Red's tonight. And this afternoon, Leah and I were going to go over some new songs. I wrote one about an artist who loves abs."

"That's going to help a lot with the morality police, thank you. And if you can't tell, my tone is sarcastic."

"I could tell," said Todd.

"I don't mean to get ugly, but I've got enough problems without you writing unflattering songs about me."

"I'm flattered you like abs," said Todd. "Because I've got an awesome six-pack."

"This is not the conversation I want to have with you." I rapped on the folder in my lap. "Listen, I've got to figure out how Max is involved with this whole hijacking. If he's guilty, then Miss Gladys will be happy because that's a big wallet to sue. But if he's innocent, I am not going to let him take some other perp's fall."

"I thought you liked busting Mr. Max."

"For misdemeanors that pull our town into the world of clandestine gambling. This is a whole 'nother ball of felonies."

We fell silent, and I watched our town zip by. Halo was no Mayberry, but I still loved her crumbling sidewalks connecting homes to local businesses. The family doctor no longer made house calls, but he was always at the Halo High School football games. And you could call his wife if you needed to lawyer up for a divorce or a DUI. This was a town of decent people and even if they were a tad judgmental—about artists who painted classic nudes, for example—their judgment came from fear of corrupting the small town peace and solitude that was becoming harder to find in this era.

"I need to know who was supposed to drive that Dixie Cake truck," I said. "Something happened when the original trucker was arrested and the other driver took his place."

"How are you going to find him?"

"I'm sure the Sheriff's Office knows, but they won't tell me. The Gearjammer. Too bad Casey is working. She'd distract the truckers enough that they might spill their secrets."

THIRTY

A serious party crowd packed the Gearjammer on Saturday nights. Marshall Dobson, the smoking dispatcher, held his previous spot at the bar with his dispatching female friend. I scanned the crowded, smoky bar for other familiar faces. Dona and her friends wiggled before the jukebox, groped on the pretense of dancing. The room swam with cowboy hats, trucker hats, and farm caps. If you had a thing for bald guys, you would go to some trouble finding them in the Gearjammer.

I figured to try the couple again and slid between Marshall and his female cohort. My head and shoulders cleared the bar, but I had to stand on my toes to get the bartender's attention.

"You came back," said Marshall. He stubbed out his cigarette and scooted his stool to give me room. "You remember Marge? Where's your boyfriend?"

"Luke's my ex-boyfriend," I said. "I'm here by myself tonight. My sister had to work and everyone else thinks they're too good."

"Too good for you or the Gearjammer?" asked Marge. Tonight she had rolled her hair into horizontal sausages and backcombed her bangs. Her arms also reminded me of sausages. Thick and heavy links, like she spent time putting in fences and chopping wood. Arms good for brawling.

"Too good for me," I said quickly. It wouldn't do to insult the establishment's patrons. "I'm an artist and word has gotten out I'm controversial."

"What, like *Piss Christ* kind of stuff?" said Marge.

I shook off my surprise at her knowledge of contemporary art. "No. Classical representations of a nude male."

"I saw that poster hanging in the library," she smiled. "Round of shots for my girl. Give her your seat, Marshall."

"That's okay," I said, happy that my dateless state had made them friendlier. "I'm planning on mingling tonight."

Marge elbowed me in the ribs and winked. "Good plan. Looking for another hot model?"

That pleasant thought stumped me for a second, but I recovered. "Actually, I'm still trying to figure out what happened with that hijacking."

I tugged the composite drawing from my pocket and unfolded it. "Have you seen this guy?"

"No." Marge took the copy and studied it. "Never seen him before. How about you, Marshall?"

Marshall glanced at the sheet of paper. Sliding off his seat, he waved at the empty stool. "Go ahead and sit. I've got to use the gents' room."

I watched him walk away and a feeling of anxiety unfurled within my core. "Marge, y'all know more about this hijacking than you admitted the other night. The cop is not here. Will you talk to me?"

"I don't have a problem talking to you. But I'm not in the good ol' boy network, so I don't know if I can help you."

"The trucker driving the hijacked truck was shot, but he was standing in for someone else. Do you know the guy who was originally going to drive that truck?"

She shook her head. "Not me. What are you thinking?"

"I think the real driver had an arrangement with the hijacker and didn't get a chance to call it off. When he didn't show at the designated spot, the hijacker tracked down the truck, found the new trucker, and shot him. Maybe because the perp panicked. Maybe because he needed whatever was in that truck. Possibly the new driver threatened him."

Marge snatched the shot glass sitting next to her beer and downed it. "Shit, that's a mess."

"You think it's a possibility?"

"I hate to say yes, but yes." She sipped her beer. "Most of these truckers are good guys. Family men. But you get renegades who find easier ways to score more money. Trucking doesn't pay that well, especially now that gas prices are so high."

"You ever heard of Max Avtaikin?" I said. "On the radio or even around town?"

"No," she shook her head. "Sorry, I can't help you more."

I opened my mouth to thank her when I felt hands on my waist. I yelped an angry curse and spun around. Zach's dark eyes gleamed below his cowboy hat. His toothpick rolled around his smile and he moved his hands to the bar, pinning me in a detached embrace.

"You came back for me," he said. "I was hoping you'd bring your sister. I got a look at her the other day at your house. Man, can she rock a pair of shorts."

I shoved him out of the way. "What were you doing at my house?"

"Happy hour."

I muttered a few unflattering words about Cody and his liberal use of my studio for a party den.

"Let's dance." Zach grabbed my hand and pulled me onto the dance floor. He began to shuffle his feet and wave his arms to *Sweet Home Alabama*.

I stood and watched him, then strode up and put my arms around his neck. He stopped shuffling and waving to clamp his hands on my waist.

"Before you get any ideas," I said. "I am in this position so we can talk privately."

"Hey now," he said, pulling closer. "I like the sound of that. I knew older women were the ticket. Young girls just laugh at me."

"Probably for the way you dance," I said. "And I want to talk to you about the hijacking, not whisper sweet nothings. I need to know who was supposed to drive the Dixie Cake rig. I think he had a deal with the hijacker."

"Ernie Pike." Zach's hat brim touched my forehead. The tooth-pick slipped between his lips and reappeared in the corner of his mouth. His whisper barely registered in my ear. "I went to happy hour hoping I could find you. Ernie Pike is getting heat from the cops. And he's on suspension for the DUI. He's looking for squeal-ers."

"Squealers?"

"I'm worried about you, Miss Cherry. Your name's been flashed around town quite a bit the past few days."

"Crap." A rush of anxiety overtook me, and I leaned my head against Zach's chest. We continued to sway. "Zach, I've been show-ing the hijacker's picture around the bar tonight."

"Maybe not a wise choice." Zach slid an arm up my back, pressing me against his chest.

I pulled back. "Zach, I wouldn't play knight for me. You're like-ly to get your ass kicked by your trucker friends or worse."

"What kind of gentleman would I be if I let anything happen to you?"

"A smart one. This is my rodeo, Cowboy. You've got a life of truck stops ahead of you, and I don't want to see it ruined by my interference as a snitch." I stepped out of his embrace and pulled the drawing from my pocket. "Before I go, have you seen this guy before?"

Zach studied the picture and shook his head. "No, ma'am."

"Good," I said and gave him a quick kiss on the cheek. "Stay sweet, Zach."

I spun away from him and saw Marshall Dobson flag me. I pushed past dancing couples and sauntered to the bar.

Marshall pointed his cigarette toward the door. "I'd get if I were you. Folks didn't like your cop boyfriend asking questions and they like it from you even less."

"Is Ernie Pike here?" I asked. "I want to know if Ernie Pike works for Max Avtaikin. And if he knows the man in the drawing."

"Ernie Pike ain't going to talk to you. He'd chew your bones for breakfast."

"You tell Ernie Pike not only is he never driving a truck again, he's going to be charged with conspiracy, aiding and abetting, or as an accessory to a murder. Maybe all. If he confesses and gets this murderer put away, he'll get a reduced sentence or a plea bargain."

Marshall sucked on his cancer stick and blew a column of smoke in my face.

I tried not to blink.

"That so?" he said.

"Yep. But if Ernie Pike's the one who's been tailing me, I'll make sure he gets stalking charges attached to his file. He lays a hand on me and he's never getting out of jail. My uncle is the sheriff."

"If Ernie Pike lays a hand on you," said Marshall, "you won't be alive to press any charges."

THIRTY-ONE

I took Marshall's advice and shoved through the crowd toward the front door of the Gearjammer. Trucks of all varieties crammed the lot. I had wedged Casey's Firebird between a Super Duty pickup and a Ram Laramie. A BMW would stick out like a sore thumb. And it did. The small silver car had parked at the edge of the lot behind a gigantic, unhitched Kenworth double sleeper. I slunk into the shadowed corner between the doorway and building.

Streetlights and a full moon brightened the Gearjammer's parking lot. Curiosity more than fear kept my back glued to the wall and my focus on the Beamer. What was the purpose of watching me? Waiting to find me alone? It found me in odd haunts like here or Max's, yet I never saw the hatchback around my house. Before the Gearjammer, I had stopped at the farm to snag one of Pearl's casseroles for Miss Gladys. Had the BMW found me between the farm and the Gearjammer? That was a twenty-five minute drive.

The casserole now rested in a cooler next to the locked box holding my daddy's old Remington Wingmaster shotgun in the Firebird's trunk.

Since Miss April's warning at the Sweetgum Estates, I had taken to carrying the shotgun on my local errands. Forget the diamonds. A firearm is a girl's best friend. Diamonds won't do you any good if you can't defend them from armed robbery.

Unfortunately, a firearm locked in the trunk of Casey's car didn't do me any good either.

The door to the Gearjammer banged open, and I jumped. Zach strode out, looking left and right. He pivoted and spotted me.

"I hoped you were already gone," he said, drawing into my corner. "But I was also afraid they found you."

"Who found me?" I cleared my throat to take the panic out.

"Couple guys who want to protect their asses," said Zach, tossing his toothpick to the ground. "They're waiting behind that big tractor with their tire thumpers."

"Tire thumpers?"

"Just to scare you, probably." Zach tipped his hat back. "I overheard some townies talking about it inside. Can't believe they wouldn't go out and defend you. What kind of man lets a girl walk into something like that?"

"The kind of men who think I deserve what I get. I don't want you to get hurt, Zach."

"Now you're insulting me." he yanked on the brim of his hat and grabbed my hand. "Where's your ride?"

"The Firebird. Second row."

"Is that the one Cody overhauled? Sweet."

He guided me toward the rows of trucks. Two men strode out from behind the Kenworth, carrying clubs. The largest man measured his steps by whacking a sawed-off baseball bat into his palm.

"Shit," said Zach. "They were waiting all right."

"I'm going to get my gun," I said. "Will you be okay if I make a run for it?"

"Go." He waved me behind him.

I darted between the trucks, fumbling with the car key. Squeezing between the Firebird and the huge Laramie pickup, I watched the men approach Zach. My brother's buddy stood rigidly, his hands held out at his sides.

"Get out of here, rookie," yelled the large man.

"No, sir," said Zach.

"We just want to talk to that girl," said a heavy, older man holding a tire iron. "We want a look at that picture she's been flashing around."

"I didn't recognize the guy in the drawing," said Zach.

"Why would you, son?" asked the old hand. "Get back to dancing with the ladies. We'll be just a minute with this one." He jutted his chin toward me.

I scooted from the narrow alley between the vehicles, rounded the Firebird's trunk, and jammed the key in the lock. The trunk lid popped open, blocking my view of the men, but I could hear the shuffle of footsteps.

I leaned over, reaching for the gun box. My hands grasped the metal, and I righted myself, hauling the box against the rim of the trunk.

The footsteps moved closer, combining with a scuffle that sounded like shoving. Zach started to argue, and I flinched at the crack of wood on skin. My fingers flew over the tiny combination dials. The box snapped open. My hand grasped polished wood. The gun case fell into the trunk, and I slammed the lid shut. At another crack of smacked wood, I hopped backward, swinging the shotgun onto my shoulder in a practiced arc.

"Hold it right there," I yelled, squinting through the sight. I trained my eye on the older man who stood before the hood of the Firebird. Behind him, the large man let his baseball bat fall into his palm with a sharp thwack.

The older man bent over, laid his tire iron on the ground, and rose with his hands held in the air. Zach watched him, then lunged to grab the tire iron.

"You want to talk to me?" I said. "Talk. Who was Ernie Pike supposed to meet to hand off his haul? I want the guy's name in the sketch."

The old hand shook his head. "Don't know what you're talking about, honey."

"I ain't your honey," I said. "I've got an elderly woman sucking oxygen through a tube who's counting on me to find out who murdered her grandson."

"Her grandson is the one who stood in for Ernie?" asked Old Hand. "Real sorry to hear about him."

"Doesn't matter who he was," I said. "I want the name of the guy who shot him."

"You tell your old woman that it was a big mistake," said Baseball Bat. He swung the bat at his side, keeping his eyes on Zach. "The crew was expecting Ernie to stop somewhere else. When they realized it wasn't Ernie, someone got a little excited."

"Shut up, idgit," said Old Hand and spat on the ground.

Baseball Bat swung his club up. "I told you to stop calling me that."

Old Hand looked over his shoulder at Baseball Bat. At the sight of the raised bat, Old Hand fully turned to face him. "Stop acting like a rookie, and I'll stop calling you names."

"Zach," I called. "Car."

Zach took a running three steps and slid behind Old Hand and over the hood of the Firebird. He landed in the tight passageway next to the Super Duty truck and held up his free hand.

"Keys," he said.

I tossed the keys underhand. Zach caught them, still grasping the tire iron. He unlocked the driver's door, slid inside, and revved the engine. With the gun still mounted on my shoulder, I slipped in the narrow alley between the Super Duty and the Firebird.

Old Hand glanced behind him. "This isn't over, girl."

Baseball Bat dropped his club to his side. "Your grandma isn't getting anything from Ernie or anybody else. Ernie's not squealing, no matter what. The cops got nothing and so do you."

"How about Max Avtaikin?" I said. "What's he got?"

"Who in the hell is Max Avtaikin?" said Baseball Bat.

Old Hand waved to shut him up. "If you're talking about the Atlanta crew, they won't be as nice as us. They won't care about that shotgun either. Think about what happened to that driver, girl. That crew doesn't ask questions, they shoot first."

Beside me, the Firebird rolled backward. "Who's the Atlanta crew?" I said. "Ernie's with the Atlanta crew? Max Avtaikin, too?"

"Pow pow." Baseball Bat shot me with his fingers. "Keep your mouth shut and forget about this."

I stepped away and the Firebird jerked back. The driver door swung open.

"Get in," said Zach.

I lowered the Remington and dove across his lap. The door hung open as Zach spun the wheel to the left and popped the clutch into first gear. I scrambled off his lap to the passenger seat. Zach floored the accelerator and we jerked forward with the door swinging.

"Grab the wheel," he said and leaned out to snag the open door's arm rest.

The door swung shut and he tore through the parking lot. We passed the gigantic Kenworth, bumped out the entrance, and onto the street.

The BMW had taken off during our tussle with the truckers.

After refusing his plea for a post-scuffle make out session, I dropped Zach at his house and headed northeast, toward Halo, on zigzagging country roads. Now I had Ernie Pike's attention. I didn't think a trucker would drive a BMW, but I didn't want to take chances.

On Max Avtaikin's street, Luke's truck remained on stakeout duty. I didn't wave or stop to talk. He had abandoned Jerell to the system before I could work out a better solution. Instead, I flipped Luke the bird to express my feelings over his disloyalty.

Maybe I should have taken up Zach's offer, just to tick Luke off.

I whipped the Firebird into the drive before Max's closed gate and honked. The gate didn't move. I stomped from the Firebird to the intercom and pressed the talk button.

"Bear," I said to the intercom. "You've got to talk to me. I can tell something's coming down on you."

He didn't respond, but I could feel him listening.

"Do you know Ernie Pike? How about an Atlanta crew who jacks trucks?"

Nothing.

"Know a Sweetgum hustler named Regis Sharp?" I waited. "No? Thought that was a stretch. What about the fact that your SipNZip is stocked from the back of a U-Haul? But Little Anatoly and Sam don't know you from Adam. I thought that very strange since you're their employer."

I swore a growl emanated from the small black box.

I had written the name from Max's file on the composite sketch. I pulled the drawing from my pocket and checked my scribble. "Do you know an M. Hawkins? You should. They had something to do with your immigration. By the way, I didn't know you went to Emory. I love the Michael C. Carlos Museum and the Visual Arts Gallery."

The intercom refused to comment.

"I'm trying to help you. Do you understand? I won't stop until I know the why and how of your involvement." I kicked the intercom stand. "Dammit, I don't like this. I know you didn't hijack a truck. The blond dude did. I know you didn't kill Tyrone. What would be the point? You didn't even know about the hijacking."

I paused on that thought. "They can't charge you as an accessory if you didn't know about the hijacking or the murder. I can attest to that. But according to Luke this is bigger than the hijacking. This has to do with you owning the SipNZip, doesn't it?"

No reply from the squawk box.

"So maybe you're organizing hijackings to fill the SipNZip. Maybe you're a big time crook and just when I started to trust you, your true colors are showing." I centered my serious expression in the tiny camera. "That goes against my instincts. And instincts are about all I've got left."

Walking away from the camera, I leaned against the gate and stared at the silent box. "I know you think you're protecting me. I'm so far beyond that. I'm wading through a very dangerous swamp full of trucker gators and tweaker piranhas."

The rumble of a car motor drew my attention away from the icy reception blowing out of the intercom. Shawna's Mustang pulled around the Firebird and shone a light on my lean against the gates. She stuck her head out the car window.

"Trolling for handouts?" she said. "Mr. Max doesn't want any more to do with you than anyone else in this town."

I pushed off the gate and strolled to her car. "I don't have your photos."

"Of course you have them. You think I'd just wait around while you decided what to do with them?"

"If I had the pictures, don't you think I would have given them to you by now? Or have already used them against you? I'm appealing to your sense of logic here, Shawna."

"One of you Tuckers will use them," she sneered. "There's no doubt in my mind. Maybe you don't have them, but I'm positive one of you does. And I know you're the only Tucker who would stop your siblings."

She tapped her horn three times and the gate swung open. "You bring me those photos and I will stem this tide of hatred against you. I can turn it around."

"No you can't. It's gotten out of hand, and you know it," I said. "You've got all these women riled up with your own dirty mind."

"Next up is the men," Shawna smirked. "You think husbands and fathers are going to want you painting pictures of dingles in their town? I'm taking the photos 'round to Sunday services tomorrow. And I'm inviting Mr. Max to do the circuit with me. I heard he needs to reach out to the community. Perfect timing, really."

She gunned her motor and flew through the gates.

I kicked a piece of gravel and stomped back to the Firebird. I could handle a couple beefy men at a trucker bar, but this ridiculous woman almost made me cry.

I should have pulled the shotgun on Shawna.

THIRTY-TWO

The next morning sunlight glanced off the dusty aluminum siding and heated tar paper roofs in the Sweetgum Estates. Feisty pit bulls charged their fences as I rolled past. Unsure of when Nik would show to pick me up for my Sunday painting session, I decided to haul butt to the Sweetgum Estates first. I had avoided Miss Gladys the day before. Now I avoided the good Christians of Halo who were about to get Sunday schooled on nekkid *Greek Todd*.

God should smite Shawna just for proposing that idea.

I had stopped at the Tru-Buy and loaded up on groceries and tabloids for Miss Gladys. No BMWs appeared, nor hostile truckers. Luck was on my side.

I parked Casey's Firebird before the Coderre trailer and glanced at my traveling companion, the long, metal shotgun box on the seat next to me.

After last night's scare, I was no longer flying solo anywhere. However, I couldn't carry the shotgun and bags of groceries. And leaving a gun box in the front seat was akin to placing a "Rob Me" flag in the windshield. I left the gun box in the trunk and hauled out the groceries, all the while feeling the eyes of the neighborhood junkie coalition on my back.

Carrying the food, I struggled up the rickety wooden steps to the trailer door. With plastic bags looped over my arms and Pearl's casserole dish clamped between my fingers, I knocked on the door with my shoulder and waited. After several minutes of silence, I grew nervous. What if Miss Gladys had fallen in Jerell's absence? Or something had happened to her oxygen tanks?

Setting the bags and casserole on the steps, I tried the door knob. The door swung open.

"Miss Gladys?" I called, forcing my voice from hesitancy to hope.

I picked up the groceries and carried them inside the house, glancing around the shoddy room as I did. The video games and magazines had been pushed off the coffee table and onto the floor. The cabinet doors under the TV hung open and more video game equipment had been strewn across the rug. I dropped the groceries and pulled out my phone.

Luke's line clicked over to voicemail, and I left a hurried message explaining what I'd found. Unsure if a messy house warranted a 9-1-1 call, I thought about my Remington in the trunk when I heard a weak cry from the back.

"Miss Gladys?" I called again.

The pitiful sound came from the bedroom at the end of the trailer. I abandoned thoughts of the shotgun and hurried down the hallway. Taking a deep breath, I turned the doorknob and pushed. The thin plywood door wouldn't budge.

"Ma'am?" I knocked on the door. "Are you hurt? I'm calling an ambulance if you can't get to the door."

The door whipped open, and I stumbled back in surprise. A wild-haired woman with bloodshot eyes and a knife greeted me.

"Who are you?" she said.

"Miss Gladys," I screamed through the intruder. "Are you in there? The police are on their way."

"You didn't call the police," said the woman, jabbing the knife toward my face. "You called a Luke."

I skipped back holding my hands before me. "Luke's a deputy in the sheriff's department. He's on his way. He'll bring back up."

The woman lunged, directing the knife toward my midriff and backed me into the wall. "You're just saying that because I got a knife. You know where Tyrone hid his money?"

"Miss Gladys," I hollered. "If you can hear me, make a noise so I know you're alive."

I heard her feeble call from the bedroom and felt my resolve strengthen.

"Who are you?" I left my hands in front of me, slid my boot between the woman's legs, and slowly turned my body on an angle. A self-defense move Uncle Will taught me. "You a Coderre or just some Sweetgum junkie looking to score off a sick, old woman?"

"Latisha Coderre," she said. "I'm protecting our assets before the Sharps descend upon our family like the locusts in that Bible story."

"Tyrone's dealer?" I kept talking, my eyes on Latisha's knife. My right hand drew back.

"Yes," she said impatiently, raising the blade toward my neck. "They already messed with Destiny and she told them to come look for Tyrone's money here. They're coming to clear out the trailer."

"The trailer of an old woman and a child?"

"The Sharps don't care. Tyrone owed them. There's lots of people in Sweetgum who owe the Sharps money. They don't want people thinking that dying is a way to get out of a debt."

"The Sharps sound real charitable."

Latisha's knife hand relaxed while she tried to puzzle out my sarcasm.

"Listen, can you lower your knife?" I said. "I want to check on Miss Gladys and make sure she's okay. I was bringing groceries."

"Yeah, okay."

As her hand dropped, I rammed her arm with my shoulder. The knife fell to the floor, and I dove to snatch it. With the knife in hand, I jumped to my feet and turned on Latisha.

"What the hell?" I screamed at her. "What kind of person are you, holding knives on a dying woman? Go sit on that chair." I pointed to a chair next to the kitchen table.

"I thought you was sympathetic," Latisha moaned, rubbing her arm. "The Sharps are coming. Any minute. I'm trying to find the money and hide it before they get it."

"The hell you are. You're robbing an old woman." I glanced around the room. No handy skein of rope lay nearby. I didn't have time to paw through the cupboards. "Stay here while I go check on Miss Gladys."

"Don't get caught when the Sharps come. They killed Tyrone."

"How's that?"

"That's what Regis Sharp told Destiny. They followed Tyrone and all he had was a little wire, so they killed him."

"Just wait there," I waved at the chair, yanked my phone from my pocket, and rushed toward the back bedroom. Miss Gladys lay on the floor, gasping. I found her oxygen tank in the bathroom, rolled it back to the bedroom, and slipped the tubes into her nose. While rubbing her back, I called for an ambulance and followed that with a direct call to Uncle Will.

Hearing a crash in the other room, I left Miss Gladys to peek down the hall. Latisha had fled. She had been replaced by another woman and two men. They stood in the living room surveying the mess. One man with dark, slicked back hair held a pistol in his hand.

"Holy shit." I crept back to the bedroom and fastened the door. I glanced down at Miss Gladys and began to clear a path to shove the dresser in front of the door.

Sirens wailed in the distance. I blessed my phone and hunkered next to Miss Gladys. Pain and fright deepened the lines in her face.

"They'll kill us," she said. "Tyrone didn't have no money."

"The police and ambulance are on their way. You're going to be fine," I whispered. "We'll get out of here."

Through the door, I could hear an agitated conversation between the Sharps. The sirens grew louder.

"I better get Tyrone's money quick, old woman."

I jumped and Miss Gladys whimpered. The deep voice had resonated through the thin outside walls of the trailer. My Remington could have blasted a hole through that wall and easily taken him. For that matter, so could his handgun.

"I don't care where you get the money, but you better find it. I know you've got it, Miss Gladys," said the Sharp. "Everyone knows you've been stashing Tyrone's take before he could spend it. You get it."

Miss Gladys's brown eyes rolled white. I held my breath, afraid to speak, fearing the bullets that could penetrate the thin walls. As the sirens grew, the dogs flew into a mad frenzy of barking.

"Don't think I didn't see you, Blondie," said the voice. "I've watched you all week. You keep your mouth shut about this or you're in for a world of hurt."

THIRTY-THREE

"I don't think my life could get much worse," I told Uncle Will. We sat in his Crown Vic, watching his officers process the crime scene. They strode throughout the trailer park, banging on doors and rounding up the idiots who tried to flee. In an abandoned trailer, another deputy questioned meth-heads coherent enough to speak. My ex-deputy was noticeably absent.

Will nodded thoughtfully. "Getting caught in the middle of a drug feud is pretty bad."

I hadn't mentioned my trucker escapades. At this point, I figured one more threatening stalker wouldn't make a difference. The Sheriff's Office would put a watch on me either way.

"At least Miss Gladys is in the hospital," I said. "I won't worry about her safety now."

"And Jerell is tucked away with a family," he added. "That's good."

"Do you know where Jerell is?" I could tell by Will's face even if he did know Jerell's whereabouts, I wouldn't learn the answer. I felt my eyes smarting again. I bit my lip hard and glowered at the trailer. "Do you think Regis Sharp killed Tyrone?"

"It's a possibility," said Will. "They could have arranged a meeting at the rest stop. Wouldn't put it past them. Maybe Tyrone thought he could give Sharp wire instead of money. Words were said. Sharp shot him. Maybe out of anger. Maybe to make an example out of Tyrone."

"Is Sharp a suspect?"

"Most definitely. I want that bugger anyhow. His men are in and out of prison on possession or intent to distribute. Regis Sharp is hard to catch. I'd need a weapons match, though. You say he had a Ruger?"

"That's my best guess." I fell forward to lean my head against the dash. "What am I going to do? A BMW has been following me around town. You think that's Sharp?"

Uncle Will rubbed his forehead. "Why didn't you tell me this earlier, hon'?"

"I told Luke a few nights ago. Everything happened so fast."

"I want you out of town. Are you still working that job in Buckhead?" He noted my nod. "I'll pay for a hotel up there. I can bring in Regis Sharp and hold him on your testimony. I know a judge who is dying to get rid of this sonofabitch."

"I don't want you paying for a hotel. The lawyer offered to room me anyway. I turned him down because he's a control freak and his decorating hurts my eyes. And I had stuff going on here."

Which I didn't anymore, I thought sadly. The Coderres had been dispersed. I couldn't find the photos and Shawna's plan had advanced past the stopping point. My siblings had taken over my studio. Max had abandoned me. Ernie Pike wanted to permanently shut me up. And now Regis Sharp had his eye on me.

"Did you check into that guy, Sam, at the SipNZip?" I asked. "The one who looks like the hijacker?"

"Sure, hon'," said Will.

"Max Avtaikin owns the SipNZip."

"Yes, I know." Will's attention had reverted to his deputies and the Ziploc bags of goods they stacked on the trunk of a car. "You should get going now."

"I can't take Casey's Firebird to Atlanta. I'll have to call Nik to pick me up. I don't know where he is."

"Don't worry about that, sugar."

"I should go visit Miss Gladys in the hospital first. Check on her. And I'm supposed to give Miss Wanda some posters."

"I'm giving you an escort," said Will. He glanced in the rear-view at the sound of a vehicle rolling to a stop behind us. "Here he is. No arguments. Run your errands and then he'll drive you to Atlanta."

I twisted in my seat to glance out the back window and spun back around to glare at Uncle Will.

"You do have a choice," Will smirked. "Luke as your babysitter or sit tight in the drunk tank until I can take you to Atlanta myself."

"That isn't a fair choice. I've done nothing wrong."

"I know, hon'. I just want you safe until we get Regis Sharp."

"Thank you for taking me to see Miss Gladys." I spoke with my chin lifted and eyes fixed on the bug splattered windshield.

If I had sat any more rigidly, my shoulder blades might have slashed the truck's leather bench. "And I appreciate you swinging by the farm so I can say goodbye to Grandpa. Although I'm not sure he cares."

In Luke's pickup, we had chased my errands in unnatural silence. The kind of atmosphere that makes your neck prickly, legs twitchy, and mouth ready to spew any word that hops out of your brain.

I knew Luke well enough to know this silence meant some intense feelings gripped his psyche. I tried to ignore that knowledge. Mixed with my wounded pride were other hurts like rejection and a seething anger at Luke for calling DFACs on the Coderres. Of course, if Jerell had been home when the house had been ransacked by Latisha and the Sharps...

I couldn't let myself think about that possibility.

"Thank you also for taking me to your momma's house to drop off those posters," I continued in the manner taught to me by my Grandma Jo. I waited out Luke's no comment before persisting. "I believe Miss Wanda was pleased with the posters. You might not realize that in creating those signs, I have done the equivalent of career hari kari. Except less bloody."

"The posters looked fine to me," said Luke. "Don't know why you're making such a big deal about them. Just a photo of a Greek statue and some words."

"It's not the execution that will ruin me. Lord knows I should be able to hand letter a piece of poster board after four years of art school. And I did save myself embarrassment by replacing Shawna's Photoshop of my paintings by replacing them with photos of the original Greek statues."

I paused and blew a disgusted sigh from my nose. "Why can't you see Shawna is trying to ruin me with this Concerned Citizens Committee?"

"I do my best to ignore this ridiculous feud between you two. That's what keeps me sane. Y'all put me in the middle, and I'm trying to step out of it."

"Have you ever asked her why she hates me?" I glanced at his stiff grip on the steering wheel and then to his stony profile. His jawline could chop wood. "Why she goes to such lengths to humiliate me? You know she's taken Mr. Max to shop the churches today with abstractions of my paintings?"

"I try to avoid the subject of you when I'm around her. And I'm around her a lot. She's always at my mom's house. That's why I didn't get involved at Avtaikin's house last night."

I pressed a hand to my temple and shifted my body to look out the window. Pastures interspersed with forests flew by. A fox carrying a critter in his mouth paused in a ditch to wait out our passage.

"Why are you worried about Shawna when you were practically held hostage today?" Luke ground out the words. "You should be worried about Regis Sharp, not Shawna."

"I agreed to get out of town, didn't I? I let Uncle Will talk me into driving around with you, for goodness sakes."

"You want to drive yourself around? After what happened today?"

I twisted to face him. "You're blaming me for this? I brought a sick, elderly woman groceries. No one else was looking out for her. I can't be scared of people like Regis Sharp when someone like Miss

Gladys is alone and ill. She would have died if I hadn't been there. And Jerell would have nobody."

"I know." He pulled his hand off the wheel to rub his eyes.

"Are you crying?"

"No," he said roughly. "Of course not. And I don't think it's your fault. If anything, it's my fault."

"How is this your fault?" I pulled my knees onto the seat. "What's going on with you?"

"I can't talk about the investigation." His glance flashed a hint of dull silver. "It's beyond our department. Don't ask me anything about the hijacking."

He looked away, but not before I caught a wet gleam.

"I screwed up," he said. "First with not putting a tail on Tyrone Coderre. Then for not putting somebody in Sweetgum to watch that trailer. I got Tyrone killed and put Jerell, Miss Gladys, and now you in jeopardy."

I kept my thoughts to myself while I watched him hammer the steering wheel and curse greater obscenities than those used by the sailors who caroused the riverfront of Savannah. When he had finished, I laid a hand on his thigh. After a long minute, he slipped his hand in mine, crushing my fingers in his grip.

We continued toward the farm in silence, our hands speaking for what could not be said. As we neared the lane, Luke slowed his truck, and I squinted at the object parked further down the road.

"Wait," I said, pulling my hand from his to point. "There's that hatchback parked down the road. That idiot. Parked on the side of a county road."

Luke flipped me his phone. "Dial 9-1-1 and repeat what I say to the dispatcher."

"I can't believe this," I said, punching the buttons on his phone. "Spying on my Grandpa's farm in broad daylight? How did he think nobody would see him? So stupid."

"Quit complaining about their surveillance techniques and tell the dispatcher 10-80, pursuit in progress. Requesting assistance now."

THIRTY-FOUR

As Luke backed out of the farm lane, the BMW pulled into the road and accelerated.

"Hang on," said Luke. "I want to get those plates. Keep the dispatcher on the line and report as soon as we read them."

"Got it," I said, leaning forward in my seat.

The Raptor's motor revved with the power of eight cylinders, but the little Beamer flew down the road ahead of us. Fields flew by. Cows lifted their heads to watch us pass.

"I'm not getting beat by a hatchback," said Luke. "Keep your eyes on that license plate. The Sheriff's Office knows our location. We'll keep with them until the first responder arrives."

"Yes, sir."

The BMW approached the junction for the local highway, careened into the right turn lane, and disappeared behind the stand of trees lining the highway.

"Shit," Luke muttered and gunned toward the stop sign.

I grabbed the door handle with my free hand and grasped the phone to my ear. "Just a minute, Mindy," I told the dispatcher. "We're fixing to take a tight turn on to the highway. Stay on the line, but I've got to hold on."

Cars flashed by on the highway. Luke slowed to ready for the turn. He glanced left and began to take the corner. I screamed. A goliath combine, the head lifted and man-sized tires rolling, began its left turn toward our county road. Cutting across our lane of traffic, it drove directly into our truck's path. From his high perch, the farmer shouted words better not repeated. Luke braked and reversed onto the county road. The combine continued its sluggish path, the tire brushing near Luke's front fender. I placed a hand on my heart to settle the wild thumping.

"Dammit," Luke said. "Friggin' farmers. He was in my lane."

"How did you not see a combine? Even in a car chase you need to look both ways."

He shot me a look that momentarily shut me up and cranked onto the highway. In the distance we heard the wail of a siren.

"Finally," he muttered. "Still wish I had those plates."

He sped up, tailing the minivan ahead of us. The minivan flashed their brake lights, causing another string of curses about soccer moms to spill from Luke's lips. He waited until we rounded a curve, then zipped into the left lane, passed the minivan, and slipped in front of her as a pickup pulling a horse trailer came at us. He surged toward the next vehicle, an old Buick sedan. Her turn signal had been left blinking and the Buick canted toward the middle lines. This time, Luke cut right and passed the grandma on the shoulder with the help of a driveway.

"I don't see the BMW anymore," I said. "You think they got that far ahead or did it turn off somewhere?"

Behind us the sirens grew louder. We pulled to the side as two county patrol vehicles flew past us.

Luke full lips pursed into a pout. "Damn, I wish I was on duty."

"Let's follow them," I said. "If that's Regis Sharp and they've got him, then I can go home."

Luke shook his head. "You think I'm taking you to an apprehension? That's the last thing the officers need."

"Might as well take me home, then. Either way, I can't go to Atlanta now."

He swiveled in his seat. "What are you talking about? If they didn't nab Sharp, you have to go to Atlanta."

"If Regis Sharp is driving that BMW, he knows where my family lives. How can I go to Atlanta and leave them in danger?"

"We make Casey and Cody hole up at the farm. Your Grandpa has a personal armory of hunting weapons. He and Cody can protect Casey. Even Todd McIntosh will be good for something. I'll stay at the farm and watch over them myself."

"Casey can handle herself, that's not the point. I can't just run away. Luke, that car watched the farm. I can't let him do that."

"Are you crazy? Sharp is looking for you. He wants to use you to get Mrs. Coderre to tell where Tyrone hid his money."

"Tyrone didn't have any money." I strummed the seat with my fingers. "How can I convince Regis Sharp of that? Maybe I should go talk to Latisha Coderre again. Spread the word by community grapevine."

"Do you hear yourself? This can't be solved with gossip. Regis Sharp runs a drug trafficking network. He doesn't give two craps whether Tyrone has money or not. He'll shake anyone down to get something from them to protect his reputation as a bad ass."

"He has a lot in common with Shawna," I said. "Sounds a lot like what she's doing to me."

Luke ran his fingers through his hair and pulled on the curls. "Lord, you are frustrating. Give me my phone. I want to know if they caught the BMW."

I handed him the phone. "Might as well tell them I'm not going to Atlanta while you're at it."

From inside my satchel, my phone buzzed. I reached inside and glanced at the caller ID. "Crap," I said. "It's Rupert. I'm going to have to go to Atlanta."

"Rupert," I said. "Today's not so good for me."

"My dear, this is exactly why I wanted you to stay up here. We discussed this as part of your contract. When I'm free, I need you to be free."

I swallowed my scream of frustration and tried for politeness. "I have a family emergency."

"I suppose I could come to Halo, then."

"No," I checked my shout. "Not a good idea."

"How long will your emergency take? I have a guest coming and I want him to see what you've done. You took your sketches with you."

I knew he'd look at those sketches. "When are you expecting your guest?"

"For dinner. I will send Nik to pick you up."

I thought about my ruined local career and birds in bushes. Rupert was not just a loony control freak. Rupert was a manipulative micromanager.

"What's going on?" asked Luke. He had finished his conversation and tucked his phone back into his pocket.

"I have to work in Atlanta today. I'll send everyone to Pearl's house to keep them safe. It's almost worth it, just to turn the tables on Pearl."

"Good idea. And you'll be safer up in Atlanta. You should spend the night up there."

"Rupert would love that." I pinched my lips in disgust at the thought. At least I could return Max's stolen folder before anyone checked.

Luke narrowed his eyes. "Maybe I should go with you. In case Regis Sharp finds where you're staying. If he gets wind your employer is rich, who knows what will happen."

"Give me a break. Nobody around here knows Rupert Agadzinoff except for Max Avtaikin."

Luke folded his arms. "If you come back, you're sleeping at Pearl's, too. They didn't find the BMW."

"Dammit. We should have stayed on its tail. Forks County Sheriff's Department is not winning any awards this week," I shook my head. "I don't know which place would be worse. Rupert's or Pearl's?"

"Doesn't McIntosh have anything to say about this?" said Luke. "Why aren't you calling Todd?"

"Why in the hell would I ask Todd's permission?"

"You'd make a terrible wife," Luke shook his head.

"What a thing to say to someone who has a violent drug dealer looking for her."

"Sorry," said Luke. "Look, if I were Todd, I'd want to know what was going on."

"He can stay with Pearl, too. I'm not leaving him alone at my house if that's what you're worried about."

"Fine. I'll take care of it. Everyone goes to Pearl's house. You don't need to worry about them. Happy?"

I shrugged.

"Now can you worry about protecting your own butt?"

"I still think I should go talk to some people in Sweetgum."

"I'm driving you to Atlanta myself." Luke jammed his gearshift into drive. "Lord, woman. You are a huge pain in the ass."

THIRTY-FIVE

Luke's face rearranged into his cop mask as we approached Rupert's house. Although Luke grew up with more money than I did, the upper middle class wealth he experienced living in a Branson household couldn't hold water with Rupert's net worth. He eyed the Tara knock-off while parking in the circular drive before the house.

"What kind of law did you say this guy practiced?" asked Luke.

"Immigration. That's how he knows Mr. Max. Filed his citizenship papers or what have you. Although I don't think they like each other too much."

I pouted, thinking of Max's betrayal to my cause.

Luke grunted, tapping his steering wheel while he continued to stare at the house.

"Thanks for the ride." I reached behind his seat to grab my duffel bag of clothes.

"I'm going in with you," he said, snatching the duffel bag. "I'll get your canvases out of the bed."

I picked up my satchel of sketching supplies and another tackle box holding my paints. "Do you want me to question Rupert about Max? Any kernels I can pick up for you to aid you in your stakeout of our local gangster?" I already knew his answer and ignored the look Luke gave me. "Just tell me this. Is it a personal vendetta against the Bear or is he really in trouble with the SipNZip? Max wouldn't tell me."

"I'm a cop. We're not allowed personal vendettas."

"Right," I snorted. "Well, whatever you're doing, Max saw fit to throw me out and is no longer speaking to me so my already ruined reputation wouldn't be further dirtied by his police surveillance. He is very touchy about the authorities."

"What a guy," said Luke. "Protecting your rep by tossing you out. A real gentleman."

"Stop it. Anyway, he's not gentlemanly enough to help me do a show anymore. He's doing one with Shawna."

"Like any man, Avtaikin probably offered to help because he thought it was a way into your pants. And got tired of you not noticing his advances because you've been too busy competing with Shawna and investigating the SipNZip."

"So now he's trying to get into Shawna's pants? You men amaze me. What is the big deal with sex that you would go to such lengths?"

Luke focused on snapping the duffel straps together, pretending the language I spoke wasn't English.

But I had noticed Max, I reflected. And had thought about his "maneuvers."

Red and Leah were right, I was worse than a guy. I needed to douse my warped brain with Lysol. Or my libido. If either were possible.

"Never mind," I said. "How did you know I was investigating the SipNZip?"

"Heard about your call to Sheriff Thompson regarding the employee who looked like the hijacker composite. He had me check on it." Luke said the last lines with an annoyed glower. Checking on my crime tips was considered a lower totem sort-of job, I guessed.

"Sam," I said. "Although I don't think he's the hijacker. He's much taller than Tyrone described."

"I agree," said Luke. "His real name is Samuil Rybak. The Department of Labor is checking his background."

"Department of Labor? Why?"

"He's an immigrant." Luke yanked open his door and scooted off his seat.

I slithered out of the truck, pulling my bags and boxes after me. "You need the Department of Labor to do background checks on recent immigrants? I didn't know that."

As usual, Luke left my question unanswered and focused on the task of pulling out several stretched and wrapped canvases from the bed of his pickup. I left him to his job, walked up to the house, and rang the bell. Miss David answered. Today's monochromatic color choice was cream. Maybe she lightened her wardrobe for the weekend.

"Don't you ever get a day off?" I said. "It's Sunday."

"You're here on the weekend," she replied. "Why would you expect less of me?"

"Believe me, if I had the choice, I wouldn't be here. Just point out the room you want to stash me in and I'll stay out of your hair."

She smirked. "I intend to do just that. I was surprised by your sudden change in plans. Rupert is thrilled to keep you here. He's very selfish that way, but it does make it easier on him to have you at his beck and call."

I snorted. "I guess you know all about that."

Behind us, the door swung open. Miss David took a step back as Luke plowed into the foyer, carrying the duffel and canvases. He leaned them against the wall and let his eyes wander the foyer until they finally landed on Miss David.

"That's Luke," I said. "He wants to case your joint, but he's not a criminal. Just a hyperactive cop."

Her eyes widened then dropped to their look of world-weary ennui. "You have interesting friends."

"Speaking of friends, what happened to Nik? We can't get a hold of him."

"We've been wondering the same. Mr. Agadzinoff is not pleased." Miss David betrayed her own annoyance with an elegant sniff. "Nikolai's been gone since yesterday."

"He's probably drowning his sorrows in a bottle of vodka somewhere. He thinks he's in love with my sister. Do you know if he put my truck back together?"

"I have no idea. Now, I will show you where we will keep you, Miss Tucker." She turned and strode to the large staircase.

I glanced at Luke and winked a grimace. "Crazy English," I whispered. "You think they're going to have me for dinner, too?"

Thankfully, Rupert's guest room tended more toward French Provincial than Rococo. I sat on the four poster king sized bed raised to a height that forced me to walk up a dainty staircase to reach it. We're talking serious princess and the pea.

I wanted to revel in the satin sheets and thick goose down duster printed with red and gold paisley, but I had a stolen folder to return before my keeper buzzed me from his infernal intercom and forced me to paint his likeness.

Not that I didn't appreciate his patronage. Or the fact that my room had a giant flat screen, a private bathroom with a full body spray shower (which I had already given a whirl), and the kind of soft rug that makes your toes giggle.

Before he had returned to Halo, Luke had eyed the shower and bed, then tested my lock.

"Keep your room locked. It's a cheap ass lock, so use this, too." He pulled a rubber wedge from his pocket and tossed it on the bed. "I borrowed it from your Grandpa Ed, so you'll need to give it back to him. Shove it under the door, as tight as you can."

I picked up the stopper and glanced at him. "You worried?"

"You're in a strange man's house. Of course, I'm worried." He glanced around the bedroom again. "Keep your phone on and in your pocket."

"Goodness, Daddy. It's not my first slumber party, you know."

He had left muttering words about background checks. I had focused on the full body shower, which turns out, is not such a great experience if you're short unless you like getting smacked in the face with a water jet. After drying my body in the fluffiest towel imaginable, I readied to slip downstairs and sneak Max's folder back in the file cabinet.

"Miss Tucker?" Miss David knocked. "Mr. Agadzinoff wants you downstairs."

As she talked I shoved the file into my satchel and tossed it around my shoulders. I couldn't lock my room from the outside and didn't want to take a chance of someone searching through my things and finding the folder.

"One minute." I smoothed out my skirt, fluffed my damp hair, and pasted on a smile. Yanking on the rubber doorstop, I slipped it in my bag before opening the door. "What's for dinner?"

"I have no idea." Miss David glanced over my formal dinnerware with a pained expression. I had on a skirt. The fact that it used to be a man's t-shirt and tie-dyed likely offended her monochromatism. "You can leave your things in this room. You won't need them for dinner."

"That's all right." I patted my satchel. "I might see something worth sketching. You never know."

"During dinner?"

"I've been known to doodle while I eat." I shut the door behind me and traipsed down the hall. "Who all is coming to dinner?"

"Usually Mr. Agadzinoff's brothers. Sometimes his nephews and their families. Tonight there's a special guest."

"Who's the special guest?" I hoped it was some famous Atlantan like Elton John or Tyler Perry.

"Mr. Agadzinoff said he's to be a surprise. You're to meet him in the office."

THIRTY-SIX

Miss David left me at the office door, strode down the hall, and disappeared through a doorway. The woman really needed to get a life outside Agadzinoff's home. Her twenty-four-seven living-with-the-boss lifestyle made her edgy and irritable. Unless she liked living with the boss and she just found my presence irritating. I contemplated the thought of Rupert and Miss David getting busy for a horrifying second and then realized I had the perfect opportunity to replace the file.

A murmur of voices hummed behind Rupert's door. He wouldn't miss me for a few minutes. I scooted toward Miss David's office. The foyer was empty. The red room's French doors closed. I took a quick glance out the front window, checking for the approach of dinner guests. Noting an HMV in the drive, I darted back to her office. I cracked the door and slipped inside the dark room.

The overhead lights were off and the curtains drawn, but a desk lamp had been turned on. Light puddled on the desk. Stacks of piled files glimmered under the glare. Behind the desk, a dark shadow moved. I froze against the door. The person behind the desk cranked the gooseneck toward me, throwing the light in my direction and leaving themselves in darkness.

"Who are you?" said the voice.

"Are you Miss David's assistant?" I asked, knowing Miss David needed no assistance. "She told me to wait in the office. Why is it so dark in here?"

Keeping my back against the door, I fumbled against the wall for the switch.

"Do not turn on light," said the voice. "Who are you?"

"I'm an artist hired by Mr. Agadzinoff to paint his portrait. Who are you?"

"His nephew. Go. You are in wrong room."

"Does he know you're in here?" I asked. "Does Miss David know you're going through her files?" I could hear the stolen folder in my satchel screaming "hypocrite," but I ignored it. "I believe if they knew you were in here, you wouldn't act so stealthy."

"Stealthy?"

"Mysterious. With the light shining in my face and the dark room and such."

"You don't know what you talk about. Get out."

"Why are particles and verbs so difficult for y'all?" My hand found the light switch.

For a long moment, we blinked out the sudden brilliance in silence. I gasped. The man standing behind the desk in a shiny, jade green track suit with an orange stripe had the heart shaped face, small eyes, and long nose of the hijacker. The long, blond hair was now black.

"Holy shit," I said.

"What?" The hijacker touched his hair then the gold chain around his neck. "What is wrong with you?"

"Nothing," I recovered. "I'll leave you alone."

"Why are you in here?" He circled the desk.

My hand grasped the door handle. "Like you said, wrong room. But you were acting suspicious, so I wanted to see what you were doing."

He pointed at me. "I acting suspicious? What about you?"

"What about me?" I turned the door handle until I felt the pop of the latch dislodging. "Miss David told me to go to the office. I thought she meant this office."

"Let's see if this is truth." He strode forward and grasped my arm.

"Hey! Get your hands off of me." I kicked his shin.

He dropped his grip.

I turned the knob, yanked on the door, and ran down the hall to Rupert's office.

"What is your problem?" he yelled.

I didn't think but pulled on Rupert's door and sprang into his office. Rupert hopped up from his chair behind his desk.

I barely glanced at the large man sitting in the chair across from him. Charging forward, I slammed my hands on Rupert's desk.

"Someone is going through Miss David's files. He says he's your nephew."

"What?" exclaimed Rupert and pulled his attention to the doorway where the hijacker stood. "Yuri. What's going on?"

"He's really your nephew?" I said and flinched. A hand snagged my wrist. I glanced at the hand and followed it to the body sitting in the guest chair. "Bear. What in the hell are you doing here?"

Max tugged me away from the desk toward his chair. His icy blue gaze sliced through me. "Why are you here? You work with Rupert?"

My gaze toggled from Max to Yuri, and back to Rupert. "Why is Mr. Max here? That's your nephew?"

"Ask her what she is doing in Miss David's office," said Yuri.

"Wrong place, wrong time, obviously," I said, feeling the guilt from Max's file weighing down my messenger bag. "But your nephew's going through the file cabinets. I thought you should know."

Should I tell him Yuri's also suspected of armed robbery and murder? Max's painful squeeze on my wrist told me to shut up. Maybe Rupert didn't know. Maybe he did.

But Max knew. He saw my composite drawing. I gave him an angry "you could be charged with accessory, conspiracy, and/or aiding and abetting" look. Max was no better than Ernie Pike. I let my eyes dance with the words I wanted to convey aloud. The Bear's return look told me to keep my big mouth shut.

Rupert sighed deeply. "Yuri is my black sheep. He's always in trouble. What can I do? I am his uncle." Rupert's voice slid off its jovial tone and into irate. "I let him stay here and he repays me by sneaking around when he should be convalescing in his room."

Rupert pointed at Yuri. "*Začyni dzvery.*"

Yuri shut the office door and slouched against it, pulling a phone from his pocket. He began to text, unconcerned with his uncle's anger.

I shook my head to find some focus. I needed to call the police. Rupert harbored a fugitive, whether he knew it or not. My phone was in my bag, but I needed to get out of the room first.

"I should tell Miss David about her files," I said.

"Miss David left for the evening," said Rupert. "I'll let her know."

Max still had a grip on my hand. I yanked, but he held tight. The long lines in his face hardened and the small scar above his eyebrow pulsed. "Rupert, why is Miss Tucker here? Does she know what is happening in Halo?"

"What's happening in Halo?" My stomach lunged and took a quick dive.

Rupert strolled to the gold and brass credenza. "Maksim's business is in trouble. The Department of Labor is harassing him about his workers. I believe the Feds just had a bust of the Sip-NZip."

"Max doesn't even know his workers," I said, then turned on him. "Do you?"

Max's lips tightened. His clutch on my wrist began to cut off my circulation. I tugged, then kicked his chair. I mouthed "let go." He ignored me. I abandoned Max's vise grip and refocused on the trouble in Halo.

"Are you his lawyer?" I asked Rupert. "Or are you representing the workers?"

Max snorted.

Rupert strolled back to his desk with a glass of vodka in his hand. "It will be one or the other, Maksim."

"I can't believe your lack of compassion, Bear. Even if you let Elena manage the place, you should check on your workers," I said. "Do you know they work twelve hour shifts almost every day? And they live together in a two bedroom apartment? It's like they're indentured servants or something."

Max ignored me, keeping his gaze on Rupert. "They chose to come to this country. It's not my business."

Yuri looked up from his phone. "*Cherry Tucker vedae Elena?*"

Rupert flipped a hand at him. "Keep out of this, Yuri. Stupid nephew. *Idyët.*"

Max glared at Rupert and turned reproachful eyes on me. "Again. Why is she here, Rupert?"

"A bad time, I know." Rupert tossed back his vodka. "Miss Tucker is painting my portrait. I know you admire her work, so I sought her out. Not everything happens as planned. She needed a place to stay. How could I refuse?"

Max glanced at the Christmas tree and easel. "Rupert, you seek to undermine me in strange ways."

"I would like you to let go of my hand," I said, coming to my senses. "Obviously, y'all have legal things to discuss. I'll go back to my room."

"Yuri," said Rupert. "See Miss Tucker to her room."

"Room?" Max's eyebrows flew to his hairline. "No, you stay here where I can keep eye on you."

"I knew I should never have trusted you," I hissed. "I thought you were trying to protect me. You were just messing with me to cover your own ass. Not to mention my pants."

"This is too much," laughed Rupert. "Just what is going on between you two? The way Max spoke of your works, I had thought you meant something to him."

"She has been trying to have me arrested ever since we met." Max's grip tightened and I yelped. "I am always her first suspect. Maybe she is prejudiced against our people?"

"He's been corrupting our town with back room gambling since he moved to Halo. Can I help it if I have a nose for crime detection?" My gaze fell upon Yuri. I silently begged my eyes to quit with the Freudian slips.

"Noses get cut off," said Max. "I have tried to warn you."

I wiggled within his grip. "Were those the maneuvers you meant?"

With a disgusted sigh, he released my hand.

I teetered back, falling on top of my satchel, and felt my phone crunch under my tailbone. I scrambled to standing, flipped the satchel to my front, and rubbed my sore back.

Rupert giggled. "You are both too much. This day that began so badly has improved tremendously."

"Rupert, this is your house," I said. "Max might want me around, but I'm asking you if I can leave."

Rupert glanced at Max and then to the Christmas tree and easel.

Surely, he didn't want me to paint. I massaged my back and tried not to hyperventilate. I needed to call the police and report Yuri. I had no idea if Yuri was operating alone or with Max and Rupert.

"I am undecided on how to proceed," said Rupert. "My plans have been upset."

"I can paint tomorrow," I said. "I'm fast."

"I had imagined you before your easel. I would stand in my suit before the tree." Rupert skimmed a hand down his custom fitted, blue suit. "Maksim would walk in and see us. I pictured your anger, Maksim. It made me laugh."

"I see," said Max. "Rupert, you misunderstood my relationship to Miss Tucker."

I felt my eyebrows twist into a what-the-hey arc. This pissing contest had warped Rupert's brain. "Mr. Rupert, I'm not a hairdresser. You don't cheat by stealing your friend's portraitist."

"Miss Tucker said you were financing a show for her," said Rupert. "You have her paintings."

"I was wrong," I said. "Max is financing a show for my mortal enemy. An Amazonian two-faced blackmailer who, with the Bear's help, has destroyed my career and run me out of town. Just so he can get into her curvy jeans." I balled my fist and socked Max's shoulder. "Disgusting pig."

"Goodness," said Rupert. "I truly was mistaken."

"I know. I can't even look at him. So, I'm gonna go." I flipped the satchel to my back and marched to the door.

Yuri looked up from his phone, smirked, and didn't move.

"Excuse me," I said. "I need to leave."

Yuri pursed his lips and shook his dyed head.

I turned around and stared at Rupert. "Your nephew won't move."

"Let her go," Max said. "Anyway, Yuri and I should talk."

I bit my cheek to keep from exclaiming any "ahas" or "double-crossers."

Rupert waved his hand and Yuri stepped to the side.

"Don't go far," said Rupert. "Dinner is in a few minutes."

"Not hungry," I said, but my stomach betrayed my words with a sound like an ice road trucker backing through a forty foot drift.

With a foreign exclamation of shock, Yuri jumped to the side and opened the door.

I traipsed through the doorway acting the air of someone who had no idea the person standing before them had robbed and killed another man at gunpoint. The door swung shut behind me. I glanced right, then ran left to Miss David's office.

Before I called the police, I wanted to see those files.

THIRTY-SEVEN

Miss David's office door stood open. I raced inside, grabbed the first file, and glanced at the name. Samuil Rybek. I tossed it to the side and looked at the next. Anatoly Navitski. I pawed through the rest, but the names meant nothing to me. Perhaps they worked at other SipNZips Max owned. If the Department of Labor was involved, someone had blown the whistle on the workers. Not surprising, considering the terrible hours they worked. Not to mention the illegal stocking of food from possibly hijacked trucks. Max and Yuri must have been working together.

My gut hurt. So did my heart.

I snagged Little Anatoly and Sam's files, shoved them in my bag, and took off again. Flying out the front door, I danced in the circle drive and tried to jog my brain into a quick plan of action. The gargantuan Hummer sat in the driveway. One of Max's many vehicles. I tried the door handle. Locked.

"Why are you trying to run? Call the police, you idiot," my brain screamed.

I pulled my phone from my satchel and glanced at the house. Atlanta police would arrive quickly to make Yuri's arrest. They might bring in the Fulton County Sheriff's Department, too. A lot of back up would be needed for a man who shot an innocent truck driver and a witness in cold blood. Rupert and Max could be held in a standoff situation. Panicked, desperate men took hostages. Happens all the time, particularly in domestic violence situations.

Oh hell, I've got to get the innocent people out of the house, I thought. Did Rupert have any more servants?

I ran toward the garage and dialed Luke's number.

"Can't talk. We found Sharp. You're safe," said Luke and hung up.

"Shit," I screamed at the phone. "I am not safe." The garage doors were shut. I kicked the door and cussed Nik for not showing up on the day I needed him.

I dialed 9-1-1 and chugged my little legs back up the hill toward the front door.

"What is your emergency?" said the dispatcher.

"I'm at Rupert Agadzinoff's house. His nephew, Yuri, is the perp who hijacked and killed the driver of a Dixie Cake truck as well as Tyrone Coderre, a copper thief."

"Slow down. What is your emergency?"

"Too long to explain. There's a suspected felon at 4201 Northside Drive. Possibly armed. Could turn into a hostage situation. Send a team."

"A crime has taken place?"

"Mr. Agadzinoff is harboring a fugitive and doesn't know it. This is taking too long," I shouted. "I've got to get people out of this house. Call the Forks County Sheriff's Office and get the back story. Just send a team to this address."

I shoved the phone in my pocket and catapulted the steps to the front door. Cracking the door open, I peeked inside. Yuri mounted the grand staircase, a gun in his hand. Most likely on his way to visit my room. I pressed a hand over my heart to shove it back in place and waited for him to turn the corner on the landing.

Slipping through the door, I ran down the hallway with my satchel hammering my back. At Rupert's office door, I paused and listened, but couldn't hear talking. I continued down the hall and pushed through the kitchen door, taking no time to admire the luxurious modern design. I found the door to the garage, smacked the buttons to open the doors to all three bays. My poor truck remained gutted.

"You're still here?" said Max. "Why can't you do anything simply?"

I screamed, and he clamped a hand over my mouth.

"Quiet," he said.

I bit his finger and his hand flew off.

"Get your paws off of me," I said. "You've been yanking me around all week, figuratively and literally. Where's Rupert? The police are on their way."

"I thought as much knowing you," he said. "Rupert is resting."

"What do you mean resting?"

"Yuri left the room. I took care of Rupert. Come on."

"Surprised you didn't pull a gun and blow them away."

"I left Glock at home." He pushed me into the garage. "Now."

"I'm not going anywhere with you."

"No more arguing," said Max. He grabbed me around my waist, threw me over his shoulder, and jogged down the steps of the garage and out to the driveway.

I kicked and pounded his back with my fists, but my struggles couldn't match his he-man strength. The bloop-bleep of his car alarm rang, and he tossed me into his Hummer. Before I untangled my limbs, he climbed into the driver's seat and cranked the engine. I scrambled to sitting and slid to unlock my door. Max hit the power lock, floored the beast, and cut across the circle and down the driveway. He sped out of the drive and down the street.

"You're kidnapping me," I yelled and leaned over to hit him.

He trounced the brakes.

I launched forward, ramming my nose into the dashboard.

"Put on your belt," said Max, cranking the wheel. "I'm taking you home. The police will find me soon enough, but first they'll have Yuri."

"You double-cross your own partners? Snake." I slouched against the seat, holding my nose. "I hope Miss Gladys strips you blind. I can't wait to testify at your trial."

"I'm sure you do," Max cut his eyes toward me. "You have to answer for your own part in this, you know."

"What part is that? The part where I tried to help an old woman and orphan and have nearly gotten killed for it?"

"You betrayed me," Max's voice rocked the vehicle. "Your dedication to finding me guilty brought this on. I had once thought you mischievous prankster, much like my sister who sought to get me in trouble with my mother."

"You worked for crime bosses back in your country. Of course your sister wanted to get you in trouble," I shouted.

"I worked as dealer in casinos," he yelled. "No proof of criminal organization. You read my file. You should know."

"I can't read your stupid file. It's in cryptic."

"Cyrillic," shouted Max. "You are the stupid."

"Forgive me for not knowing your foreign language, foreigner," I yelled. "I'm American and you're in America."

"No, stupid for working with Rupert."

"Dear Lord in heaven, I was just painting his picture. What is it with you two? Did he lose a million dollars in your poker palace and never got over it?"

Max jerked his head to glance at me. "Not one million."

"Dammit to hell, Bear. This is why I don't like your underground games."

"This is more than poker," he grunted and fixed his eyes back on the windshield.

"More than poker. More than a hijacking," I mimicked in a nasty drawl. "What's more important than two dead men, a shut-in threatened by a drug dealer, and a child taken from his home?"

"I did not know about the hijacking. Or murders."

"I know that. So what are you doing with friends like Yuri? You knew who he was when I showed you the composite drawing. Did you make a deal with Ernie Pike?"

"Who is Ernie Pike?"

"Why doesn't anybody know anybody?" I squeezed my palms against my temples. "Did you have an agent to give the hijacking orders?"

"I did not order hijacking. I tell you I know nothing about it."

"But they are supplying your SipNZip with jacked goods."

"It's not my SipNZip," he shouted and whipped the wheel to the left, pulling us onto an interstate ramp. Three police cars screamed past us, heading in the opposite direction. "Only in my name."

I dropped my hands and stared at him. "What do you mean, only in your name?"

"I need focus on driving. Look for police and Rupert." He stretched his hand to the radio, chose a thumping dance station, and turned the volume to earsplitting.

"Turn it down and talk to me," I shouted and reached for the volume. "Stop avoiding me."

He swatted my hand. "You are very frustrating woman," he yelled. "Big pain in ass. No more talking until Halo."

THIRTY-EIGHT

Twilight painted Halo in a cool, dioxazine mauve glow as we pulled off the interstate and onto the local highway. Max sped past the SipNZip while I pointed out the yellow tape crossing the doors and the multitude of vehicles parked in front.

I turned off the radio. The electronic tempo still throbbed inside my head. "Are we going to your house or mine?"

"Neither," Max grunted. "Your family lives outside Halo? I want to avoid town streets. Too many police."

"Take me to the farm. If the sheriff caught Regis Sharp, my family will show at the farm soon enough. Grandpa will need to feed his goats."

He followed my directions in silence. I hoped he had pondered the right thing to do during our musical interlude. As we pulled into the farm lane, I scanned for errant goats. The Hummer zipped up the pockmarked farm lane and stopped in the clearing before the house.

Max turned off the engine, but left his lights on. Goats bleated from behind the fence and several sets of ghostly eyes blinked in the glare from the headlights.

I patted Max on the arm. "You'll feel better once you tell the authorities what you know about Yuri. You'll protect Little Anatoly and the other SipNZip employees from any involvement with the hijacking crimes, especially if they were just doing what they were told. Protect yourself, too."

Max shook his head. "You don't understand. We will be deported."

"For the hijacking?"

"Maybe some arrests for hijacking and selling stolen goods. I don't know which SipNZip peoples do the hijacking." Max sighed and rested his head against the seat. "All will be arrested for illegal immigration."

"You're not legal?" I said. "I thought you had a green card."

"I thought I did, too," he said. "Until Rupert blackmailed me."

"What do you mean blackmail? Isn't he your lawyer?"

"You remember the audit, no?" he said. "Your poking at the bingo caused the government to look at my finances."

I nodded. An uncomfortable heat spread through my body and prickled my neck.

"This brings interest in my citizenship. I am forced to call that *mu`dak* scum Rupert."

"I thought Rupert helped immigrants."

"He get us through your doors for big price. If you can't afford big price, you work it off in place like SipNZip until you do. I paid that sonofabitch. Always he tries to get more money out of me. Sometimes using people against me."

Max's voice shook. "I told you not to work for him. Rupert uses extortion by hiring you. To make me worry what will happen to you."

"How was I supposed to know? I thought y'all were playing whose grass is greener."

"Never the mind. During audit, Rupert told me he has proof that can cause me problems with the United States government."

"Deport you?"

"I don't know if he is telling truth or bluffing. So much paperwork." Max waved his hand through the air. "So I was blackmailed by this *zlačynny*, Rupert. 'How much you want?' I asked.

"'I want you to buy some convenience stores so my people have a place of employment for their green card applications,' said *mu`dak* Rupert.

"I don't have anything to do with the store," continued Max. "It's franchise under big corporation. I just have to purchase the land and put store in my name."

"So if there's any trouble, the blame falls on you," I said.

Max nodded. "But I can't report anything for fear they will check into my paperwork. We take old gas station, renovate, and it's SipNZip. I step away."

"You've got to report all this to the sheriff."

"Too late."

"You don't have a choice," I said. "Are you going to live on the run? I thought you enjoyed your palatial southern monstrosity and the local gentlemen's lax morality on high stakes gambling."

"If I go back to home country, my old boss will kill me."

"Literally?" My voice pitched high.

Max cut his eyes away from mine.

"Yuri was going through Rupert's files when I caught him." I pulled my satchel off the floor and hauled it onto the seat. "I don't know what he planned to do with them, but if Yuri felt desperate enough to steal the files, there must have been a reason."

Max shook his head. "You need proof of Rupert's hijack organization. These files just have citizenship paperwork. What does it matter?"

"I don't know, but I grabbed Little Anatoly and Sam's files. I also have yours." I placed my hand on the satchel and gave him my most serious look. "I know reading your papers was an invasion of your privacy, but you weren't telling me anything."

"I am confused," Max tapped my satchel with a finger. "You wanted me to make confession for a crime I didn't commit, yet you have committed robbery by stealing these files."

"I had planned to return your file," I said. "So it's more like borrowing without permission."

"I do not believe this is legal term."

"Do you want the files or not?"

"I am in enough trouble. Do I also want possession of stolen files?" Max opened his door and stepped onto the gravel drive.

"I will leave you here and find some place to go."

He circled the front of the vehicle and reached for my door. I slid to the edge of my seat before he opened it, taking advantage of the Hummer's height to look him in the eye.

"I am trying to help you, Bear," I said. "Even though you let me down and sought the pants of an Amazon. But in the interest of catching the man who killed Tyrone, that's all flushed under the bridge."

"I am truly confused by your assistance. And your idioms."

He took my hand to help me slide off the seat, but I held tight, willing him to continue.

"I cannot tell if you want me arrested because of your anger or out of concern for me," Max's eyebrow scar lifted. "If it is anger, I have told you my feelings for the Shawna Branson. Your jealousy both piques and astounds me. If it is concern, you have a very odd way of expressing your friendship."

"I suppose it is confusing," I said. "But I do like you. In the past six months, you have grown from my personal chigger to more of a pesky honey bee."

"I am still confused," he said, and jerked. The Hummer rocked, and the air burst with a booming explosion. The giant jeep dipped, and Max's hand slipped from my grasp. He hopped back, lost his balance, and fell. As his body slammed to the ground, his legs went in two different directions, under and out.

I righted myself in the seat and stared in shock at his blown front tire. "Bear!"

He collapsed onto his back. One hand stretched for my ankle as he writhed in the gravel.

The air cracked and a shot winged the open door.

Max's arm dropped to the ground.

I kneeled on the floor of the Hummer and reached over the side. "Get in the car, Bear. Hurry."

The window exploded. I yanked my hand inside as the door slammed shut. Tiny pebbles of glass showered my bent body.

Beneath me, Max bellowed a painful cry.

"Bear," I screamed. "Are you shot?"

"Not hit. Rolled under car." He spoke in gasping phrases. "You crawl to other side. Stay down."

"Do you have your phone? Call 9-1-1."

The air cracked again and the ground rocked below me. I scrambled over the Humvee's ridiculously large console and squeezed under the steering wheel. The explosive thwack of gunfire sounded as another bullet zinged through the passenger window, slamming into the backseat window column. I cowered against the accelerator, holding my ears. Plastic exploded inside the car with the next shot. Dust blew up in my face and my ears rang. I opened my eyes and peered above the seat.

A quarter-sized shred in the passenger door convinced me to get the hell out of the Hummer.

I stayed low, flipped the latch, and pushed the door wide. The light from the cab spilled onto the gravel. I followed the spill, sprawling into the rocks below. Gun fire cracked the silence. Above me, the driver's door swung shut. I blinked at the sky above me. Lights swarmed my vision. Time slowed. I heard my name called. My chest tightened, then air exploded from my lungs. My brain cut back on, and I slithered under the Hummer.

"Cherry," Max repeated. "Are you shot?"

"No," I said. "Your door has a big hole in it, though. And the window is blown to hell."

I rolled onto my stomach and squinted into the darkness at Max's mammoth shape. "Where were you hit? How bad is it?"

"Not hit. I slipped when the first bullet hit the tire. My knee," he said. "Hurts like the hell. Who is trying to kill you?"

"Kill me? I thought they were trying to shoot you." I arched my neck and peered into the gloomy farm yard. "Where are they?"

"They were behind the house," said Max. "Moving closer now."

"We're sitting ducks," I said. "Where's your phone?"

"In the Humvee." He shifted and his left hand reached through the shadows toward me. "I will crawl out. You get in jeep and drive away. The tire will hold."

I grabbed his hand. "No, sir. I am not leaving you to be shot up. My Grandpa has an arsenal of hunting guns in his house. Just give me a second to figure out how to get us both out of here."

"No." His hand crushed mine. "Absolutely no."

"Maybe Regis Sharp escaped. Or it's Ernie Pike. Sharp had a Ruger, so I'm betting on Sharp."

Our argument was cut short by the remote sound of a car engine slowing on the highway and turning onto the gravel farm lane. Footsteps smacked the gravel as the shooter ran back toward the house.

"You stay where you are," I said. "I'm getting out and flagging that vehicle before it comes any closer. It could be my family. Don't move."

I scooted out from the Hummer and kneeled beside the rear tire. The vehicle's lights bobbed on the potholed road. I ran diagonally, toward the cover of the big oak that grew alongside the path. I didn't recognize the car, but continued my run toward it. The vehicle slowed to a stop. As I drew nearer, I made out the sleek hood and large grill of a very expensive Jaguar.

Definitely not any of my relations.

The back window rolled down, and I heard Rupert call my name. I wavered between heading toward the car and back toward Max and the shooter. Behind me the lane split, running toward the out buildings. The house was closer. I began backing toward the oak.

"Miss Tucker," called Rupert. "Is that Maksim's Hummer?"

So much for the Atlanta police.

"Did you follow me here?" I called, looking over my shoulder. I couldn't see any hint of the shooter. The vehicle may have scared them away, but I placed my back against the tree, blocking my body from the house.

"I've been here before, remember darling?" said Rupert. The Jaguar pulled up behind the Hummer and parked. Rupert leaned out the window. "Miss Tucker, I need to speak to Maksim. He attacked me. Then the police came to my house looking for a fugitive.

I had already left, but they reached me by phone. I need to call them back with his whereabouts."

"Max isn't available right now," I said, peering around the tree.

"The police are looking for him, my dear."

"I figured as much. Still, can't help you."

I heard the whir of another window rolling down. I glanced over my shoulder. Yuri waved from behind the Jag's steering wheel. His gun pointed at Miss David, who sat in the passenger seat. She did not wave and kept her eyes fixed on the Hummer.

My brain squeezed out a few phrases best not spoken aloud. My mouth tried an "Oh, crap."

Rupert laughed. "You do have a way with words, Miss Tucker."

I gave him a tight smile. "And you have a strange sense of humor. Why are you letting your nephew hold a gun on Miss David? She's kind of prickly, but certainly not worth shooting."

Another snort of laughter ripped from Rupert's belly. "This was for Maksim. He abandoned her once when she decided to work for me rather than stay with him. I thought she might change his mind about talking to the police."

"Max and Miss David were an item?"

She turned to look at me, her cool gaze gouging fresh wounds into my chest.

"He cares for me as much as he does for you, it seems. If you know where Maksim is, tell Mr. Agadzinoff so this *mu'dak* can remove his gun."

"Yuri put down your weapon. Max isn't here," I said, then worried Max might pop up and prove me a liar. Of course, with a blown knee, he couldn't pop. But he could holler.

"If Max were here to save Miss David, I'm sure he'd not lay around worrying about his own ass, even if that was the more intelligent option. I think he'd know he couldn't do any good jumping up to save you," I called loud enough for Max to hear and shifted to peer around the tree toward the house. "He's got enough chivalry to make a stand, but your timing is not good."

"Why you look at house?" said Yuri.

"I have all kinds of people trying to kill me," I said. "I told you it was a bad day, Rupert."

Behind the house, the goats bleated a warning. I watched for movement in the area beyond the Hummer's headlights. The sky darkened by the minute, giving the shooter easy cover.

Rupert laughed. "My dear. You are too much."

I glanced over my shoulder at Rupert. "Seriously, though, someone is trying to kill me. Have you not noticed the Hummer is shot to hell? You should take off."

Yuri leaned out the window to get a better view of the Hummer. He turned around to look at Rupert. "It is true."

"Maksim's not here," said Miss David. "Let me go."

"Get in the Jag, Miss Tucker," said Rupert.

That was not the option I wanted.

THIRTY-NINE

"So Miss David and Max," I said, wondering how long I could hedge a conversation from behind a tree. "Did you hire me to do your portrait thinking Max would get jealous? Because it's not like that between us. In fact, you're better off hunting down the Real Artist of Forks County, Shawna Branson. Particularly if you don't really care about art."

"I had hoped you working for me would make him squirm a bit," he admitted. "Anything to keep Maks in place. He's very difficult to control."

"If you're worried about Max squealing about your SipNZip scheme, don't. He hates the police. I'm the one who can give up Yuri, not Max."

"Give up Yuri?" said Rupert. "What do you know about Yuri?"

I knocked my head against the tree, hoping some sense would seep in. I had confessed my knowledge of a crime they hadn't suspected I knew. Idiot. When I peeked from the tree, Yuri had his gun directed at me. Miss David scrambled from the car.

"She is unnecessary if Maksim is not here," said Rupert. "But Yuri is very interested in what you know about him."

I strode out from behind the tree, praying Miss David could get in the house and not be killed by Yuri or the mystery shooter. I also prayed for the man underneath his big-ass jeep to keep still and for my own hide to stay in one piece. I threw all those thoughts toward heaven and hoped most of them stuck.

"So what now?" I said, stopping in front of the car. "Secret's out. I know Yuri held up that Dixie Cake truck, killed the driver, and then killed Tyrone, the witness. I called the cops and reported the fugitive. Max and Miss David had nothing to do with it."

"When I cannot find you in the house, we leave," Yuri said. "Police is too slow. Where are files? Where is Maks?"

"And here I was looking for a BMW, not a Jag. This is not my day, but I guess I'm getting my comeuppance." I raised my face to heaven, waiting for my prayers to fall back toward earth and smack me in the head. "Lord Almighty, I swear I did not mean to agitate all these women with Todd's nudity. If I had lust in my heart, I never meant for it to come out of my paintbrush."

"What is she saying?" said Yuri to Rupert.

"Get in the car, Miss Tucker," said Rupert, "Or Yuri might shoot you."

I edged toward Rupert's door, then rounded the back of the car and ran. Every woman who has ever watched Oprah knows you never get in the car. Rule number one in a kidnapping or carjacking. I hated abandoning Max, but I hated more the thought of not reporting his location and my brains exploding over the back of the car. Or worse, giving up his location in fear of said brain explosion and watching his brains explode instead.

Through the screen of the porch, I could see Miss David crouching behind a rocking chair. "Unlock the door," I yelled. "Get in the house."

Behind me, I heard the slam of a car door and the cursing of Yuri. His gun cracked, but I didn't flinch.

Officially desensitized by violence.

Miss David peeked out from behind the chair, then dropped back.

"Get out of there," I yelled, still twenty yards from the porch. "There's a key in the empty PBR can on the windowsill."

She turned to look and reached for the beer can. The gun fired and shot through the window above her. The beer can flew from her hand and she dropped behind the chair.

I didn't risk a look over my shoulder, but could hear Yuri walking toward the house.

"Open. That. Door," I screamed.

The can rolled toward the front of the porch. Miss David scrambled out from behind the chair. Yuri fired again. The screen tore off the door and the bullet thwacked the side of the house. Wood dust filled the air. Miss David screamed and ran back toward the chair.

My Grandpa would be sore ticked about all these holes in his screens.

"That chair is not going to keep you from getting killed." My legs pounded across the weedy centipede lawn and hit the stepping stones to the porch. "Get that key."

She shook her head.

Gasping, I pounded up the porch steps, grabbed the screen door, and ripped it from the eyehook latch. I pounced on the can and shook out the key.

"Get up," I wheezed and canted toward the door.

Miss David screamed again and pointed. I imagined she pointed at Yuri, but I was too busy fumbling with the lock to look. I heard the gun fire. I ducked as splinters and wood dust from a shutter rained on the porch floor. I reached for Miss David's arm and yanked her toward the front door.

Yuri's feet smacked the stepping stones before the porch. I pushed the lever on the door and shoved it open. Miss David fell inside. I catapulted over her. I heard the bang of Yuri's feet on the wooden steps.

"Close the friggin' door," I yelled.

She pushed it shut with her feet. I lunged to turn the deadbolt, then grabbed her hand and pulled her away from the door.

"Push stuff in front of windows," I said and shoved her toward the back of the house. "No. Call 9-1-1."

Yuri's gun fired. A bullet blasted through the wood above the door handle. Miss David screamed and ran toward the back bedrooms.

I sprinted through the kitchen to the mud room and gun cabinet. The tall, wooden cabinet had drawers above and below a glass plated door to the rack. Grandpa kept it locked, but the key hid on a nail behind the dryer. Yuri's gun fired again, hitting another window. I snagged the key, unlocked the drawers, and grabbed a box of ammo.

My skirt had no pockets. Of all the times not to wear jeans.

I folded my top up toward my bra, bound the loose material into a knot, and dumped some of the cartridges into the fold. Neither comfortable nor practical, but I ignored that fact and opened the cabinet door.

Skipping over the Browning and Marlin, I grabbed the Winchester Featherlight, the rifle Grandpa had used for my deer hunting education. I knew this gun. Knew I could load and drop rounds quickly. Knew the recoil and my range.

I tried not to think about why I might need to use those rounds.

Taking a deep breath, I walked out of the mud room and through the kitchen. As I walked, I slid the bolt back and loaded the gun with three cartridges from my shirt. I lost two bullets to the floor from hands that wouldn't quit with the shakes, but by the time I reached the doorway to the living room, the rifle was mounted on my shoulder.

And Yuri was gone.

"Miss David?" I yelled. "Did you call 9-1-1?"

I heard a rambling in her foreign tongue from a back bedroom. "Just stay back there."

Keeping my back against the walls, I moved toward the front porch windows. Otherwise intact, each window had a spider web of cracks spiraling from the bullet hole. Grandpa had secured the house with some nice double panes.

I hoped Grandpa had insurance to cover bullet holes.

Kneeling before a window, I peered into the darkness. The dome light in the stolen Jag shone on empty seats. The back doors were open. The headlights of the HMV and Jaguar still brightened the lane. The Jag's beams spotlighted Rupert and Yuri dragging a body from under the Hummer.

I yanked open the front door, yelled over my shoulder for Miss David to lock it, and flew off the porch. I stopped in the yard, wished I had night vision, and aimed at the dirt several yards away from the men.

"Stop right there," I yelled. "Get your hands off of him."

The rifle cracked, the ground exploded near the men, and I felt the wincing pain of recoil in my shoulder. Quickly, I slid the lever back to release the bullet and pushed the next round into the chamber. This time I aimed at Yuri's body.

Rupert and Yuri rose from their crouch, holding their hands up. In the lane next to the Hummer, Max lay unmoving. Behind the fence, goats screamed and brayed. I could hear them galloping in the paddock, stirred into a frenzy by the gunshots.

"Keep your hands where I can see them. Police are on their way."

"Calm yourself my dear," said Rupert. "We are carrying Maks to safety. He needs medical attention."

"Did Yuri shoot him?" I called, startled by the bite of pain in my throat and eyes. "Get away from him. Keep your hands up."

"I'm not dead yet," called Max. "Get the Beretta from Yuri."

Keeping my rifle trained on the men, I slid-stepped toward them as they backed into the Jag. I reached behind Yuri and snagged the pistol he had shoved into his back waistband. My experience with handguns was limited to Uncle Will's gun safety courses he made all the Tucker kids take. I checked the safety and shoved it into my skirt. Returning the rifle to my shoulder, I backed toward Max.

"Artist," he said, struggling to sit. "You impress me with your courage. And your fashion sense."

"Like the midriff look, huh?"

I gave Max the Beretta to make him feel better and gently pushed him down. "The police'll bring an ambulance. You shouldn't move. I can tell you're in a lot of pain."

Max gave me a hint of a smile, and I stroked his cheek. Behind me, I heard the gallop of hooves. Tater rushed toward me, braying.

"Not now, boy." I rose with the Winchester mounted, but held a hand out to Tater. He nudged his horns against my hand and took a hunk of my skirt in his mouth. "Where did you come from? Perfect timing as usual."

I shoved him off, and he bent his head to investigate Max's prone body.

"Leave the Bear alone," I said to Tater, nudging him with my hip, and refocused on the men standing in my farm drive. "So who's the great mastermind? You're arranging fake hijacks to fill your gas stations with black-market food. What happened, Yuri? When the wrong driver didn't stop in the designated place, did you follow the truck and shoot him?"

"He pulled gun on me," said Yuri. "Self-defense."

"He thought you were holding him up. That's armed robbery."

"*Idyët*," said Rupert.

"What about Tyrone? Was that self-defense, too? You shot him in cold blood. I know Tyrone didn't have a gun on him."

"Who is Tyrone?" said Yuri.

"The witness. The guy hanging from the pole who saw you take off your ski mask after you shot the Dixie Cake driver." My voice shook with anger.

"*Idyët*," repeated Rupert.

"Yuri didn't shoot witness," said a female voice behind me. "I did. Put down your gun."

FORTY

"Elena," cried Yuri. "You are here."

I spun around. Elena, the crabby SipNZip clerk, held a hand-gun that matched Yuri's. "What are you doing here? You're the shooter?"

"Put down your rifle and give me Yuri's gun." She gripped her gun in both hands with her arms extended and legs planted. "I am master shot."

"You missed us," said Max.

"Let's not agitate her. She did do a job on your Hummer. And Tyrone."

I laid the rifle on the ground and took the Beretta from Max's fist to lie next to the Winchester. Tater bleated and nibbled at the Winchester's walnut stock.

"Kick them toward me," she said. "Away from Maksim Avtai-kin."

My Grandpa would whip my butt if the gravel scratched his Winchester 70 Featherlight, but I complied. I did have the gun-to-my-head excuse.

"Where's the BMW?" I said. "That's your vehicle isn't it? You've been following me? Yuri didn't know about me, how did you?"

"Shut up and sit next to Maksim."

The bullets inside my shirt clinked as I dropped to the ground beside Max. I laid my hand against his tensed shoulder.

With his body pointed toward the Jaguar, Max couldn't see Elena. "I could have taken care of this," he muttered.

I knew he wished we'd taken his gun-to-the-window approach the night she parked outside his house. "Bear, she wouldn't have told us anything and Luke would have arrested you for threatening her," I whispered.

Max stared into the darkened sky, gritting his teeth.

"Still don't know how a SipNZip employee could afford a BMW," I said. "You must be making money hand over fist from robbing. That's all you are. A bunch of bandits."

"BMW was a gift," Elena smirked.

"From you, I suppose." I cast a scathing look at Rupert.

He grinned, held up a hand, and let it drop. "She's managed her operation well. A reward. I have found women like Elena and Miss David more reliable than the men."

Yuri strode past us to Elena and tried to hug her. "Baby."

Elena shoved him away. "Not now. You let this `suka take your gun?" She spat on the ground.

"I get the feeling you don't like me," I said to Elena. "Have you been planning to kill me or is this a spur of the moment decision?"

"You identified Yuri in his picture. And you are very busy talking about it. I heard you in SipNZip and saw your fast car." She pointed the gun at Max. "Plus you are meeting with this one many times. I watch you and decide I don't trust you."

"You've been spying on the farm, too." My skin prickled at the thought of Elena stalking my family. Tater nosed me, and I wrapped an arm around his scratchy neck.

"You gave this as your home address on SipNZip application." Elena's gun didn't waver as she spoke. "But you do not come to the farm often. Tonight I am lucky. I park behind barns and wait. Two birds at once."

"You are so good, baby," said Yuri. "My hero."

Max's hand grasped mine. "Tell her I already made deal."

"What deal?" I said and gave Tater a shove as he tried to bite Max's hand. I angled toward his ear. "You didn't make any deal."

Max turned his head and glowered at me. "I lied to you. I was leaving you here to meet agents."

Rupert slid from his lean against the Jag to crouch next to Max. "You already spoke to the agents? *B'lyad.*"

"What agents?" I said.

"The Special Agents with Department of Labor," Max closed his eyes and forced the words. "They want Rupert, Rurik Agadzinoff. He owns conglomerate of gas stations. He puts illegals in stores. Fakes invoices. Products sold from black market. Hijacks trucks for products. I find out he is not real lawyer when IRS looks into my bingo."

"*Zatk `nis,*" yelled Rupert and slammed a fist into Max's knee.

Max's body levitated with pain. At his scream, Tater reared back and galloped away.

"Agents will get Rupert on tax evasion, money laundering, visa fraud," Max coughed out a laugh and closed his eyes. "It's too late. I gave testimony already."

"I thought you were worried about deportation," I said, lying the back of my hand against the Bear's cheek.

"My visa is real," his voice hissed from his throat. Max's eyes fluttered opened and found me. "Filed illegally. Rupert paid off someone in Citizenship Immigration Service."

"The name on the folder?" I said. "Is that the C.I.S. worker who took the bribe?"

"It's not too late, Rupert," said Elena. "We can still get away."

I looked up and found the barrel of the Beretta aimed at me again. "Yes, it is too late. The police are on their way. The Feds have already taken the SipNZip."

"No," said Elena and pushed Yuri. "Get in car, Yuri. You, too, Rupert. I will take care of them."

"Find out where the files are first," said Rupert.

Rupert rose, kicked Max in the ribs, and scurried to the car. I glanced toward the house, wondering what had happened to the 9-1-1 call. Then realized my sheriff's department wouldn't careen into the driveway with sirens screaming and blueberries spinning if they knew we were replaying the Shootout at the O.K. Corral. They knew the farm and how to approach us.

Maybe they were watching us now, waiting for their opportunity to move in.

Or maybe Miss David had been too freaked out to call 9-1-1.

I found Max's hand and squeezed. Unless a sharpshooter had a bead trained on Elena, it didn't really matter.

He tugged on my hand. "Get me a gun," he mouthed.

How in the hell did he think I could do that? The Beretta and Winchester still lay on the ground on the other side of Elena. She held a sleek and scary piece of metal pointed at us. However, her focus was on Yuri, still standing behind us and giving Elena a litany of his love and devotion. Or pointers on how to kill us and what to do with our bodies. It was hard to tell in a foreign language and the Jag's lights shown on his back so I couldn't see his face.

I dropped Max's hand and inched toward Elena. Come on Cherry, I thought, what's the difference if she shoots you from a few feet compared to one yard? Cops do this every day.

Well, maybe not the cops in Halo, but I found my risk-taking brain cells easily fueled by pep talks.

The sound of small hoof beats galloping across the grass-lined clay distracted Elena for a moment. Rupert leaned out the window and yelled at Yuri to hurry up his dissertation on love. Or death. The giant, white goat sailed into view just as Yuri finished with a rude gesture at Rupert. Startled by Tater's reappearance, Elena tipped up her pistol.

I pushed from my squat, launching myself at the guns. Elena spun around to face me. I scooped up the Beretta and underhanded it toward Max. The chunk of metal thumped the ground. Elena yodeled a string of curses and pointed the gun. Tater leapt at my accessible form sprawled on the ground and landed on my back with a kidney crushing blow. Elena fired. And another gun fired.

And then it really went to hell.

What sounded like an army of vehicles roared into the lane. No sirens or lights, but they sprayed gravel and dirt all the same.

Some went right and left, tearing across the farm yard in different directions and ripping through the ratty remains of Grandma Jo's azaleas. Spotlights blazed and flashed.

My back felt broken. I lost focus on anything but pain.

FORTY-ONE

It took two men to get the heavy goat off me. Then I had to continue to lie face down in the gravel while the EMT made sure my spine hadn't really been snapped before they could roll me over and put me on a cart. Luke knelt at my side, holding my hands and wiping my face while I bawled for that stupid goat who loved to ram my truck and chew my clothes.

"I let him out of the pasture," I sobbed, "just to spite Pearl. And look what happened."

"He took your bullet," said Luke. "I'm not sorry."

Which made me cry harder.

"Tater's tough," Luke's voice dropped to apologetic. "He's hurt, but alive. Please don't worry about the goat, darlin'. Let's get you fixed up first."

I pushed up on my elbows so I could watch the EMTs loading Max into onc ambulance. I blew him a kiss and he sent me a tired smile. Elena went into the second, while I waited for the third ambulance to arrive.

Rupert and Yuri had already been deposited in police cars and whisked away. The Department of Labor's Special Agents had gleefully snapped up Rupert, while our boys in brown had stolen Yuri to the Forks County Jail. Miss David left with one officer from each department.

"Miss David said she stayed with Agadzinoff because she thought he'd protect her from deportation," said Luke. "Her real name is Natalya Davidovich. She worked as the middle man between Rupert and the crooked Citizenship employee."

"Rupert said Max abandoned her."

"She didn't look abandoned to me," said Luke. "She looked like she enjoyed living in Buckhead."

"You're so cynical. I think she loved Max and he cared for her. Someday maybe he'll tell me that story."

Luke cocked a strong look at me. "What was with the kiss blowing thing?"

"We thought we were going to die together. The man is in pain. Max and Tater saved my life."

"Judging by the bullets jiggling around your bra, I think you did plenty to help him." Luke pulled on my shirt's knot, causing the remaining two bullets to spill onto my skirt. He watched them fall and glanced back at me. "Next time I go hunting, would you carry my ammo for me?"

His attempt to make me smile failed.

"What took you so long to come?" I said, starting a fresh cascade of tears. "If y'all had gotten here sooner, Tater wouldn't have gotten shot."

"Honey, the vet's doing emergency surgery. Please don't worry about Tater."

"I can't help it," I sobbed. "Stupid goat."

"We had a great response time, considering we couldn't understand the caller and had to get the teams coordinated on the fly. The dispatcher heard the gunfire and used the landline to get your location."

"Miss David is not as cool-headed as she'd like to appear," I mumbled, noting that jealousy made me unappreciative.

Luke interrupted that thought. "She did fine. Not everyone charges into a situation with guns a'blazing like you. And what kind of idiot lunges at captured weapons when someone's pointing a forty-five at their head?"

"Since childhood, I've been trained by a sheriff to handle crisis," I sniffled. "The worst thing you can do is panic."

"You should panic more," Luke's voice betrayed his hostility. "Maybe then you'd stay out of these situations. Thank the good Lord we were able capture Regis Sharp without your help. That fool tried to take on Miss April and got caught in a landslide in her trailer while she called for help. This time we had plainclothes waiting. And I had Ernie Pike picked up, too. You may have grown up around a sheriff, but some of us have had real training to serve and protect."

"There's the Luke I know," I said, noticing his confidence had returned. Mine reared its ugly head as well. "And I'll have you know, if I had stayed hidden in the house with Miss David, Max would be dead and those three would have gotten away. Everyone would think the Bear had ordered the hijacking and was keeping illegals in his store as cheap labor. He told Elena he had flipped, but I know he hadn't spoken to y'all. He doesn't trust cops. And thanks to me, they now have those files with the name of the corrupt C.I.S. worker."

In the glare of the task-force lighting, Luke's eyes appeared as burnished as new quarters. I caught a tremble in his hands as he brushed a wet strand of hair from my cheek. "The Special Agents have been gathering information about Agadzinoff for months. They've been checking on the SipNZip ever since it opened. They didn't need you playing Die Hard to catch Agadzinoff."

"So Tater sacrificed himself for nothing."

"Tater did good," Luke sighed and brushed a kiss on my forehead. "When that goat gets out of surgery, I'm chaining it to your leg."

FORTY-TWO

Squatting on the floor of my closet, I flipped a pair of Cody's drawers out of my laundry basket with an irritated huff. The rumble of voices in my living room grew. I didn't need to look at the clock to know the subject of their discontent.

"Hurry it up," Casey hollered from the room next door. "This shindig is for you. I know there's such a thing as fashionably late, but you're going to make Shawna real happy if we don't make it."

I stopped pawing through my laundry to yell back. "I'm looking for something for Jerell. I got him a Special Agent cap."

"I saw a hat in Cody's gym bag," called Todd.

"I didn't take your damn hat," yelled Cody. "And I'm not wearing any tie, so don't try and make me."

"I can't find anything in this house anymore," I said, echoing my daily complaint for the last month, and tried to show my anger by stomping in my teetering heels without success.

"What in tarnation is taking you so long?" Pearl said, appearing in my doorway.

She wore her cruise ship dress, a spangled shift that thankfully covered her goat tattoo. I didn't like any reminders of Tater, who now hobbled on three legs because of me.

"I'm looking for something," I tried not to sound impatient. I owed much to Pearl. For a week, Grandpa wouldn't look at me. He had kept himself busy calming goats who refused to milk after a gun battle and dealing with the legalities of a shot-up house. Pearl said he couldn't stand the thought of someone shooting at me. Oddly enough, Grandpa's withdrawal had brought Pearl and I closer.

"Ed's coming later tonight," she said. "He had to chat with the insurance folks about getting the porch rescreened first."

"I understand," I said, although I wondered how long he could avoid talking to me about what had happened. "I hoped he could see the paintings that made everyone so upset. Then maybe he'd know the *Greek Todds* weren't that big of a deal."

"He believes in you, honey," Pearl thumped the door. "I'm looking forward to seeing that sweet Mr. Max. Harassed by the authorities, tore up his knee, and now doing this show for you. The man is a saint."

"The Bear is nowhere near a saint," I lectured. "He's likely to take a chunk of profit from this charity show for Miss Gladys. Never mind I could use some philanthropic support now that Rupert's bank accounts have been seized and his deposit for the incomplete portrait bounced."

"I thought you liked Mr. Max," Pearl frowned. "How on earth he got Shawna Branson to give gallery space for you, I'll never know."

"Shawna misunderstood the Bear's intentions. She thought the show was for her and not me. And he allowed her to think that until the last minute while he attended the Concerned Citizens meetings with her." I studied my toes. "And allowed me to think he was interested in Shawna's pants for a while."

"What would he want with Shawna's pants?" Pearl scoffed.

Casey snuck into the doorway beside Pearl. "Who wants Shawna's pants?"

"Not Mr. Max," said Pearl. "He's a sweetie."

"I thought you said he was interested in some David chick," said Casey.

"I don't know what to think." I stared at my Tutu-pink nails. "He gave me some mixed signals, but I have been known to misinterpret men's advances. Luke Harper, who I have not seen for weeks, did as well. I thought we had a moment."

I cast a glance at my bedroom door. "They are both making Todd's loyalty look awful good."

"Boo-yeah," Todd hollered from the living room. I could sense his fist pump and high five from Cody.

"Which means nothing," I yelled back. "If I wanted to be with you, I wouldn't have annulled our marriage."

Casey snorted. "Marriage isn't so bad."

"You married a man so he could keep his visa."

"And for the sex." She waggled her thinly waxed and penciled eyebrows.

"If you weren't married, I'd smack you," said Pearl. "What a thing to say."

"I am still not talking to your husband either," I said. "Nik never fixed my truck and now I have no vehicle while Rupert's house remains bound in crime tape. And if Nik had told me Rupert was keeping him as an indentured servant, I would have reported it to the authorities and saved everyone a lot of grief."

"Not his fault. Can I help it if Nik didn't trust you? And he was too busy driving me to Panama Beach? The man swept me off my feet."

"I feel sorry for Nik when you're feet finally touch the earth," I said. "And I feel sorry for the rest of us until y'all move out of my house."

"According to Grandpa, this is not just your house," Casey swiveled a metallic red hip and planted a hand on it. "And Nik is used to living like sardines in old, drafty houses. He's European."

"Come on, Casey," said Pearl, astutely judging our brewing combat. "Leave her so she can find the whatnot for the little boy."

Casey whirled from me and slammed into her honeymoon non-suite. Pearl dusted her capable, goat-tending hands of us and strode to the living room to wrangle the boys. The front door banged open. I jumped, then chastised myself for acting nervy. The din in the living room grew louder.

I blew out my irritation with Casey and continued my search for the hat. Cody's gym bag lay in the hall. I shook out a jumble of tools, clothes, and a book. No hat. I picked up the novel and flipped through the pages. The last time I had seen Cody with a book had been high school and even then, the binding had remained fresh.

Several photos had been stuck between the pages. I pulled out an old snapshot, but before I could examine it, I glanced up and saw Luke standing in my hallway, studying me. In his hand, he held a box wrapped in white paper and decorated with a white bow. He wore his snug jeans and his cop mask with the serious, undimpled expression. My heart did a short dive, and I silently lectured myself on the stupidity of excitement over nothing.

"What's that?" I said.

"Wedding present," he replied and handed me the box. "From my mom."

Still holding the photo, I shoved the book under one arm to take the gift. "This is unexpected. Casey will be thrilled, though. Thanks."

"Mom heard about the wedding. Congratulations." He shrugged. "Took me a while to get over here, but you know why."

"No, I don't know why," I tipped a shoulder. "Except I figured you really don't want to see me."

"You're married. What do you expect?"

"I'm not married. Casey's married. To Nik and his green card," I gasped. "Is that what the town thinks? That I got married again? Why doesn't anybody tell me these things?"

"You're not married? Todd's been living with you."

"I told you we're friends. He's been out of work." I pointed to the air mattress on the floor of my bedroom. "That's his bed. Not mine."

Luke lunged, and I dropped the wedding gift and book. The snapshot fluttered in my hand, but before I could release it, Luke pulled me into the bedroom, slammed the door shut, and pinned my body against the door. His face hovered over mine.

"Tell me this again," his husky voice rang with bitterness, "because for the past few weeks I was under the impression that you were Todd McIntosh's wife."

"Who gave you that impression?" I said, tilting my chin up. "Did you ask my Uncle Will or Red or anybody I know? Because they would have told differently. I would have, too, if you would talk to me."

"I didn't want to talk to anybody you knew. I've been avoiding the subject of Cherry Tucker all together." His breath smelled of mint and liquor, like he had fueled himself with liquid confidence before appearing on my porch. "I just now found out this art show thing is for you."

"That means you've been talking to Shawna." My eyes narrowed. "I would love to not have to tell you I told you so. But I told you so."

"I'm not talking to her either. My momma told me about the show and your marriage," he pounded the door with a fist and stepped deeper into my personal space. "Why is Shawna doing this to you?"

"Because she hates me." And you love me? I couldn't think those words, much less say them aloud. "And she would like to humiliate and hurt me any way she can."

"You are both hurting me." He leaned his forehead against mine.

"How am I hurting you?" I had trouble focusing. His eye color had deepened from cool Payne's gray to charcoal.

His hand stroked my face. "You scare me."

"How do I scare you?" My mouth bumped against his thumb.

He drew a gentle line over my bottom lip. I scrunched the snapshot in my palm and allowed my hands to slide up to his shoulders.

"I don't know. You just do," he said and replaced his thumb with his mouth. His kiss pulled the breath from my body, and when I found myself teetering on my toes, he nudged his leg between my thighs to hold me upright.

"Wait," I panted when we pulled back for air. "Are you mad at me or not? Because I might still be mad at you. You're a horrible communicator. You don't listen to me."

Before I could give more reasons for our failures, he captured my mouth again and did more personal space invasion. I moaned as his hands became reacquainted with my body.

"Slow down," I begged. "I've got to go to the show. Come with me and we'll make up later."

"I can't," Luke pulled away, sighing. "I thought you were married."

"I know," I said and ran happy fingers through his curls. "But I'm not. I never really was."

"What I mean is, I started seeing someone else."

While I searched for my jaw on the floor, Luke yanked my bedroom door open and stepped into the hall.

"I'll fix this," he called, hustling through the crowd and out the front door before I could find my tongue.

Heads poked out of doors to gape at me, but I ignored them.

"What the hell," I said to his retreating back and glanced down at the crumpled snapshot still fisted in my palm. I smoothed it, took another hard look at the photo, and felt my mouth go dry and my knees weaken.

"Momma?" I whispered. Why did Cody hide a picture of our mother? The photo was candid, taken from a distance and blurry, but I knew her immediately. I tore my gaze off the pretty blond and searched my memory for the identification of the other person in the photo. A handsome, dark haired man who had an arm slung possessively around my momma's waist. A man who was not my daddy. Someone I had seen in another photo recently.

Billy Branson.

These were Shawna's friggin' missing photos?

"What. The. Hell."

READER'S DISCUSSION GUIDE

1. Cherry sketches a composite of the hijacking suspect because she's the only artist the Sheriff knows. Have you ever been asked to do a project outside your experience but still within your skill set?

2. Whenever Cherry gets "distracted" by a man, she blames it on her mother. Do you agree or disagree with her reasoning?

3. Have you ever known someone who sought to cover their own embarrassments by making other people look worse? How does Shawna compare to your example? How did you handle it?

4. The story of the SipNZip was loosely based on an actual Department of Labor Special Agent case. What real crime stories have you heard that might make for good fiction?

5. Several different characters complain that Cherry talks too much and gets involved in things that are not her business. Do you think these flaws negatively or positively influence her character?

6. Cherry says she and Luke "carried baggage that didn't fit through one another's doors." Why can't Cherry and Luke just move on in one direction or the other?

7. Have you known anyone like Pearl who began a relationship with someone with a preexisting family? Are the grandchildren's feelings fair toward her? How would you mediate their dispute?

8. What do you think Shawna's pictures represent? Why are they so important to Shawna, and will they mean to the Tucker kids?

10. Which character do you most relate to or you feel you're the most similar to? And which character do you wish you could be more like?

LARISSA REINHART

Growing up in a small town, Larissa Reinhart couldn't wait to move to an exotic city far from corn fields. After moving around the US and Japan, now she loves to write about rough hewn characters that live near corn fields, particularly sassy women with a penchant for trouble.

Hijack in Abstract is the third in the Cherry Tucker Mystery Series from Henery Press, following *Still Life in Brunswick Stew* (May 2013) and *Portrait of a Dead Guy*, a 2012 Daphne du Maurier finalist. *Quick Sketch*, a Cherry Tucker prequel to *Portrait*, is in the mystery anthology *The Heartache Motel* (December 2013).

She lives near Atlanta with her minions and Cairn Terrier, Biscuit. Visit her website larissareinhart.com or find her chatting with the Little Read Hens on Facebook.

Henery Press Mystery Books

And finally, before you go...
Here are a few other mysteries
you might enjoy:

In Case You Missed the 1st Book in the Series

PORTRAIT OF A DEAD GUY

Larissa Reinhart

A Cherry Tucker Mystery (#1)

In Halo, Georgia, folks know Cherry Tucker as big in mouth, small in stature, and able to sketch a portrait faster than buck-shot rips from a ten gauge -- but commissions are scarce. So when the well-heeled Branson family wants to memorialize their murdered son in a coffin portrait, Cherry scrambles to win their patronage from her small town rival.

As the clock ticks toward the deadline, Cherry faces more trouble than just a controversial subject. Between ex-boyfriends, her flaky family, an illegal gambling ring, and outwitting a killer on a spree, Cherry finds herself painted into a corner she'll be lucky to survive.

Available at booksellers nationwide and online

Visit www.henerypress.com for details

In Case You Missed the 2nd Book in the Series

STILL LIFE IN BRUNSWICK STEW

Larissa Reinhart

A Cherry Tucker Mystery (#2)

Cherry Tucker's in a stew. Art commissions dried up after her nemesis became president of the County Arts Council. Desperate and broke, Cherry and her friend, Eloise, spend a sultry summer weekend hawking their art at the Sidewinder Annual Brunswick Stew Cook-Off. When a bad case of food poisoning breaks out and Eloise dies, the police brush off her death as accidental.

However, Cherry suspects someone spiked the stew and killed her friend. As Cherry calls on cook-off competitors, bitter rivals, and crooked judges, the police get steamed while the killer prepares to cook Cherry's goose.

Available at booksellers nationwide and online

Visit www.henerypress.com for details

LOWCOUNTRY BOIL

Susan M. Boyer

A Liz Talbot Mystery (#1)

Private Investigator Liz Talbot is a modern Southern belle: she blesses hearts and takes names. She carries her Sig 9 in her Kate Spade handbag, and her golden retriever, Rhett, rides shotgun in her hybrid Escape. When her grandmother is murdered, Liz high-tails it back to her South Carolina island home to find the killer.

She's fit to be tied when her police-chief brother shuts her out of the investigation, so she opens her own. Then her long-dead best friend pops in and things really get complicated. When more folks start turning up dead in this small seaside town, Liz must use more than just her wits and charm to keep her family safe, chase down clues from the hereafter, and catch a psychopath before he catches her.

Available at booksellers nationwide and online

Visit www.henerypress.com for details

DOUBLE WHAMMY

Gretchen Archer

A Davis Way Crime Caper (#1)

Davis Way thinks she's hit the jackpot when she lands a job as the fifth wheel on an elite security team at the fabulous Bellissimo Resort and Casino in Biloxi, Mississippi. But once there, she runs straight into her ex-ex husband, a rigged slot machine, her evil twin, and a trail of dead bodies. Davis learns the truth and it does not set her free—in fact, it lands her in the pokey.

Buried under a mistaken identity, unable to seek help from her family, her hot streak runs cold until her landlord Bradley Cole steps in. Make that her landlord, lawyer, and love interest. With his help, Davis must win this high stakes game before her luck runs out.

Available at booksellers nationwide and online

Visit www.henerypress.com for details

BOARD STIFF
Kendel Lynn

An Elliott Lisbon Mystery (#1)

As director of the Ballantyne Foundation on Sea Pine Island, SC, Elliott Lisbon scratches her detective itch by performing discreet inquiries for Foundation donors. Usually nothing more serious than retrieving a pilfered Pomeranian. Until Jane Hatting, Ballantyne board chair, is accused of murder. The Ballantyne's reputation tanks, Jane's headed to a jail cell, and Elliott's sexy ex is the new lieutenant in town.

Armed with moxie and her Mini Coop, Elliott uncovers a trail of blackmail schemes, gambling debts, illicit affairs, and investment scams. But the deeper she digs to clear Jane's name, the guiltier Jane looks. The closer she gets to the truth, the more treacherous her investigation becomes. With victims piling up faster than shells at a clambake, Elliott realizes she's next on the killer's list.

Available at booksellers nationwide and online

Visit www.henerypress.com for details

DINERS, DIVES & DEAD ENDS

Terri L. Austin

A Rose Strickland Mystery (#1)

As a struggling waitress and part-time college student, Rose Strickland's life is stalled in the slow lane. But when her close friend, Axton, disappears, Rose suddenly finds herself serving up more than hot coffee and flapjacks. Now she's hashing it out with sexy bad guys and scrambling to find clues in a race to save Axton before his time runs out.

With her anime-loving bestie, her septuagenarian boss, and a pair of IT wise men along for the ride, Rose discovers political corruption, illegal gambling, and shady corporations. She's gone from zero to sixty and quickly learns when you're speeding down the fast lane, it's easy to crash and burn.

Available at booksellers nationwide and online

Visit www.henerypress.com for details

ARTIFACT

Gigi Pandian

A Jaya Jones Treasure Hunt Mystery (#1)

Historian Jaya Jones discovers the secrets of a lost Indian treasure may be hidden in a Scottish legend from the days of the British Raj. But she's not the only one on the trail...

From San Francisco to London to the Highlands of Scotland, Jaya must evade a shadowy stalker as she follows hints from the hastily scrawled note of her dead lover to a remote archaeological dig. Helping her decipher the cryptic clues are her magician best friend, a devastatingly handsome art historian with something to hide, and a charming archaeologist running for his life.

Available at booksellers nationwide and online

Visit www.henerypress.com for details

THE AMBITIOUS CARD

John Gaspard

An Eli Marks Mystery (#1)

The life of a magician isn't all kiddie shows and card tricks. Sometimes it's murder. Especially when magician Eli Marks very publicly debunks a famed psychic, and said psychic ends up dead. The evidence, including a bloody King of Diamonds playing card (one from Eli's own Ambitious Card routine), directs the police right to Eli.

As more psychics are slain, and more King cards rise to the top, Eli can't escape suspicion. Things get really complicated when romance blooms with a beautiful psychic, and Eli discovers she's the next target for murder, and he's scheduled to die with her. Now Eli must use every trick he knows to keep them both alive and reveal the true killer.

Available at booksellers nationwide and online

Visit www.henerypress.com for details

FRONT PAGE FATALITY

LynDee Walker

A Headlines in High Heels Mystery (#1)

Crime reporter Nichelle Clarke's days can flip from macabre to comical with a beep of her police scanner. Then an ordinary accident story turns extraordinary when evidence goes missing, a prosecutor vanishes, and a sexy Mafia boss shows up with the headline tip of a lifetime.

As Nichelle gets closer to the truth, her story gets more dangerous. Armed with a notebook, a hunch, and her favorite stilettos, Nichelle races to splash these shady dealings across the front page before this deadline becomes her last.

Available at booksellers nationwide and online

Visit www.henerypress.com for details

CROPPED TO DEATH

Christina Freeburn

A Faith Hunter Scrap This Mystery (#1)

Former US Army JAG specialist, Faith Hunter, returns to her West Virginia home to work in her grandmothers' scrapbooking store determined to lead an unassuming life after her adventure abroad turned disaster. But her quiet life unravels when her friend is charged with murder – and Faith inadvertently supplied the evidence. So Faith decides to cut through the scrap and piece together what really happened.

With a sexy prosecutor, a determined homicide detective, a handful of sticky suspects and a crop contest gone bad, Faith quickly realizes if she's not careful, she'll be the next one cropped.

Available at booksellers nationwide and online

Visit www.henerypress.com for details

KILLER IMAGE

Wendy Tyson

An Allison Campbell Mystery (#1)

Philadelphia image consultant Allison Campbell is not your typical detective. She's more familiar with the rules of etiquette than the rules of evidence, prefers three-inch Manolos to comfy flats and relates to Dear Abby, not Judge Judy.

When Allison's latest Main Line client, the fifteen-year-old Goth daughter of a White House hopeful, is accused of the ritualistic murder of a local divorce attorney, Allison fights to prove her client's innocence when no one else will. But in a place where image is everything, the ability to distinguish the truth from the facade may be the only thing that keeps Allison alive.

Available at booksellers nationwide and online

Visit www.henerypress.com for details

CPSIA information can be obtained at www.ICGtesting.com
Printed in the USA
BVOW08s1724090714

358659BV00014B/244/P